'The Jenson Ro:

The Last Gateway

By

Alan Hendrick

Copyright © 2022 Alan Hendrick

ISBN: 9798831858679

All rights are reserved, including the right to reproduce this book in any form.
The right of Alan Hendrick to be identified as the author of this work has been asserted by him in accordance with the Copyright, Designs and Patents Act 1988
This is a work of fiction, and any Names, Characters, Places, and Incidents are fictitious and a product of the Author's imagination. Any similarity is coincidental.

'That's the thing about books, they let you travel without moving your feet '

– Jhumpa Lahiri

Let's travel together:

Facebook - Alan Hendrick
Instagram - alanmhendrick
TikTok   - @alanhendrick1

In loving memory of Tony Fitzpatrick

Chapter 1

Grace felt special walking past her father. He held the door firmly open as she slid in past his overstretched arm, gliding beneath like a sailboat cruising below a steady archway.

'Good evening, Miss Harper,' the waitress said, appearing out from behind the partition.

Grace's face beamed with red uncertainty. Ambivalence masked by embarrassment. She did like being welcomed by her last name. She felt important. She felt special. But she also hated what was happening, the set-up, the attention. This seemed to be a festive night where all eyes would be on her.

Her mother had been acknowledged by 'Miss Harper' on numerous occasions, so now turning sixteen, Grace felt this was an introduction into adulthood, even though it was two years premature.

But to Grace, this was an important birthday. Although, not yet reaching the heights of maturity, her parents believed this was a 'coming of age' affair. Sweet sixteen was a sign of 'New Blooming'. Grace couldn't help but feel like a young woman. Turning sixteen was a big deal, and these little gestures added to the overall experience.

'This way Miss Harper,' the waitress said. 'You can bring your family,' she added, smiling at Grace's father, who in return, gave a thankful wink. He appreciated how his daughter was being treated so far.

Grace felt like the star of the show, walking in through the tables full of activity, while the rest of her family followed behind.

They received a few stares and quick glances from other diners, but this wasn't unusual. Grace and her family were black. Most people were not rude nor ignorant to the colour of their skin. They were just intrigued, especially when a large family of six had just walked in.

It would probably be different if it were a smaller group, but consisting of herself, her mother and father, her younger sister, and two younger brothers, walking anywhere together, they would always receive attention, a real impact wherever they went.

This strangely produced an extra 'self-worth' to her birthday night. She really felt like all eyes were on her, and that she was a "somebody", somebody who had just turned sixteen.

This was her favourite diner in town. She loved the whole American vibe, with all the banners and old-style retro pictures, along with the fixtures and furnishings that dated way back, mimicking a funky sixties joint. And the smell. That meaty aroma of fried chicken, and the burning fat from the greasy fries, every oily particle wafting inside each nostril with every sniff. Even though she had been here on so many occasions, she knew this was a night she would never forget.

'Can I get you some drinks first while you look at the menu?' The waitress asked.

'Can I have a vanilla milkshake please?' Grace asked, turning her head to her father as he held onto the back of her chair. 'Thanks dad,' she added as her father helped inch her in towards the table. And leaning over, after pushing her in, he whispered into her ear.

'Remember Gracie, this is your special night, so you order whatever you want, anything at all, and as much of it as you can eat!'

'Thanks dad.' Grace said again. She knew this wouldn't be the last time she would be saying those words tonight.

Her father kissed the top of her head and walked around the table to help his wife settle in the younger ones of the family.

Now seated and all the drinks given out, the waitress returned with a pen and notepad in hand.
'Anybody got any allergies?'
Most of the table nodded, or said no, except for Grace's two younger brothers; they didn't quite understand the question.
'Mum, can I have chicken nuggets and chips?' Alex asked.
'Everybody ready to order then?' The waitress suggested.
Her thumb clicking the pen in preparation, but not at all hinged by the potentially lengthy order.
'Hang on Alex. It's your sister's birthday so she should....'
But before their mother could finish her sentence, Grace interrupted.
'It's okay Mum, let everyone else order. I still haven't decided yet.'
Grace's mother, a heavy-set strong woman, now looking at her strangely. Any other special occasion when they came here, Grace always knew what she wanted. She was a creature of habit. But maybe this time she would try something different? Her mother shrugged it off and turned back to Alex.
'Okay Alex, you can go first.'
Alex was the youngest of all the children. He was only four years of age. Grace adored him with every bone in her body. And every time she looked at him her heart would just melt like butter, oozing the soft dairy all around her arteries, clogging them up with adoration.
Being the eldest, Grace could vividly remember holding Alex as a baby in her arms. This tiny little boy

who couldn't fend for himself, and now look at him, ordering his own dinner.

'Can I have the same?' Alex's older brother Freddie asked.

Freddie was only two years older. He looked very much like Alex, only he had lost his puppy fat and had stretched out to become a skinny laced kid. Grace didn't seem to share the same adoration for him. Even though she loved him, she felt he was one of those annoyingly perfect older brothers who didn't want anything to do with childish behaviours.

Grace could see the disgruntled look on Freddie's face as his little brother had managed to order his food before him. This would no doubt lead to an unprovoked quarrel later. Something they would have to deal with when Freddie's resentment would kick in.

'Okay, and yourself?' The waitress asked as she turned towards Ebony.

Ebony was twelve. A young, shy, twelve. She kept herself to herself. Grace would try to include her in things, but she would nearly always refuse. They had an average relationship, but it could be better. This was something Grace had hoped would change in time.

'And now for the birthday girl?' The waitress continued.

'Can I have the rack of ribs please?' Grace replied, glancing over at her mother.

Her mother smiled back at her, now knowing that she had never intended to pick something new. Grace had a tendency not to steer off course. She had planned to order the ribs. She just simply delayed her choice to allow her siblings to go first. After all, she didn't want the night to be all about her.

~~~

'Happy birthday to you....
Happy birthday to you....
Happy birthday dear Grace...
Happy birthday to you.'

It wasn't as sharp as a harmonic choir, but as her family and some staff members joined in, with the addition of a few random revellers, it was construed quiet well. It did help that Grace's mother was in a gospel choir and was able to take lead vocals.

Dinner was well and truly over. And placed down in front of Grace was a giant slab of her favourite dessert. The sweet confection with its soft centred texture, allowing the foamy cream to sit on the surface whilst the ripest of strawberries decorated every inch.

Grace could feel the heat from the sixteen candles, all glistening in front of her face as her mouth began to salivate at the thought of eating this amazing pavlova.

'You ready?' She asked looking around the table and preparing to blow out the candles.

'Make a wish.' Her father whispered next to her.

Grace closed her eyes. A quiet void allowed her mind to think. A few seconds later she opened her eyes. Without any hesitation, she creased her lips together and began to blow.

'What did you wish for?' Alex asked, shouting from across the table.

'She can't tell you, otherwise it won't come true,' his mother retorted.

'But I want to know.'

'You don't need to know everything,' Freddy barked. And there it was, the unprovoked attack on his brother.

'Who wants a slice of cake?' Their mother asked, picking up the napkins and trying to deflate the situation. Preparation for the sweet fluffiness had finally begun.

'Well excuse me while I go to the toilet,' Graces father said. 'And no pavlova for me please, I couldn't eat another bite.'

'Just a small piece dad, it would be rude not to have some of my birthday cake.'

Grace's father smiled. 'Okay, but just a small bit.'

~~~

Not a single spoonful of cake was left when the bill came out. All the other siblings were too young to notice but Grace was old enough to read her father's facial expression.

Looking over at her mother, she could tell the signs of an expensive bill.

She felt guilty, but this guilt didn't run deep. She had asked for no presents this year. So, this expense would be the only suffering her parents would have to endure. She knew her parents didn't have much money. And even though it was a special birthday and having dinner in here was going to be costly, she realised it could have been a lot worse. For at least this way, everybody got a share of the present, each one savouring the spoils of her birthday.

Grace watched her father disappear over to pay. But just then, the recalling of her wish had provoked an uncertainty. For Grace was a 'Dreamer', an average dreamer with no powers. But with every imaginative bone in her body, she would always wish to be exceptional. She had always imagined herself to be more. An average girl wanting to be 'less average'. And this wish was just another frail attempt to cast a spell out in the universe. A spell that someday she hoped would be answered.

Chapter 2

As soon as the car came to a stop, Grace reached in towards the middle of the front seats and softly spoke.
'Thank you so much for a great night. It was the best birthday ever.'
She kissed both her mother and father on their cheek as her siblings were motionless in the back. They were so stuffed from eating the tiny banquet they had fallen straight to sleep. It could have been a mixture of brimming stomachs and the long drive home. A forty-five-minute drive, mostly through dark country roads off the beaten track. But it was getting late, and darkness had fallen.

Grace opened the front door whilst her father carried in the sleeping body of Alex, a struggle showing on his face,
'We need to put him on a diet,' he said. His knee's buckling as his wife effortlessly stepped across the threshold with the light and scrawny body of Freddy.
'Goodnight Grace and Happy birthday,' Ebony said. She sheepishly hugged her sister before following her parents up the stairs. She had still not fully woken from her unexpected slumber.
Grace walked into the dark kitchen and turned on the light. She then marched over to switch on the kettle.
She proceeded to take out two cups, knowing her parents took great pleasure in having an earthy night cap.
Squeezing the tea bags and adding the right amount of milk for each, she scooped up the cups and set them over on the kitchen table. And just in time, as she could hear footsteps coming back down the stairs.

'Ah perfect timing,' she said, bestowing this kind gesture.

'Close your eyes Gracie,' her father directed even before she had turned around.

Not having much time to follow his instructions as her initial reaction was to turn. She saw both parents standing in the kitchen doorway. And in her father's hand, there sat a little white box with a yellow ribbon. A jewellery box signifying a special gift inside.

Grace's face dropped. But not to the delight of her parents. She looked appalled.

'That better not be for me?' She advised, opposition in her tone.

She wasn't trying to sound ungrateful, but she knew her parents fell short of a penny or two, especially considering they had a small business to run and four mouths to feed, along with their own.

Her father chuckled whilst her mother proudly smiled. But Grace continued her disapproval.

'No. I won't accept it. What did I say about presents?'

'Calm down Gracie! It is for you, yes, but don't worry, we didn't spend a penny. I promise.' Her father replied.

He then calmly stepped forward, his hand offering this gift in the hope his daughter would eventually accept. Both himself and his wife smiled, a gratification in their gaze, watching and waiting for their daughter's approval. And when she took hold of the box, they waited for her reaction as she began to dismantle the neatly wrapped present.

'It was your great grandmothers,' her father continued. 'It was passed down to your grandmother, and then to my mother, and then she gave it to me. But it's a little feminine, so you can probably understand why I never wore it. I was saving it up for a special occasion.'

Grace untied the bow and shredded the wrapping. Now sitting in her hand, was an un-opened box, taunting her with its antique presentation. She hesitated. She took one last look at her parents. Her displeasing stare soon transformed into a gentle smile. She removed the lid. And there, revealing itself, perched on the backdrop cushion, was a gold necklace with a pendant figure.

Grace found it unique but couldn't quite make out if she liked it or not.

'It's lovely,' she said, thinking she had to say something, even if she wasn't sure about it yet. 'Are you sure you want me to have it?'

'Of course we do,' her father insisted. 'It has been passed down through the generations. It's yours now.'

Grace's mother began rubbing her husband's arm in recognition of this proud moment. It was an important moment in his family's history.

'What about Ebony?' Grace asked.

'Don't worry about your sister. She'll get something special too when she turns sixteen. It's a goddess holding a moonstone,' her father explained, watching on as his daughter detailed the pendant.

'And she's holding an amber moonstone,' he added. 'Some people believe it increases magical properties. These pendants were often worn by our ancestors.'

'Wow…dad. It's BEAUTIFUL!' Grace declared.

She stepped forward and hugged him. The detailed report had convinced her. Her mind was now made up. She loved it.

'Here let me put it on you,' her mother offered. She carefully took it off her hands and shifted behind to put it around her neck. 'There, now let's see it?'

Grace turned around, facing them both and holding the pendant out in full view. She was overwhelmed.

'This is the best gift ever, thank you both so much,' she said, kissing both parents again on their cheeks.

Grace always over appreciated things. She was so grateful for everything, just like her father.

'Right, I'm off to bed,' she said. 'I've just made you both a cup of tea, so goodnight and I'll see you in the morning. Love you both. And thanks again for everything. Sleep safe.'

'Love you too,' her mother declared. 'Sleep safe.'

'You too, Gracie,' her father said. 'SLEEP SAFE,' he called back as Grace had disappeared out of the kitchen and was already on her way upstairs to her bedroom.

~~~

Grace stepped foot into her bedroom. She marched straight over to her wardrobe mirror, excited to take a proper look at her new necklace. She was smitten. She had now realised she loved it. Still wearing the charm, she moved closer to the mirror, admiring it even more so. She couldn't help but feel so thankful.

She was still feeling so elated about her whole birthday, she couldn't sleep. After brushing her teeth and getting into her pyjama's, she lay on top of the bed with her earphones in, listening to the music on her phone.

Even though she was ready for bed, she still hadn't taken her necklace off, gazing into the fine detail as she held the pendant out from her chest.

Bopping her head to her favourite tunes, unawares to herself, her eyelids began to droop. She soon drifted away into a profound slumber, and within this slumber, something happened. A face she had never seen before appeared.

Chapter 3

Sterling and Loretta Harper had just finished their cups of tea Grace had made them. They were simply chatting about the day and general family life, both realising their biggest accomplishment was raising four beautiful kids.

'Do you want another cup?' Sterling asked his wife as she still grasped her hands around her empty teacup.
'Oh no, thank you,' she replied, removing her hands from her cup and placing them down beside his.
They looked into each other's eyes and immediately knew why they were both grinning.
'Thank you honey,' Sterling said, stretching over to the corner of the table to give his wife a smooch.
She looked surprised.
'What are you thanking me for?'
'For, well, just being you….and giving me the most wonderful children in the world.'
Loretta smiled. Even though her husband was tall and very masculine, she always loved how he never quite fitted the description of this. He was as soft centred as they came. She loved how tender he was, how sentimental he came to be. And what she loved most of all was that, even though she knew this, he always seemed to surprise her with frequent divulgements of his compassion.
'Come on, let's go to bed,' she said putting her hand into his and slowing leading him up the stairs.

~~~

No sooner had they shut their bedroom door and started kissing, were they interrupted by screams.

Sterling quickly pulled their bedroom door back, nearly taking it off its hinges. His force revealing how frightened he was. Having a family full of dreamers with no powers proved very unnerving.

He was about to dart into the direction of the boy's room, when his wife halted his approach. She held him back. And then, he realised the screams were coming from Grace's room.

'It's Grace!' Loretta insisted, charging towards the bedroom.

As Sterling too charged for the bedroom, he managed to get there first, pushing the door open.

He could see his eldest daughter tossing in the bed and shouting.

Without hesitation, he leapt onto the bed and held onto her shoulders.

His wife switched on the light.

Sterling, now managing to steady Grace, but her body seemed unresponsive. He could not wake her.

'GRACE! YOU NEED TO WAKE UP!!!' He demanded. An uncertainty in his voice. He was scared. He knew she was still sleeping, and he was unsure of what was happening within her dream.

'GRACE?' Her mother called out. Her cry, signalling fear also as she watched on from the foot of the bed.

Grace's father began to shake her body uncontrollably, disfavouring any safeguard for his daughter's protection. It was taking too long for her to wake. Something was not right. And if it meant a morning of heated patches to sooth the whiplash, then that was the chance he was going to take. For in the Dreamworld, every second counts.

Suddenly Grace's screams ceased. And with the vigorous vibrations, she slowly opened her eyes.

'Grace, you okay?' Her father asked.
'I'm okay dad.' She replied, her anxious panting conveying the terror.
Her father began to investigate any wounded signs she may have sustained in her dream.
'Are you sure you're okay?' Her mother asked. 'Was it a bad dream? Did anything hurt you?'
'No, I'm fine.'
But Grace looked confused.
'Let me see if you were hurt. What happened?'
'I'm okay Dad. I wasn't hurt honest…it was somebody else.'
'If it wasn't you, then who was it?' Her mother asked.

Just then, Grace's father jumped up to go check on their other children. But as he turned to face the door, he could see all three of them lined up in the entrance, their sleepy eyes staring in, curious, and looking around for answers.
'NO DAD,' Grace yelled. But then she saw the queue of wondering eyes. 'It wasn't any of them. It was a boy. He seemed to be about my age. But I've never seen him before.'
Grace's parents remained silent, waiting on their daughter's every word.
'It was so vivid. It was as if I was there with him, inside his dream. I was there for a reason. But I don't remember why. It was so real though.'
'What happened to this boy? Is he okay?' Her mother asked.

'No mum, he's not okay. He died. He was right in front of me, and he died!'

Torment took root, like branches of a wilting tree, each shoot, holding her down. Grace couldn't move. She couldn't quite comprehend what had just happened.

'I couldn't save him.'

'It's not your fault sweetheart. Some people just can't be saved from this.'

'How did he die?' Her father questioned.

'I'm not sure. I don't really remember. It all happened so fast.'

'The main thing is that you're okay,' her mother declared. She reached in and gave her daughter a big hug.

'That's true,' her father reassured himself as he walked back towards his other children. 'We'll check the papers tomorrow, see if anyone died in their sleep last night.'

Grace nodded her head as her hand dipped onto her chest. Her heart was still pounding. Each beat, still hammering with panic. And just then she realised she still had her necklace on.

Unclipping the back, she reached over and placed it on her bedside locker.

Unexpectedly, a memory distorted her vision.

'JENSON!' She called out. She moved away from her mother's hold.

'What?' Her father asked.

'His name. It was Jenson. I remember screaming his name moments before he died. He was just lying there on the ground. But his name, it was Jenson.'

Chapter 4

Jenson awoke from his dreamless sleep. It was a Friday morning, but he wasn't going to school. In fact, he hadn't been back to school ever since it all began. Two weeks had passed, and the devastating marks had left a wound so great, nothing would ever be the same again.

His body slumped out of bed. His hands gripping onto the edge, wishing the fall were greater. He had surrendered his confidence, suffocating any air for it to breath. He had no conviction left. And like a relentless habit, he stood up and headed towards his sister's bedroom.

He opened the door, imagining her to be in her bed. But she wasn't. He had hoped for some reason, everything that had happened to him over the past few weeks was all, well not a dream, because dreams don't exist in his imagination, but a nightmare, a series of unpleasant thoughts, causing him to hallucinate. He was waiting for somebody to jump out and say 'Surprise', 'it was all a joke'. But that day would never come.

He stood there in the doorway, gazing over at the perfectly made rainbow bedsheets that hadn't been slept in ever since that morning, the morning he had received the phone call from his mother.

'Is this it? He thought to himself. *'Am I never going to see Robyn lying in her bed again? The irritating sniffling, the constant whining about walking to school, her fictional dreams.* What he would give just to talk to her one more time.

Suddenly he felt a hand on his shoulder. It was his father's hand.

'You okay Jenson?' He asked, now standing there beside his son.

You could cut the atmosphere with a knife. An eerie silence loomed as nobody spoke for a few seconds. They were both just as miserable as each other.

'I know you've been finding it difficult, we all have,' his father said, eventually stubbing out the silence with a large fictitious cigarette butt. 'You can't keep blaming yourself Jenson. There was nothing we could have done.'

Jenson's eyes began to fill up.

His father could see this and supported his son's plunging headline. He gathered him in closely.

Jenson's father wasn't the softest of men, and a hug was something he didn't do very often. But for this occasion, he needed to do it. If not for his son, then for himself. Something, anything which meant keeping his family from the self-destructing path they were on.

'Thanks dad. I'm sorry, I know you have a lot on your plate as well.'

'Jenson, you don't have to apologise for any of this. You do know your mother and I both love you so much, and we are here whenever you want to talk?'

'I know dad, thanks.'

'Go on, get yourself ready. It's going to be a long day.'

'Is mum up?'

'Yeah. She's been up since the crack of dawn. You know what she's like when it comes to dealing with funerals.'

Jenson's incisors bit down hard, just shy of breaking skin, but holding tight onto the loose tissue inside his jaw. He returned to his bedroom. His dad was right. It was going to be a long day.

~~~

Now dressed, and in his finest suit and tie, Jenson grabbed his phone and left the room. The last time he donned this outfit was about a year ago for his grandfather's funeral. It was an occasion just like this one, but not quite on the same scale.

He stepped into the bathroom. An image stared back at him, but he didn't feel it was his. He was numb. He felt as if his whole insides were emptying out. Each organ pouring itself into the sink. He, just like his mother, was struggling to cope. Funerals were hard at the best of times. But this day was certainly going to be an emotional rollercoaster, a ride Jenson seemed destined to never get off.

He suddenly remembered not long ago, when he stood there in the same spot, that Friday morning getting ready for school, the morning before it all happened.

'How had it come to this?' He questioned, his head nodding with pure resentment. He could feel nothing now. Spending the last two weeks crying, but for some reason now, looking into the mirror, he was emotionless.

Collecting himself, he knew he had to move. He scooped some hair wax out of the styling tub and began to massage it lightly into his scalp. No song playing this time. No beats whirling around in his head. No looping tongue whistling along to his favourite tune.
A knock startled him.

'Yes?'

'You nearly ready?' His father asked from the other side of the bathroom door.

'Yeah, I'll be done in a minute.'

'Okay. Myself and your mother will be downstairs.'

And with that, Jenson could hear his father's footsteps trudging down the stairs.

Before Jenson trailed his miserable body down, he walked back over to his sister's bedroom and opened her door one last time. The pink empty room had a despondent feel. This time, however, Jenson did not stop and peer in from the doorway. He stepped in and walked over to Robyn's desk, snatching her once favourite teddy bear, and stepping back out.

It was a brown fluffy 12inch bear, dressed in a miniature white t-shirt with a printed picture of their family on it. The picture had been taken when Robyn was only a few days old.

Jenson was five at the time, holding her in his arms while his mother and father were at either side helping to prop Robyn's limbs. Robyn loved this teddy. It was her very first toy. She cherished it so much.

Jenson held the teddy bear in his hand and just stared at it. He could feel a sensation flow back into his body. He was becoming emotional again. It was all part of this rollercoaster he would endure all day. His eyes began to water again as he looked down at this happy moment in all their lives. The moment his sister had come into his life!

'JENSON?' A voice called up from downstairs. 'We're going to be late.'

'COMING DAD.' Jenson replied, wiping his eyes with the sleeve of his suit jacket.

As he came to the bottom of the stairs, he passed his father, who was on his way out to the car with a big wreath in his hands.

'Your mother is in the kitchen,' he said.

Jenson could see the rear presence of his mother as she stood at the kitchen table, staring out the back window.

He stepped softly into the kitchen and stood directly behind her.

'You okay mum?'

His mother turned round, wiping her eyes. Jenson could tell she had been crying, and possibly crying all morning. Her eyes were puffy and red.

'Oh Jenson.' She responded.
She scrambled towards her son, wrapping him in her arms, and holding him tighter than ever. Even tighter than she had the night they were reunited on the front lawn.

They never said another word to each other. They just stood there embraced until Jenson's father came back in. They didn't have to say anything. They both knew exactly what the other was thinking. Sure, Jenson's mother was the same when his grandfather had died. She kept to herself and tried to be the strong centred woman she was, but then throughout the day, she would have moments of weakness, erupting into a volcano of tears, revealing her vulnerability.

'We'll get through this,' Jenson's father said, reaching out and holding onto them both.

Jenson's mother spotted Jenson clutching onto Robyn's favourite teddy.

'She loved Bobby.'

'I know I didn't ask, but is it okay if I bring it?'

'Yes of course,' she replied. 'That's a lovely idea.'

~~~

Jenson looked around him as they stepped out of the house. This was the first morning he hadn't seen any of 'Payton Whites' henchmen sitting in a blackened jeep, waiting to follow them.

They had been following him and his family since this all began, in hopes they would lead them to Davrin. But truth is, nobody had heard or seen Davrin since that night.

Jenson was a little relieved to be honest. Because the day that was in it, he felt he wouldn't have been able to hold back. Today, he would have targeted the car and let whoever was in it, have it. Today, he was in no mood to confront the people who did this to his sister. Today, he should have been celebrating Robyn's birthday.'

Chapter 5

There was no talk of the ceremony, or the body, or the people attending the funeral. They all sat in silence as they drove to the church, each gazing out of their window and watching Stem jeeps patrolling the area.

Stem had become even more brazen within the last week, taking people in broad daylight. The new drug didn't seem to have the desired effect they wanted. People were still able to dream. And as for the deaths this so call drug caused, they were just covered up and ignored as usual. They were too strong a force to be stopped. Nobody could go up against an army of soldiers.

~~~

Driving in past the church gates, Jenson could see a small gathering of people waiting over by the doors.

They continued in, swinging left to park up beside the church.

Jenson noticed Chloe walking towards them. He hadn't even opened the door when she edged up and stood right behind him. Her face was just like his mother's earlier in the house, red puffy eyes, swollen from her cries.

She just reached in and hugged him tight as he exited.

Jenson could then see Ellie and Callum walking slowly towards them, with Wardy and Henry trailing behind.

'Hey Jenson, how are you holding up?' Ellie asked as the others greeted each other.

'I'm okay.' Jenson replied, not knowing what else to say.

Callum, a man of few sentiments, had just lightly slapped Jenson's arm without even saying a word.

Jenson knew this was his way of acknowledging the sad occasion.

They all looked up one by one as they saw the men removing the coffin from the back of the hearse.

Jenson felt a drop of rain on his forehead as he looked up to the darkening sky. He took a deep breath and dipped his head. He hated funerals, especially when the body came. He couldn't look at it.

'The heavens are opening up,' his mother stated, coming over and linking her son's arm.

This intrigued Jenson. His mother, the biggest atheist in the world, had never believed in a higher being, apart from the day of a funeral. She had always hoped that her last frantic efforts of worship would help convince any feeble soul the right of passage.

The skies began to open, flicking its unwanted residue down on top of the assembling crowd. And in one hurrying motion, everybody bundled over towards the church entrance to find some shelter from this sudden downpour.

The funeral director was ushering everybody to go inside the church. It was too wet and dangerous to be lifting a coffin. It was now left to the professionals.

'This is slightly bigger than our church,' Callum sarcastically commented as he entered the church.

Chloe jabbed her elbow into his ribcage. She figured this would grab his attention and prevent him from offering another inappropriate comment. She knew he always tried to combat awkward silence with 'off the cusp' humour. She did however agree with him. The churches interior was a cut above the one they had stayed in. He was right. It must have been at least twice the size, and with all its grandeur. It was beautiful!

It was a Catholic church, not that any of them could tell the difference, or even cared. It was decorated beautifully. Royal red carpet, with rows of dark wooden perpetual benches, veiled in white, and gold fabric designs at each end, all leading up to a three-tiered pulpit, a designed altar worthy of being the focal point of any church.

'Chloe?' Callum whispered, watching her continue up towards the front. He had no other choice but to follow. The advancing crowd, pushing forward, and making it difficult for him to stop.

Chloe knew Callum was uncomfortable. He never went near the top of the church for any ceremony. He always stayed down the back, especially considering how much he hated religion. Chloe wasn't far off him, but she figured as a mark of respect, she would reach as far up as she could without being too intrusive on the family. She did however gain a sense of enjoyment as she kept walking. Not trying to be happy on this sad occasion, but she knew this action would deliberately aggravate her brother. And five rows from the top, she shifted in alongside Ellie, Wardy and Henry, as her brother followed. They were now too close to the family for Callum to say anything inappropriate.

Now sheltered and standing in the rows, the crowd were waiting to be seated. A brief pause with an unwanted chit chatter was followed by the chiming of a bell. And everybody dropped in unison as singers in the choir stalls stood up and began to croon.

The religious hymn resonated beautifully around the church aesthetics when the coffin was brought in with the few brave heads turning around to see it.

Ellie stood there facing the front of the church. Funerals made her sad. Not that they made anyone happy, but they especially made her sad. It always caused her to relive her mother's passing. What she would give to have her back.

She took a second look at the priest as he came out from behind the altar. He was dressed in an ankle length white garment with a long narrow golden scarf-like cloth. He looked godly and virtuous, but this wasn't the reason she began to scrutinise him. He was a lot older than her, a clean-shaven face with mid-length brown and grey hair, falling perfectly at either side of his face. She recognised his face. And then it hit her. She knew him. The last time she had seen him he wasn't as groomed. He was in the hospital looking quite scrawny. He was unshaven and looked tired. It was 'Bill'. She couldn't remember his second name or even if he had given it to her, but she was certain. He was the older gentleman she had met in the hospital, the one who kept talking about his dying friend whilst Chloe was being chased by Payton White. It was definitely him.

She then remembered how rude she had been to him, especially considering he had just given his friend his last rites, a fellow churchgoer who he probably knew for years.

Bill's eyes caught her glare. She immediately panicked and tried to alter her observation. But maybe this was all in her head because Bill raised his arms and began his service, as if he had never seen her before.

'One of life's hardest battles is to lose somebody, no matter how young or how old they may be. I know some of you sitting here have lost your faith in God. I won't judge…. I have questioned my belief also, and not so long ago. But we must ask ourselves why? Why this person, God? A verse from Corinthians 5:6-8 states……..

.......So we are always of good courage. We know that while we are at home in the body we are away from the lord, for we walk by faith and not by sight. Yes, we are of good courage, and we would rather be away from the body and at home with the lord. So, I do believe God has a plan. And in him, we must trust.'

Ellie could feel the sincerity in his voice, for she knew he had just lost somebody he loved also. This was the first time she attended church in years. And for the first time, she willingly sat back and listened to the whole sermon, taking in every single word.

Chapter 6

'That was lovely, wasn't it?' Chloe said, sweeping the tears from her eyes.
'Yes, it was,' Ellie replied. Her gaze lingering ahead.
'You okay? You do know it's over?'
'Yes, sorry, I was miles away there.'
'Are you coming or what?' Callum prompted from the end of the aisle.
Chloe made a face. She looked at Ellie in embarrassment. Her brother's sudden and loud outburst was uncalled for.
'I am going to kill him when we get back home.'
'You all go on ahead,' Ellie retorted.
'You not gonna see Jenson before he goes off?'
'Yes. I'll follow you out. I just have to do something first.'

~~~

'There he is,' Callum acknowledged, now standing outside the church. Wardy and Henry had both disappeared into the gathering crowd. Each one having to go back to work.
Chloe followed her brother's direction and noticed Jenson standing alone. He didn't seem to be talking to anybody.
They immediately poked through the emerging crowd to go speak to him.

'That was a beautiful service, wasn't it?' Chloe remarked as she approached him.

Jenson just nodded with a reluctant smile. Not wanting to smile but agreeing with Chloe as it was a heartfelt and touching sermon.

'Where are your folks?' Callum asked.

'They're over with some friends of theirs.'

'It's just as well the rain stopped,' Chloe remarked, looking up at the sky.

She instantly felt gawky, as if sounding stupid that she had nothing else to speak about other than the weather.

Chloe had her head in the clouds and Callum had his dangling down facing the ground, neither one knowing the right thing to say.

Jenson could sense this, so he began to talk, filling in that awkward silence.

'How are you both? Are you able to dream safely?' Now, finally a question they could work with.

'Not really.' Chloe replied. 'We've just been careful going to sleep together. We stay with each other 'til we wake. We haven't had any trouble since that night, so fingers crossed everything is okay.'

'I don't know about you. But I am loving my sleep now. Not worrying about you stupidly running off and getting into trouble,' Callum added enthusiastically.

'It's been nearly two weeks since we had the last demon after us,' Chloe reported. 'So hopefully it stays like that. And it would be nice to know if Davrin is okay though,' she added sniping at her brother's comment.

'He's probably off relaxing on some beach somewhere, not a care in the world.' Callum stated, momentarily forgetting where he was.

'Jeeze Callum! How inconsiderate of you! After what we've just sat through.'

Callum knew instantly how horrible his words were. He knew what it was like to lose people close to him, for he had lost both parents and a sister. Chloe's response caused his face to turn a dark orange. His substituted comedy had well and truly fallen flat this time.

'So how are you holding up with everything Jenson?' Chloe asked.

'I'm okay. As well as can be expected I suppose. It's her birthday today. Robyn's ten today. We're going up to the hospital now after this. There's been no improvement. They still don't know what happened to her but at least she's alive.'

Chloe, now looking into Jenson's gloomy eyes.

'But there's still hope?' She encouraged. 'Like I mean, she can still pull through?'

'I know.' Jenson said. 'We've been told there is a chance she could come out of the coma, but it's been nearly two weeks now and nothing. No signs of improvement'. His dejected tone sounded as if his hope was diminishing.

'Well from what Robyn went through at Stem, I'm sure she's strong enough to get through this as well.' Callum declared. 'At least they found a heartbeat by the time you got home. But it must have been some scare.'

His sudden statement surprised Chloe. Her brother never really spoke in these situations, especially not like this. The sincerity in his voice. Perhaps this was his way of making up for his completely appalling comment, moments earlier.

'Thanks guys. It means a lot, especially being here at Margaret's funeral. It just makes you think what if? Anyway, I've got to go now. My mum and dad are waving me over. I brought her favourite teddy bear with me. I don't know why, but I just thought it would somehow help. We're all over the place. We should have been celebrating her birthday today.'

'I'm sure it's hard Jenson.' Chloe acknowledged. 'But I also think that having her big brother there, every day with her, is helping. I'm sure she'll love having her teddy beside her. I've heard when people are in coma's they're still aware of noises around them. Talk to her, tell her what you've brought.'

'Thanks Chloe. I'm sorry, but my dad's calling me over. Please tell Ellie I said goodbye. I'll drop in later, after the hospital. We can catch up properly.'

Jenson gave a reluctant smile. 'I'll see you both soon,' he said. And with that he disappeared through the assembled crowd.

'I feel really sorry for him,' Chloe said. Her face, trying to dissect the crowd, to see if she could still get a glimpse of him weaving in and out.

'What about Davrin?' Callum asked. 'I know it's bad what I said, I didn't mean it. And I know what's going on with Jenson and his sister is really bad, but here we are at his grandmother's funeral, and we don't even know where he is.'

'I know. It's terrible! He isn't even here for it. But he would have been caught if he had of made an appearance. There are Stem soldiers everywhere now. He probably doesn't even know Margaret's funeral is today.'

There was a silence between the pair. Each one stood there looking around at all the strangers chatting, all oblivious to what was really going on.

Chapter 7

Waiting for the small queue of admirers to disperse, Ellie sat there watching Bill shaking hands and enjoying simple conversation.

As each minute passed, she began to reconsider this meeting. Why was she hanging around waiting for this priest's attention when she barely knew him? She had only met him for a moment. It was brief encounter in the hospital, two weeks ago. And what did it matter? She would probably never see him again after this.
Even though she didn't know him personally, Ellie got the opinion that he was a good man. She somehow had a genuine concern for him. For what reason? She was unsure of. But she wanted to put her mind at rest and see how he was coping with the loss of his friend. She also felt guilty for how snappy she had been towards him. She just wanted to make amends and apologise. It was out of character for her.

Finally, the last person approached Bill. It was a stout middle-aged woman with short brown hair.
Ellie figured it was now or never. So, standing up from the bench and picking up her handbag, she began to side shuffle out of the aisle.
She saw the priest kiss the woman, a friend of Margaret's no doubt, because after Bill had kissed her on the cheek, his facial expression changed. A sadness took over from his contented profile. And his words backed these actions up.

'I'm so sorry, I know you two were really close.'
And just as their conversation ended, Bill proceeded up the steps of the altar.

Ellie took her chance. Stepping out of the aisle and approaching the altar, she smiled as she brushed past the last remaining churchgoer. But this stranger's reaction startled her. The woman looked as if she was eyeballing her. She seemed to be quietly observing her, watching her in detail. Ellie quickly realised this but didn't understand why it was happening. She was always good at remembering a face, and this was certainly a face she had never seen before.

Unknowns to Ellie, this woman turned back round to peer at her from behind, only seeing her long wavy red hair. Still looking somewhat perplexed, the woman turned back towards the church doors and exited as Ellie began to move up the altar steps.

'Excuse me, I'm sorry to disturb you. I don't know if you remember me, but I met you at the hospital a few weeks ago,' Ellie said. 'I was the brutish woman.'

'Ah yes,' the priest said, turning round and recognising her. 'I noticed you at the beginning of the sermon.'

Ellie's smile slightly dropped. She realised he had caught her staring up at him before the mass.

'I'm sorry, it was Bill, wasn't it?' She asked, looking uncertain, but hoping she could replace this awkwardness and move on.

'Yes,' Bill said nodding. 'I'm sorry, what was your name again?' he asked holding out his hand.

'It's Ellie. I never did properly introduce myself,' she said, reaching out her hand and shaking his.

Bills face suddenly displaced. His eyes began to bulge. He stood there observing her quietly, just as the woman had previously.

Ellie found this strange. After all, she didn't even know him that well. So, she simply brushed this aside and began to say what she had to say. An attempt to finish up so she could go and leave this all behind her.

'I know I was short with you in the hospital and I'm sorry for that. I was just wondering how you are after your friend's, well, you said he wasn't well at all?'

Ellie knew his friend was dying, and by now, he was probably dead and buried. She didn't want to come across insensitive again.

'Unfortunately, he didn't make it past the night,' Bill answered while curiously scanning the church interior. His eyes were not quite looking at Ellie's. His sudden fidgeting began to alarm her.

'I'm sorry but will you follow me please,' he quietly instructed. And without waiting for an answer, he started to walk over to the side of the church where the confession booths stood.

'I'm sorry, I don't understand?' Ellie asked, watching Bill, his response, seemingly frantic now.

'Please don't be alarmed,' he whispered, holding his hands out and waiting for her to follow. 'You need to follow me, please.'

Ellie was unsure. She didn't know what was going on. *Could she trust this man? What did he want with her?* Even though pockets of people stood outside the church with the last remaining choir member packing up, she felt a bit hesitant.

Bill continued walking over to the confession booths. Ellie reluctantly followed.

Three tall dark mahogany compartments stood aligned. All cold and quiet, a feature that evoked memories for Ellie. Memories of a tormented childhood resurfaced. The forced declarations her mother made her do, with a creepy old man on the other side listening through the disguised blackness of the box.

'Please step in while I get rid of everyone,' Bill instructed again.
He opened the right door, suggesting Ellie to enter. His tone a little aggressive now.

This rattled Ellie. *What am I doing?* She thought.

Ellie took another glance around. Seeing that there were still people inside the church, she felt it was okay to step inside. *But why did he want to get rid of them?*

'What is this all about?' She asked, cautiously stepping towards the opened door.
'Please,' Bill said. 'You can't do this out here in the open.'
'Do what?'
But Bill never replied.

Even though Ellie was a tad suspicious, she went with her gut instincts and hesitantly stepped inside.

Before shutting the door, Bill whispered in her ear.
'Lift up the confession hatch, there's somebody you need to speak to.'
And with that, he hurried over to get rid of the remaining people from inside the church.

Chapter 8

The confession box was blackened out with small holes overhead. Each hole allowing indirect rays of light in. With enough radiance to make out shapes, Ellie summoned the courage, knowing this time would be different. She was no longer the timid child she once was. Now seated on the small bench inside, she lifted her hand up and reached for the hatch.

Hesitant, she pulled it back, revealing a latticed opening. She was unable to make out who the occupant was in the other compartment, their shadow giving nothing away.

'Hello?' She whispered, trying to peer into the other confession box.

'Ellie…… is that you?' The voice echoed from the other side.

'Davrin?' She whispered.

Ellie's shock was concealed from the ambiance of it all. This experience had now somehow manifested a nervousness from a former time. The time she had been in one of these chambers, with strict instructions to whisper.

'Davin, is that you?'

'Yes.'

'Oh my god, Davrin! We've been worried sick about you. Where have you been?'

Unawares to Ellie, Davrin smiled. He didn't think he was capable of a smile today, not on the day he laid his grandmother to rest. But he longed for a familiar face, a person who knew exactly what had happened. He could

see her outline, divisions of her long red hair sectioned by the grille.
'It's good to see you,' he said.
'Davrin, I am so sorry about your Nan.'
Davrin went quiet.

Ellie could hear his soft whimpers. He was trying to collect himself but seemed to be finding it difficult. Ellie knew Margaret was like a mother to him, and she also knew how hard this must have been for him. She too had to attend her own mother's funeral when she was about his age. But she knew this must have been harder for him, experiencing it from the inside of a dark wooden box, hidden away like some sort of condemned creature.

'The others are outside, Davrin. We've all been worried. We didn't know if you went back to the little church to find us. Stem soldiers are everywhere now. They know who we are now and have been following us all for the past two weeks. But we don't know why because they haven't said anything to us. They just wait and watch.'
'It's because of what I did,' Davrin whispered.
'We figured it was something to do with you, but we didn't know for sure. But because of you, they no longer want Jenson and his family.'
Davrin was silent. He was taken aback. Ellie realised this from his sudden pause. She continued. She knew Davrin would have been clueless to the last two weeks. She needed to update him.
'Because of you we've been safe. Because of you, Jenson got his family back. But Robyn is in a coma. Something must have happened from all the testing. We're sorry we never found you. We didn't want to check the church too soon. We were being followed all the time. But Callum did manage to go back on his own, a few days

later, to see if you were there. But he said he found nothing.'

'I had nowhere else to go.' Davrin retaliated. 'I never went back there. The only place I knew that was safe, was here. Bill, the priest, he and my Nan were very close. This is…was my Nan's church. Bill looked after me and has kept me hidden since the night I ran away.'

Davrin began to whimper again. He was overwhelmed. Ellie wanted to jump out of the box and hug him, but she knew she couldn't. She didn't want to draw any attention to herself. Even though they were not directly followed by the Stem soldiers today, she knew they wouldn't have just left this day unmonitored. Especially since it was the day of Margaret's funeral, an important day that Davrin might have turned up for.

'I know you must be going through hell right now, but please know that we are all here for you. We want to help you.'

'Thanks,' Davrin muttered.

'We'll sort something out, leave it with me. I'll go talk to Bill now.'

Ellie slowly opened the confession box door. But just before she fully got out, she saw Bill at the end of the church talking to a man in a black suit.

She quickly became alarmed and climbed back in, sealing the door behind her, leaving just enough room to look out of the crack.

It looked as if Bill and the suited man were having a heated conversation.

Ellie couldn't quite hear what they were saying but she knew it looked bad.

'Ellie what's wrong?' Davrin asked. He noticed she hadn't left to go speak with Bill. He observed her hesitation, even from the inside of his darkened hole.

'I'm just waiting on Bill to get the last man out of the church.' Ellie answered.

But just then she let out a soft whimper. Her hand immediately shielding the volume. The suited man had just taken out a gun and smacked Bill on the side of the head with it.

'What is it?' Davrin whispered.

'Stay here! And be quiet.'

'Ellie, what is it?' Darvin repeated. He could see her peeping out through the little gap.

The suited man had already set off towards the aisle. Ellie soundlessly closed the confession door shut, unable to see anything now. A pitch of darkness concealed them again.

'Davrin, please don't make a sound but there's a man outside and he has just smacked Bill. He has a gun. I think he must be looking for you.'

Ellie quietly lifted her handbag and began rummaging inside, trying to grab anything sharp she could find.

She suddenly heard a faint scratching noise from inside the confession box.

'Davrin, what are you doing?' She whispered.

She lifted the hatch open again. She could see Davrin's silhouette for the first time. It was clearer now. He had removed the gauze netting from between the confession boxes. Now able to fit something through, Davrin held out his hand.

'Quick give me something! He'll open my door first.' He said, knowing that there were only three confession boxes, Ellie's one, his one and an empty one beside his, the nearest one to the main doors.

Suddenly the first confession box opened abruptly.

Chapter 9

'Hello' the nurse said, leaving the door open and allowing them to enter Robyn's room.

Jenson stood there in the hospital corridor, delaying his own entrance as his parents went in first. He was watching her from the doorway. Her chest compressing softly with the aid of the machine. Her coma state body, unconscious to the world, as her mother gripped her hand in hers.

'Hi baby, it's your mother here…. and your dad……happy birthday! Jenson brought you a surprise.'

Jenson's mother looked over at him standing in the doorway. This was his cue to move.

'Hey Robyn,' he bellowed from the doorway, slowly stepping inside, and approaching her bedside. 'Happy birthday!' He continued, dropping the teddy onto the bed. 'I've brought Bobby with me, your favourite bear.'

'Do you remember Robyn?' His mother recalled, refixing the position of the bear. 'It's Bobby, your very first teddy bear we got you when you were born. The one with the t-shirt. It has a picture of us all on it.'

The family watched on in hope as they have been for several weeks now, in high spirits for any indication that Robyn would wake, even though these hopes now seemed to be dwindling.

A sudden knock on the door interrupted this family moment. And as it opened, the nurse returned with a man. The man was wearing a white coat and looked like a doctor.

'Hey, sorry to disturb you, but I have somebody here that would like to speak with you,' the nurse informed.

'Hello, my name is Dr. Richardson, Tom Richardson, and I work for Stem Industries,' the man said. His fingers began to awkwardly pinch his glasses upright.

This was in fact, the same Tom that had carried out the testing on Robyn after she was abducted from her home. Robyn's whole family immediately realised this because Robyn had mentioned him when she woke. They remembered her saying how he had treated her.

What was he doing here? They all thought.

'Thanks,' Robyn's father said, looking at the nurse and nodding at her. 'We'll take it from here,' he added, assuring her that they would like to talk to this man alone. The nurse exited the room, but the door remained open.

Jenson's father quickly scurried over and closed it behind her.

Tom looked a little apprehensive, but he was oblivious to the family knowing who he was.

'You must be John,' he said. 'And Sarah, I'm assuming. And of course, Jenson.'

He then retrieved a small notepad from the insides of his white coat. Flipping it open, he continued. 'I've been briefed about your daughter's situation and who you all are.' His eyes, glancing around the room as all three of them stared back. His focus then homed in on Robyn's unresponsive body.

They all pretty much knew this was the man involved, but not one of them had mentioned anything. They wanted to hear what he had to say first.

'I don't know if any of you are familiar with the work we do at Stem Industries, but I would like to try and help your daughter, perhaps run a few tests of my own… obviously with your permission of course.'

'So you can do more damage?' John angrily asked from against the closed door.

'I'm sorry, I'm not following.'

'You're the one that did this to her, aren't you?'
'John?' His wife called out. But Sarah knew it was too late. Anger had set in with her husband.
'I'm sorry, you must have me confused with someone else.'
Tom began to panic. His footing becoming unsteady. He began to step backwards towards the wall.

John pressed forward.
'How could you do something like this? She's only a child?'
'I'm sorry, you've mistaken me. I know Stem Industries has a bad reputation, but I assure you, I have nothing to do with that side of it. I heard of your daughter's symptoms, and I am just simply here to try and help her.'
'Look, just cut the bullshit!' John barked. He was now beside Tom. 'We know it was you. Robyn told us your name. She described you to us.'

John grabbed the front of Tom's white coat. He pinned him up against the wall. His reaction presenting more aggression now.
'John!' His wife cautioned again. But John wasn't listening.
'What did you want from her, huh? Did you get it? We know what Stem Industries do to people, so don't bullshit us again or I will…'
'JOHN! STOP! PLEASE!' Sarah called out.

The room door suddenly burst opened. The nurse rushed in.
'Is everything okay?' She asked.
'I was just leaving,' Tom said.
He brushed John's grip away from his coat and exited.

The silence was like an awkward commotion. Nobody wanted to answer the nurse. But as they all watched each other, Jenson quietly slipped out of the room.

~~~

Tom had just reached his car. He was oblivious to being followed. He switched off his alarm and opened the driver's door.

Just as he got in, the passenger door opened. Jenson climbed in.

'WHAT THE HELL?'

'I'm sorry. Please, I just need to talk to you for a second.'

Tom, realising who it was, began to calm down.

'Look, I told your parent's I don't know who they think I am but…'

'Please…we don't want any trouble. We just want answers.'

'As I've said…'

'Please…you don't have to lie. We're not going to do anything. There's nothing we could do anyway. I know what goes on in Stem, and we know about Payton White. He's your boss. You were just doing your job. Robyn told us about you.'

'I told you I don't know anything.'

'She said you were really nice to her. She said you gave her jellies.'

Jenson smiled. His niceness had somehow caught Tom off guard.

'Bu….but how do you know this? I figured she never woke up.

'She did wake up. She woke up after she was dropped back home from Stem. But then, when she went back to sleep that night, she never woke up again.'

Tom fell silent. He looked remorseful.

'I am so sorry,' he said. His stare now leaving Jenson and falling to his lap. 'I never meant for any of this to happen.'

He began to shake his head.

'I'm sure you didn't.' Jenson replied. 'But we just want her back. We want her to wake.'

'I'm sorry. I told them I needed more time. But they wouldn't listen. They just wanted to get her back.'

'It's okay.' Jenson said. 'You're not like them. We know that. You were only doing your job.'

'I have to go.' Tom declared. 'I shouldn't be here. If Mr. White finds out…'

'So Mr. White doesn't know you're here?'

'Look, will you please get out of my car.'

Jenson didn't want to push Tom any further. He opened the passenger door.

'Please,' he said. He stood there edging out from the side of the car. 'You seem like a decent man. A man who wants to do the right thing. I promise you this will go no further. I promise I won't say anything to my parents. I know they are angry now, but we all just want what's best for Robyn. We really do need your help.'

Jenson stepped out of the car and gently closed the door. He didn't know where this composure had come from. But he couldn't beg anymore.

Tom's car didn't move. A hurried deliberation set in. He rolled down his window.

'I'll call back to see Robyn after work…about nine tonight. But JUST YOU! I don't want your parents here. If they're here, I can't help you. Any sign of them knowing and I'm gone, okay?'

'Yes of course,' Jenson replied.

And with that Tom drove off.

Chapter 10

Robyn didn't know how long she had been walking around this obscure and murky forest. It felt like forever. The last thing she could remember was going to sleep in her bed, with Jenson beside her. The next thing she knew, she had woken up here in the jungle, alone.

Was she dreaming? Had she been drugged and put here, just like in Stem? This place was somewhere she had never been to before, a place she never imagined ever existed. *Could it be a place where dreams are made of?* She thought. *Was she dreaming? But if she was dreaming, then why was it never bright?* The sunlight never revealed itself, as if hiding its shiny identity, allowing the terror of the dark woodland to take over. A terror that only ever existed in nightmares. And because of this, she never screamed. She was afraid to scream. She was too scared to call out for help, to call out a name, just in case the wrong person was listening.

She eventually became camouflaged amongst the forest surroundings, falling and tumbling through the filthy jungle. Dirt and debris, sticking to every crevasse of her tiny torso. And sleepless nights, all spent tucked in some tree crack, filled with hidden smudge.

From time to time, she would hear noises, frightening and chilling noises. But she would always seek refuge in some hiding place, waiting there until the sounds faded, waiting until it was safe to step back out into the darkness.

Where was she? Had she done something so wrong to be put in such a harsh and ghastly place?

Her shoes were soaked. They were saturated from the dampness of the rooted vegetation. And her dress, covered in filth. She was cold, a bearable cold, but cold all the same. And a hunger, a hunger she had never ever experienced before. But she somehow never went to the extreme and admit defeat. She never quite trusted anything to eat. No poisonous apple ever enticed her. This was no fairy-tale. And the story of Snow White had already been told.

Suddenly, walking through another endless trail, she heard a noise. And becoming accustomed to taking cover, she buried herself amongst the fallen leaves, hiding herself under the dark skylight.

The steps were heavy and loud, so whatever it was, she figured it was big.

The noise, becoming closer now. She felt even the slightest of twitches would give her location away. She remained still.

She could feel whatever it was, had passed. But just when she thought it was clear, something bit down on her lower back. A small insect-like creature had latched on.

Startled, she grabbed the insect and pulled it away from her. She managed to bring it to her front.

Suddenly, she yelped. It was a wild spider, larger than her fist. Its skin, all briskly, with a mouth full of fangs. It was trying to sink its teeth into her again.

She immediately squeezed tight, crushing the spider's body, and squirting a dark blue substance all over her face.

Just then, she realised the footsteps were returning. Her invisibility had just been revealed.

Wiping her face to uncover the whites of her eyes; possibly the brightest thing in the forest, she was overcome by a heavy weight falling on top of her.

She let out a scream and began to wriggle from beneath, shuffling the dead weight off her.

She sat up. And there, set out as a trap, was a boy's lifeless body. It was thrown on top of her with the intentions to reveal herself. The boy's body, a few years younger than Robyn. His eyes open, with a lifeless limbo staring into nothing, lying there unconscious. He was dead. All life had been drained from his soul. And the dirt was already trying to absorb his tissue.

Looking up to see what had dropped this boy, she saw two giant tattered feet. Each one, leading into thick tree trunk legs and then a large body with a big grotesque face. It was some sort of a troll.

She screamed louder this time. And without wasting another moment, she quickly picked herself up and began to run as fast as she could. Her screams, enduring this chase as she maneuverer in and out of the bush.

'LITTLE GURRRL, YOU MINE,' the Troll shouted as it scampered after her.

No match for this 20ft Troll, as the tremors indicated its pursuit. And Robyn's efforts were cut short when it plucked her up in between its thumb and index finger.

'TWO FO DA PRICE O' ONE,' it said as it watched Robyn try to wriggle free.

Robyn suddenly noticed a flash of light in the distance. But dwindling in an upside-down position, and hanging from the troll's grasp, this distraction was short lived. In an instance it was gone. The realisation of being eaten had returned. She screamed.

The Troll walked back over to the dead body and scooped him up. It continued to scramble off to wherever it was going in the first place.

'PLEASE LET ME GO!' Robyn screamed.

'NO TALK GURL.' The troll said as it clashed the boy's body against Robyn's, knocking her out cold.

Eventually getting to its destination, the Troll entered a cave.

Taking a few turns and going down some scattered tunnels, it finally came to a stop.

A dirty room with a tabletop mounted on a large rock. And smaller boulders surrounded a big fire pit.

'I EAT YOU FIRST,' the Troll said, dropping Robyn on the 'larger than normal' sized table whilst he stuck a large twig through the boy's body. If he wasn't dead, he was now.

The Troll then slumped down on one of the small boulders. A shallow tremor made its way around the room as it began to twirl its prize over the fire pit, roasting the body for that crisp perfection.

Robyn gradually awoke. The smoky fumes combined with her light-headedness forced her to look deeper into this vague snapshot. But she didn't have to focus for long. She remembered what had taken her. She saw it now, the Troll, it was lifting the boy's body up like a roasted marshmallow on an open fire. Dropping him into its mouth just before it began to chew. The snapping crunch immediately brought chills to her body, a fate she knew was inevitable. Robyn understood she would be next. She could hear every bone break with every crunch. She was petrified!

Unexpectedly, she heard loud trudges coming towards them. Something else was coming.

Still lying there on the big table, afraid to move, she turned round to see what it was. Another Troll came crashing in.

'MINE!' This new Troll said. Its outstretched arm reaching in towards Robyn. It quickly snatched her up.

Then suddenly, the Troll was knocked over with a big punch from the other one.

'NO…..MINE!!!' The first Troll said after quickly swallowing the boy's crisp remains.

Both Trolls began to fight viciously, knocking the large table over onto its side.

This crash sent Robyn sliding down onto the cold surface.

She was hurt from the high fall but managed to get to her feet. A few cuts and bruises would not stop her. She knew she had to run. This distraction had opened a window of opportunity, and now, it was her only hope of escaping.

She didn't know how she had gotten into the cave, and she didn't know how to get out. But she knew one thing. She had to keep going to avoid becoming meal number two.

Chapter 11

'Where did you go?' Jenson's mother asked him as he stepped back into the hospital room.
'Sorry, I just had to make a phone call.'
'Your father is outside trying to explain himself for what just happened. We thought it was better if he went outside to cool off. Don't want a negative atmosphere in here with your sister.'

Jenson watched his mother turn her back. She leaned in and continued to brush Robyn's hair.
'I wonder what's going through her mind right now?' She asked. 'I hope she's at peace wherever she is.'
Jenson knew he didn't need to answer this question. They both had never dreamt before, so to him, Robyn's mind was in a dark and tranquil state. Her receptors receiving adequate signals to stay alive but not enough to function properly. He believed she was at ease.
'She looks peaceful, doesn't she?' His mother added. Jenson nodded. He agreed.
But just as he made his way over, he came crashing down against the overbed table, hanging onto its edge.

'Jenson?' His mother called out.

Jenson paused for a moment. His sudden movement had caused him to lose his balance. He gripped onto the table, trying to steady himself. He didn't want his mother to panic. He meticulously tried to play it off.
'Ah it's nothing. I haven't been sleeping well. I just keep worrying about Robyn.'

His mother looked suspicious. Jenson could feel her eyes studying him.

'Are you hot?' Jenson asked, deflecting any further uncertainty. 'I'm hot. Do you mind if I open a window?'

'Jenson sit down. Please tell me what is going on?' His mother demanded. Her eyes throwing him a look of doubt. She didn't quite believe him.

'There's nothing wrong. I just got a little lightheaded. It's very warm in here.'

'Please Jenson. Don't shut me out. I nearly lost one child. Do you think I want to go through that again? I'm your mother, I know when there's something up. Now tell me what's wrong?'

'There's nothing, I'm just hot.'

But then another shooting sting rippled across Jenson's forehead. This caused him to jerk again. He let out a little grunt. He had no warning sign this time. Another migraine had just developed out of nowhere.

His headaches had eased with only a handful of attacks in the last week, but the attacks were greater now. Unable to hide this one convincingly, he carried on over towards the window, as if nothing had happened.

And then it hit his mother. She had suddenly realised what was wrong.

'Oh Jenson, I'm so sorry, it's those headaches again, isn't it? I forgot to get you your tablets. With everything going on, I just completely forgot. I'll make a call right away. And when we finish up here with your sister, we'll go straight there to get you your tablets.'

And off she went, charging outside the room to make the phone call.

Jenson didn't want to argue with his mother. He had tried his best to hide the headaches over the past few weeks. It was a burden he felt his mother didn't need. But he knew he needed this medication. And he was a little relieved that the migraines could soon come to an end.

    He walked over and sat down in the same seat his mother had gotten up from. He looked straight at Robyn. Her eyes were shut with tubes hanging from her mouth. He knew the tubes were keeping her alive. He was grateful of that. But remorse soon set in. He was back here again, the guilt plaguing every bone in his body. The same scenario, with the same outcome. If only he had protected her like a big brother should.

    'Robyn,' he said, his hand gripping hers tightly. 'If you can hear me at all, please wake up!'

Chapter 12

Robyn didn't know if she was in a cave or not, but wherever it was, she could feel the hot air rise, bringing with it, a cold draft. This coolness was a sign. It was a sign she was heading for the exit. She knew she had to keep going.

After a few turns and sudden guesses, the tunnels opened-up ahead.

The fighting tremors from the Trolls had suddenly stopped. But now came an earthquake. Trudging steps from the victorious Troll, running after her to get its winning prize.

Just about to reach the opening, Robyn was snatched up in the air.

'I CAUGHT YOU…YOU MINE.' The original Troll said.

It suspended Robyn's body, hanging her out in front, observing her as if inspecting its next meal. Satisfied, it lowered her quickly before she could escape again.

Robyn was hysterical. Her screams were mounting at the top of her lungs, but nobody was listening.

With a sudden stroke of luck, just as the Troll placed Robyn onto its slimy tongue, concealing her inside, the other Troll came charging out of the cave. It smashed into the back of the Troll, sending it plummeting to the ground.

As it hit the floor, its jaw smashed open.
Robyn somersaulted out. Submerged in a mouthful of thick gloop, she rolled along the rocky terrain.

'MINE!' The Troll said.

But just as it was about to lift the saliva drenched Robyn, the original Troll hooked its giant hand around its foot, sending it stumbling into a tree.

The ground shook again. The vibrations had sent a murmur throughout, shaking Robyn, and causing her whole head to spin. And in one last ditch effort, she quickly balanced herself.

She ran with whatever little strength she had. She could feel the pain from the cuts and bruises on her fragile body. And her legs began to weigh her down. But she kept moving.

'Psst!'
A noise sounded.
'Psst!'
There it was again.

Robyn looked over. She couldn't see anything. Her legs were churning like a pinwheel, but her head, tilting to identify the source.

A subtle glow emitted from a dark hole.

'Over here,' a girl's voice called out. It was low, but detectable over the commotion behind. And whatever it was, it was gesturing for Robyn to come towards it. And there it was, in a crack in one of the trees.

Robyn didn't know what it was. It sounded like a girl's voice, and seemingly a lot friendlier than the Trolls. She knew it was safer than where she had come from. So, she immediately changed her course and charged over to follow the flickering light.

'This way…come on, hurry,' the voice sounded again.

As Robyn continued to run, a pair of hands reached out from an opening in the tree trunk and snatched her inside.

'Hold on,' the voice whispered.

Robyn had no other choice. She quickly elevated up from the ground. And with the fluttering of what sounded like wings, they began to whizz upwards through the hole inside the tree trunk.
The tree then instantly began to tremble.

'HOLD ON!' The stranger repeated. It was her last warning before they darted up and strategically flew out through a small opening.

They must have been about 40 feet off the ground when Robyn tilted her head down. She could see one of the Trolls recklessly break the tree.
'MIIIIIIIIIIINE!' It shouted, looking up at the glowing light darting off into the sky.

Robyn began to cry. Having time now to assess the situation, she whaled. It was the first time since being here she was able to let it all out. She was unable to distinguish if they were tears of joy for being saved, or tears of terror for what had just happened. But she was lucky to be alive.
'Please don't cry,' the voice said.

When it was safe to do so, the creature slowed up and settled down, landing on the highest branch of a huge tree. They must have been 100 feet in the air.
Robyn's cry continued.
'Please, I mean you no harm,' the voice echoed from high above the treetops.
But Robyn wouldn't stop. She couldn't stop. She was overcome with emotion.

'Please,' the voice said again, pleading for a third time now. Holding onto Robyn's arms and gently shaking her, she continued. 'My name is Myral, what's yours?'

Robyn, still crying, gradually lifted her face to look at her rescuer. She only then noticed that this girl was some sort of a fairy, standing across from her with her big blue eyes. And her beautiful long dark hair, flowing in the breeze, unmasking her protruding elf ears.
'Who are you?' She asked.
'I'm Myral.'

Perched on one of the tallest points in the forest, the sun, now capable of shining, and casting a glow. An orangey red colour shone bright, illuminating Myral's grey skin. But shaped like a semi-circle, it only allowed one side of her body to shimmer. The other side was lost, concealed within the darkened twilight. And her wings, the purest of blue with the flaming sun hitting the forewing at just the right tip, causing the purple veins within to reach out and glisten in its warmth.

'What are you?' Robyn said.
'My name is Myral. I'm a tooth fairy. What's your name?'
'I'm Robyn.'

Robyn's cries had faded now. A total bewilderment took over. She was fascinated. She stood there, watching her. She then turned to face the sun, absorbing its heat, allowing the rays to penetrate her face. She closed her eyes. It was something she never thought she would feel again.
'Are you okay?' Myral asked.
'Yes. I think so. I haven't seen the sun since I got here.'

Myral looked away, now gazing at the semi-circle of light.
'You were deep in the Lost Forest,' she declared. Her gaze returning. Her blue eyes leering at Robyn, and then she twigged it. 'I've seen you before.'

Robyn returned her stare, unable to find the answer.

'I know you,' Myral repeated. 'Yes, I've seen you before. I saw you not so long ago. I never forget a face. You're his sister. I saw you asleep beside him in the bed. How could I forget that night?'

'Jenson?' Robyn suggested. She didn't know who else it could be.

'Yes, that's his name.'

'Is he okay?' Robyn asked.

'I do not know.'

'Can you take me to him?'

'I'm afraid not. You must wake up from this dream.'

'I'm in a dream? But I don't dream. I'm like Jenson.'

'But you are here now?' Myral confirmed. She looked confused.

And with that, a loud bang resonated. It was far away, but they could both hear it. It's muted roar sourcing a tremor and causing the leaves of the tree to shake.

'When two worlds collide, a human boy can save us all!' Myral declared.

'I don't understand?' Robyn asked.

'Your brother, he can save our Worlds.'

'How?'

'I'm not sure.'

'Where is he?' Robyn asked.

'Why he is in the human world of course.'

'Where am I then?'

'If you are like Jenson, something is wrong. How did you get here?'

'I don't know. I just woke up here. Where am I?'

'You are in the Land of Dreams.'

'I'm dreaming?'

'Yes….I believe so. But I don't know how you got here. If you say you are a Non-dreamer, then you shouldn't be here. And this is the Lost Forest. Humans do not reach the Lost Forest.'

'But I can't dream. Where is my family?'

Robyn appeared too broken to bear this revelation. What felt like an eternity of questioning, cross-examining every last step before coming here, she couldn't find an answer. Trapsing through the forest alone and wondering what she had done, so bad, to deserve this punishment. But now the answers had come to light. A light, awakening now from a darkened spell within the forest. All she wanted to do was to go home.

'Please don't be upset.' Myral encouraged. She could see the panic in her eyes.

'But I don't want to be here.'

Their conversation halted as another tremor rattled the treetops. The leaves now circling the two girls. And vibrations lasting longer this time. Myral couldn't risk being here anymore.

'We need to go. This is no place you want to be in for too long. I'm going to get into trouble for this, but you need to come with me.'

'Where are you taking me?'

'To my home,' Myral answered. Her hand swatting the spiralling leaves away from her pastel pixie dress.

'Can't I just go back home instead?'

'It's not that easy. Only you can get home.'

'But how?'

'I don't know. I cannot leave you here. You will not survive much longer in a place like this. My father will know what to do. Hold on!'

And just like before, Myral took hold of Robyn. The humming of her wings resonated, preparing for the ascent.

Chapter 13

Davrin clutched onto Ellie's car keys. He jumped out of the confession box as soon as the door opened. He instinctively stabbed the biggest key into the suited man's neck, falling on top of him as the two of them crashed to the ground.

Davrin wasn't much of a fighter. And even though blood oozed from his opponent's neck, the wounded man was able to get the better of him. Luck favoured Davrin as the gun fell. But a struggle pursued.

The stranger had managed to kneel on top of Davrin now, reaching for his gun. But just before he could grab it, another bit of luck enfolded.

Ellie flung her door open. She smashed the corner of it into the stranger's head. Her resurface had proved eminent.

A weighted body fell on top of Davrin. But Davrin quickly wriggled his limbs, whooshing it to the side. And watching the stillness of the unconscious frame next to him, he immediately began to move.

'Quick Davrin, come on!' Ellie said, helping him up off the ground.

But just as they started to run off, a loud bang echoed around the church.

~~~

'Did you hear that?' Chloe asked as they stood amongst the sojourned crowd outside the church.

'Yeah, it sounded like a gun shot, from inside the church.'
Chloe gasped. 'Ellie's in there.'

Both Callum and Chloe immediately ran through the startled onlookers, over towards the church front doors.

Callum getting there first, pushed in at the doors.
'Shit, they're locked. Come on!'
And with that, they both ran around the side of the church.

~~~

'The gun?' Ellie bellowed, crouching down in between the church benches. She had suggested they get the man's gun, the man they had knocked unconscious.
'Can you see him?' Davrin whispered, now looking under the row of benches. He was trying to identify where this second man was.
Ellie inched her head up and saw another suited man, a bald, larger man over at the church entrance, over where Bill had been struck in the head.
It was George, Mr White's first in command. He was pointing a gun in their direction. He had just fired the first shot.

'He's coming!' Ellie gasped.
'Stay here, I'll get the gun,' Davrin suggested. 'Here take these,' he added, handing Ellie back her car keys, the blood marks staining the tips.
Ellie secured the keys in her grasp as Davrin crawled away.

'I knew you'd show your face eventually Davrin. We don't want to hurt you,' George explained. His voice resonating up the aisle as he came walking through the centre. 'But if we have to hurt you, we will. I'd advise you both to come quietly.'

Ellie was scared. She froze. Hunched down, she didn't know what to do. But she knew he was approaching. She had to move.

She quickly began to crawl back to the end of the bench. But just as she did, George had reached the other side.

'Stop there or I'll shoot!' He demanded.
Ellie stopped. She slowly turned around.

George had now reached the other end of the aisle. He began to walk between the benches, aiming his gun directly at her, and getting closer.

'Get up!' He ordered.
Ellie held her hands in the air, slowly getting to her feet.

'Where is he?' George asked.
'Who?'
George shot another bullet in Ellie's direction, deliberately missing.

Ellie leapt. She instinctively closed her eyes.

'I'm not stupid, I saw him. Next time I won't miss. I'll ask again. Where is he?'

Just as he reached Ellie, his gun still pointing at her, another shot was fired. This time it was from Davrin. The bullet grazing George's suit jacket.

George immediately took cover, dropping to the ground and grabbing Ellie with him.

Ellie screamed.

Davrin panicked. He crouched down, trying to see where they had gone.

Within moments George revealed himself. He appeared again, this time shielding Ellie out in front. His gun abrasively pressing into the side of her head. Ellie looked in pain. The barrel of the pistol digging deep into her temple.

'Put it down boy or else she gets it.' George demanded.

Davrin didn't know what to do. He hesitated. But he knew he had to act fast, otherwise Ellie would be shot.

'Are you going to kill us?' He questioned, raising his head slightly up above the top of the bench.

'Not if you co-operate.'

Davrin could see the fear in Ellie's eyes. Her stiff body, static now as George forced her out of the aisle.

'Do you want to see your mother again?' He asked. This surprised Davrin.

'My….my mother?' He questioned. He was startled by how this man knew her. He seemed to know everything about him.

'Yes, do you not know we have her? She's been with us for a while now. We need you to come in and have some tests done. You can be together.'

'I know what happens to people in Stem.' Davrin declared.

'Well then you'll know the progress your mother has been making.'

Davrin was completely shocked. *Had his mother become well again? Or was this a trick to get him in to Stem?*

'We just want to help,' George declared. 'It'll only take a short while. And I promise you, you and your mother can go home safely after we're done.'

'I DON'T BELIEVE YOU!' Davrin shouted. 'I thought there was a cure already?'

'That didn't go to plan There is something new now. We've nearly completed a different type of cure that will help. We won't harm you. You have my word.'

'What about my Nan? Did you say that to her before you killed her?'

George pulled back the hammer of the gun. The clicking sound resonated as he forced the gun fiercely into Ellie's temple.

'You wanna be smart right now?

'No, please!' Davrin begged.

'I've called for back-up. There's no point in trying to get out of this. Either you put the gun down and cooperate, or else Ellie gets it. That is your name isn't it, Ellie? We've been keeping close tabs on you all.'

Ellie knew they had been watching them all. But the sheer mention of her name had made her panic even more.

'Okay okay,' Darvin said, agreeing to his demand. 'But please don't hurt her.'

Davrin gently placed the gun down on the bench seat. He held both hands out in front, slowly backing away.

'You're a smart kid, now start coming towards me.' George instructed.

Just as Davrin had reached them, George smashed the gun into Ellie's head, knocking her to the ground. He quickly grabbed Davrin, and spinning him round, he wrapped his arm around his neck, securing him tightly. He then pressed the gun up to his head, just as he had Ellie's.

'This way,' he said, bringing Davrin up towards the altar to leave out the back exit.

Davrin had stepped out first, out through the door behind the altar, the door leading into the back room. But just as he did, he noticed a shadow to his left.

This shadow was Callum. Callum had edged his way back in against the partitioned wall, waiting there. His hands clenching onto a golden chalice.

Callum gave a hushing signal as one finger touched his lips.

Instinctively, Davrin played along. And George was too quick ushering him out to react. He fell straight into the trap.

As soon as they stepped out, Callum swung down as hard as he could. He smacked George in the head with the chalice, causing him to crash to the ground.

And without any further hesitation, Callum smashed down again.

'Callum, STOP!' Chloe called out, standing on the opposite side of the doorway. 'You're going to kill him.'

Callum paused.

'Do you not think he wouldn't kill us, given half the chance?'

Callum adjusted himself. He was reluctant to stop. But his sister's words were stronger than any urge. He raised the chalice, blood dripping from one corner.

'DAVRIN?' Chloe said, revealing her shock. This was the first time she had seen him since his disappearance. 'Where's Ellie?'

'DAVRIN?' She called out again.

Davrin was incoherent. He seemed fixated on George's body. The blood, the chaos, it was all starting back up again. This nightmare was never going to end.

'Davrin, can you hear me?' Chloe asked, taking a firm hold of his arm.

'Yes?'

'Ellie? Where's Ellie?'

'She's inside.'

'Here,' Callum said, handing the chalice over to Davrin. 'If he moves again, hit him.' And off he went, running with Chloe to get further inside the church.

Seconds merged into minutes, each one feeling longer than the last. And what felt like an eternity, standing over the body, Davrin just watched on silently. He couldn't tell if the body was breathing. But within minutes, Callum and Chloe had returned, both at either side of Ellie, helping to prop her up.

Davrin could see how unsteady she was. Her legs, sluggishly following her body. Her balance wavering with every step.

'Are you okay Davrin?' Ellie asked.

Davrin could see she was trying to steady herself.

'Yeah, are you?'

'Yes, I'll be fine. We need to get out of here. That man said he rang for back up.'

'What about Bill?' Davrin said.

'Who's Bill?' Callum declared.

'He's the priest. He's a friend of my Nan's. He helped me.'

'Okay, you all go on ahead. I'll go back and get him. I'll meet you back at yours Ellie.'

'No Callum, they know who we are. We need to go now. We need to go into hiding. We can meet back at the church. They don't know about that.'

'Okay. Well take these.' Callum said, handing his sister the guns he had retrieved.

'Are you sure Callum?' Chloe asked.

'Yes of course, my bike is outside. Now go on and get out of here, hurry.'

And without further delay, Callum dashed back into the church.

Chapter 14

Ellie drove the car out beyond the church gates. She was trying to act inconspicuous, but her panic had taken over. Her usual consistent care had developed into a sporadic charge. She was unable to watch the road carefully. And just as she exited the church gates, something smashed into the rear side of her car, sending them spinning out of control.

Beyond the screams and panic, the car stopped. Chloe looked back to see what had hit them. It was a Stem Industries jeep. Its black exterior had crept up on them like some sort of jungle cat. George must have given detail on the target when he called it in. And now, a handful of soldiers began to emerge from the broken vehicle. The driver had swerved and crashed into the church railings. George's back-up had arrived, just as he intended.

The soldiers were revealing themselves like a unified zombie mob. Their reactions were slow. An indication that their jeep had taken an equal share of the collision.

'Are you two alright?' Ellie asked. Her engine looked busted as steam began to evaporate from the bonnet.
'I think so.' Chloe answered, tilting her body, and twisting her head around even more so. She could see the Stem soldier's approaching. 'Ellie, we need to go now. They're coming!'

'Shit shit shit! 'Ellie gasped. Giving a quick glance into her rear-view mirror, she could see them coming. 'Shit shit shit!' she repeated.

She was desperately trying to start the engine up. Her hand flicking hard against the ignition as her foot began to kick down on the clutch. But it was of no use. The gruelling sounds proved how busted the car was.

Davrin sat there looking straight ahead. He seemed unhinged. His back, shielding him from any commotion without even a flicker of an eyelid. He looked unharmed, but the shock had frozen any instinct to react. His mind had alienated every limb.

'DAVRIN? DAVRIN?'

Chloe's voice called out. She wanted him to move. She needed him to move. And in one sudden charge, she slapped him across the face.

This sent vibrations coursing through his veins. His body suddenly reacting. And unlike the car that was never going to move, Davrin had just revved up his own engine.

'HERE QUICK!' Chloe said.
'What?'
'I SAID QUICK, TAKE THIS!' she instructed further.
'What is it?'
'WHAT DO YOU THINK IT IS? IT'S A GUN!'
'What do I do with it?'
'YOU SHOOT IT!'

Chapter 15

Jenson got out of the back seat and shut the door. The sign 'Harpers Herbal Healing' hanging over the front of the shop stuck out like a sore thumb. The lettering seemed faded. Its big bold writing tarnished and taking with it any sign of glory.

As Jenson approached further, he took more detail in. He noticed the rusted chains hanging from each corner of the sign. And a dirty coating throughout. It must have been hanging there for quite some time, enduring the intensity of every storm. The small complex seemed old and rundown. A shop space below with the living quarters above, and all the windows were tainted from the dusty breeze. Autumn's rage carrying in a drifting residue, encasing the whole property like a gritty shell.

Sweeping the gravel from beneath his feet and following his parents over towards the entrance, Jenson couldn't help but consider the reason why they had used such a poor looking emporium. A shop like this, hidden off the beaten track, and abandoned in some remote isolation. *Could it be because of the illicit dealings? Had this tattered shop been the only place to help with his migraines as a child, granting him the help and protection he needed without the risk of Stem finding out?*

A light jangle noise sounded as the shop door opened. They stepped inside.

'Sorry I'll be with you in a second,' a deep male voice pronounced from somewhere within the shop.

Jenson glanced around looking at all the glass jars and bottles, the type of containers you would see in a mystical potion shop from some wizardry movie.

'Hello.' The voice said. 'Sorry about that. How may I help you?'
A tall black man stood up from the counter, holding a dark glass bottle.

'Hi Sterling.'
'Oh Sarah, hello, apologies. I didn't realise it was you.'

This friendly welcome seemed more than a formality. The monthly visits over the years to restock Jenson's medication showed visible signs of a friendship.

'It's quite alright,' Sarah answered. 'I'm not sure if you remember my husband?'
'Hello Sir,' Sterling exclaimed.
'Hello,' John replied, walking over, and shaking his hand.
'Oh, and this is my son, you definitely won't remember him.' Sarah claimed. 'He was so young the last time he was here.'
'Yes, that's right. I think he was scared of me, if I recall. The big chocolate man he kept saying.'
A humoured smile now appearing on Sterling's face.

Sarah began to smile back. She remembered how scared Jenson was of 'the big chocolate man' when they had first come to visit the shop. A child's innocent insult flattened from the start. The embarrassment had stained her thought of ever bringing him again.

'JENSON? She called out, her eyes in search of her son.

Huddled in some dark corner, Jenson turned around. A glass jar in his hand as his eyes remained fascinated with the contents. His curious exploration had caused him to wonder. Even though the shop seemed in ruins, it was something of a spectacle. It reminded him of an Apothecary in Diagon Alley, something Harry Potter would have stumbled across, only these potions were more of a 'Muggle' fit.

'Hey,' Jenson greeted.
He carefully placed down the bottle and began to walk over. His aversion to this 'friendly giant' had all but vanished, something he had forgotten a long time ago.

Sarah looked back at Sterling, noticing he had a certain stumped look on his face. He seemed to be waiting for Jenson to appear out from the shelving.

'Are you okay Sterling?' She asked.
'Yes, sorry.' He said, hesitantly. 'I just can't believe how grown up he is now.'

Sterling had forgotten about this boy, only now, retracing the missing memory. A story that had disappeared many years back, just like the shop's clientele. The name Jenson had startled him. He had always dealt with Jenson's mother, using her name 'Sarah Rose' as an alias to hide Jenson from the truth.

That light jangle noise sounded again as the shop door opened once more.

'Hey dad, sorry I'm late. I just had to…,' and with that his daughter looked up. She froze. She stood there in her school uniform, staring across at Jenson.

A detachment loomed as Jenson and his parents looked at this girl. Her sudden stiffness brought with it an awkward silence, a silence that caused them all to stare even harder.

'Hey Gracie,' her father said, interrupting this fixation. 'You go on through and get changed, and then come out when you're ready.'

Grace recovered composure. Her father's words had provoked an understanding. She began to shuffle across the shop floor. A nervous condition showing in her absent response. Her hands squeezing firmly around the straps of her schoolbag and her eyeline purposely avoiding Jenson's glare. And soon, she vanished into the back of the store just as quick as she had entered.

'You'll have to excuse my daughter,' Sterling said. 'We're not used to having people in the shop anymore. Stem frightened everyone away. People are too scared to come.'
'She looks sweet.' Sarah replied.
'That's Grace, she's my eldest. Now what can I do for you?'
'Yes, sorry. I completely forgot to get this month's supply of tablets, the one's for my son's headaches?'
'Yes, I should have them. Let me just double check your file, I'm not with it today.'

Sterling stepped into the back, dipping his head down past the doorway.

Grace stood there waiting. She was nestled in behind the shop partition.
'Dad?' She whispered.
'Not now Grace!'
'But dad. That's the boy in my dream. That's Jenson!'
'Shhh. Just go upstairs and get changed. We'll talk about this when they leave.'

Chapter 16

A white run-down campervan came bursting out of the church grounds. And driving like a manic mad man, the driver drilled the van straight into the two soldiers who were nearest to Ellie's car. It sent them flying into the air like two skittle pegs, the impact, making sure they would not return anytime soon.

It then swung round to the side of Ellie's car just as the other soldiers began to fire.

The campervan somehow strategically angled itself towards Ellie's car. The soldiers, now having difficulty in finding their intended targets, and each bullet spraying against the side of the aluminium structure.

'QUICK, GET IN!' A woman's voice called out.

Ellie recognised this woman immediately. It was the woman from the church, the one who had exchanged a brief stare at her just before she had spoken to Bill.

'COME ON!' Davrin instructed, jumping out of Ellie's car and running over to the campervan. He quickly adjusted the side door, as if knowing what to do.

Ellie and Chloe didn't ask questions. They both hopped out of the car and followed Davrin's lead. He stood there holding the side door of the camper van open.

Just as they reached him, the sound of a shot fired. Davrin let out a loud groan, dropping to the ground.

Chloe quickly turned round seeing a soldier at the end of the camper van. His gun, pointing straight at Davrin.

She immediately raised her gun. And without thinking, she fired, hitting him in the chest. The soldier immediately fell to the ground.

The smoke from the barrel carried a fright with the recoil as it washed over Chloe's face. She couldn't believe she had just shot someone.

Ellie grabbed her and pushed her into the campervan. She then picked Davrin up and did the same.

'GO GO GO!' She screamed.

All safe inside the campervan, and without any delay, the accelerator roared. The small woman in the front pressed down hard on the pedal, the wheels skidding as she swerved away into the dispersing traffic.

Ellie looked back to see the soldiers in the distance. Luckily, their Jeep appeared to have received the same fate as her car, and a pursuit, unlikely.

'Thank you so much!' Ellie said, reaching in and holding the headrest of this woman's seat.

'Don't thank me. You're lucky my husband isn't alive? He'd kill us all if he could see those holes in his camper!'

Ellie then turned round. She could see Davrin holding onto his shoulder. He had just been shot. She needed to examine the wound.

'Davrin are you alright?' She asked, noticing the blood staining his shoulder and hand. 'It looks like a lot of blood.'

Davrin didn't know what to say.

Ellie forced herself upon him. She removed his hand to establish how serious the gunshot was.

'I see they've upgraded to real guns.' The woman said.
'We need to get him to a hospital.' Ellie advised.
'Ah it doesn't look too bad. Just keep pressure on it and I'll look at it when we get home.'
'No offence, but I think he needs a doctor. Can you please take us to the hospital?'
'You don't think they'll check the hospital?'

This strange woman seemed one step ahead of Ellie. Her question implying further instruction.
Ellie didn't respond. She seemed out of her dept. *'Perhaps this out of shape, retired G.I. Jane knew what she was doing?'* she thought. But she was in no position to challenge. Her blank retaliation had no other choice but to turn around and see how Chloe was.
But Chloe looked dazed. She was staring down at the gun. It was placed neatly on her lap.

'Are you okay Chloe?' Ellie asked. She knew she had just shot a soldier.
The repercussions were trying to sink in. But it wasn't the gunshot Chloe was worried about. If a troop of soldiers had arrived at the scene, what were they going for next, and who?
'Callum?' she called out softly.
'I'm sorry Chloe, we can't go back.'

Ellie looked over her shoulder. The Stem soldiers had all vanished into the church grounds. The possibility of Callum getting away was slim. She just hoped he had escaped in time.

Chapter 17

The skies began to pour as they drove away from the city in the campervan full of holes. The stretched motorway beginning to become congested. The squelching window wipers were going that fast, their fluent motions were obliterating any raindrops falling onto the windscreen.

'We're lucky this heavy rain is cloaking all the bullet holes along the side,' the woman expressed.

Ellie could see her smiling through the rear-view mirror. Her amusement with all of this was baffling. She seemed to be enjoying it. *How could she be so calm?*
'Why did you help us back there?' She asked.
'It was my godly duty!' The woman answered, with a light chuckle.
'Who are you?'
'How rude of me. I never introduced myself. Its Tessa. Tessa Limes….as in the fruit. But nobody likes to eat limes, do they? And nobody wants to eat me, so that's another thing we have in common.'
Again, this behaviour seemed to baffle Ellie, especially when she had a bleeding passenger in her campervan.
'Please to meet you Tessa, I'm….'
'Yeah yeah I know. You're Ellie. I thought it was you back in the church. And you must be Chloe.'

Ellie was taken aback, but still managed to extend her arm and place it on top of Tessa's shoulder.
'And this is….'

'Yeah yeah, I know Dav. Me and Dav go way back. I am……well, I was a good friend of Margaret's.'

Davrin didn't say a word. He just sat there pressing the dirty rag hard against his gunshot wound.

'Oh,' Ellie muttered, sensibly feeling her loss, and looking somewhat subdued.
'Thank you for helping us,' Chloe said, looking up to see a fraction of this stranger's face. Only now realising why she had helped.
'No need to thank me. It was my pleasure! After what Stem did to my dear friend, I'd do anything to get one up on those FUCKERS! If I could, I'd burn their building down!'
This remark left everybody speechless. Even though it was an aggressive comment, it led them to believe how hungry Tessa was to see Stem's demise. It also showed them how angry she was at the loss of her good friend.

'Where are we going?' Ellie remarked.
'Just hang on. We should be there in a few minutes. Enjoy the view,' Tessa advised, again chuckling away to herself.

Tessa had taken them along the country pathways, the rain acting as a shield, restricting their vision. A yellowy haze flickering through the raindrops as Autumn reflected against the glass. And speckles of red from the seasons wilt shared this abandonment of summer. The dead leaves basking in the rainy takeover.

The camper van then suddenly came to a stop.
'Wait here!' Tessa instructed.
The engine still revving, Tessa unhooked her seatbelt. The storms rage fought hard against the door, trying to force it

shut, impeding her from leaving. She battled hard against the turbulent winds proving she was a worthy adversary. She stepped out as the door slammed shut behind her. The howling winds revealing just how bad it was outside and the threatening rain trying to leak in.

'Who is she?' Ellie asked, turning to face Davrin. 'Nothing seems to phase her.'
'She was my Nan's best friend from the church.'
'Did she know you were in the church?'
'Yes. They were helping to keep me safe. Tessa, and Bill.'
Both Ellie and Chloe could see how sad Davrin looked. After all, this was the day his Nan was going to be cremated.

With that, they all paused, turning towards the front to see Tessa battling with the door again. She stepped back into the campervan. Her clothes were covered in the rain's spit. The engine roared again, and she drove into some sort of shelter. The rain then disappeared.

Tessa got back out of the camper, with ease this time. She walked around to the side of the campervan and dragged the door sidelong towards the rear, the squeaking hinges crying out in pain from all the bullet holes.
'If Terry could only see this now,' she said.

Ellie was the first to get out of the campervan.
'Thank you again so much for what you did back there. I'm sure Terry would have been very proud of you.'

Tessa smiled.
'That's if he was ever sober enough to remember. My late husband, he was a drunken ass hole.'

Ellie was taken aback by this brash statement. This woman, a woman of divinity, a devoted churchgoer, but with the language compared to that of a serpent, with a tongue, slashing any virtue. Ellie tried to hide her shock, but it was evident on her face.

'We are allowed to curse you know?' Tessa barked. 'He was an ass hole, but he was my ass hole. Til death do us part and all that. I do have this place to thank him for though.'

Ellie didn't know where to look. She turned around to watch the others step out into what looked like a barn shed, possibly where horses once resided. This now uninhabited stable, dry, with hard mud, and straw coating the concreted floor.

'Come on, let's get inside.' Tessa directed. 'I need to get out of these wet clothes. And then I'll take a look at that hole in your shoulder Dav.'
She stepped up onto a step and pulled back a long-standing side door which led into the house.

'Are you sure we don't need to take him to the hospital?' Ellie questioned. A concern in her voice.
'There's one thing I've learned all these years around here, and that's how to fix a wound. My husband was a farmer you see. Animal wounds, human wounds, sure they're all the same.'

Chloe's eyes widened. She looked at Davrin. Her look indicated her concern at how stable Tessa was. Everything seemed casual to her, as if nothing would unhinge her carefree manner.
'Don't worry,' Davrin whispered. He had recognised the worried expressions on their faces. 'I know her all my

life. She's a bit mad, but in a good way. She knows what she's doing.'
'You know the rules here Davrin!' Tessa confirmed. She didn't quite hear what he was saying, only the mumbles from behind. 'I have one rule around here, and that's no whispering or secrets. My open house, my open rule. We have to trust one another if we're going to take down Stem.'
'Take down Stem?' Ellie questioned.
'Well who else is gonna stop them?'

An air of silence gave Tessa the response she wanted.
'Right, does anybody need anything?'

'If I could use your phone Miss Limes,' Ellie suggested, calling out and hurrying after her.
'Tessa, call me Tessa.'
'Tessa, sorry. I left my bag back at the church, just after I spoke to…'
'Bill. Yes, I knew it was you. Dav described you all very well. When I saw you at the church, well, I waited around. And lucky I did, hey?'

Ellie didn't say a word.

'But I didn't expect any of this.' Tessa added. 'I knew Stem had a price tag on your heads, but I didn't realise it was this high.'
She began to chuckle.
'Well, we're so glad you waited around. And thank you for what you did.'
'You don't have to keep thanking me. I'll be finding out how much the reward is, and if it's a decent amount, sure I'll be handing you all in myself!'
Again, another self-assured chuckle. And with Ellie not joining in, Tessa continued.

'You'd wanna wipe that look from your face.'
'What look?'
'That worried look on your face?'
'Oh, that's just me, I over think everything.'
'Try tell that to your face!'

A forced grin took over Ellie's face. She didn't quite get the level of humour Tessa was on, but she needed to try.

'I know what you're probably thinking,' Tessa said. 'This woman has gone mad. But when you live on your own for years, you get used to laughing at your own jokes. Margaret, God bless her soul, always loved adventures in her hay day. We were as thick as thieves when we were younger. She would have loved this.'
'I'm sorry Miss Limes, I don't mean to change the subject, but can I make that call by any chance?'

Tessa kept walking.

'It's down the hall at the end of the stairs. Oh, and for god's sake, call me Tessa. Teassa, Tessa, Tessa, that's my name.'
Tessa must have enjoyed her own company because she seemed like one of those women who amused herself, a crackpot with all the alone time in the world, entertaining herself out here in the abandoned pastures.

'Thank you again, I just need to call my dad. You see I left my bag back there and it has all my belongings. I need to warn him.'
'Ap ap ap, no need for explanations. Down the hall at the end of the stairs. And take as long as you want. Terry's inheritance can pay for it.'

Chapter 18

Jenson and his parents had just left 'Harpers Herbal Healing' when his phone began to ring. He sat there looking at the unknown number.
'Aren't you gonna answer it?' His mother asked.

Jenson, now seated in the back of the car. His mind reluctant to answer. But eventually the crying tones called out to him. The persistent ringing refusing to give up. He answered.
'Hello?'
'Hey Jenson,' Ellie greeted. 'Where are you?'
'Oh hey Ellie. We just had a stop off after the hospital. I was gonna get dropped off at yours on the way. I'm nearly there now.'
'Oh Jenson, please, I can't get through to my dad. He's not answering the phone. Can you please call round? He needs to leave the house right away.'
'Why? What happened? Is everything okay?'
'No, it's not. We got into trouble at the church with some Stem soldiers. I left my bag there. My purse is in it, with all my belongings. They knew who we were. I think they'll go after my dad. You need to warn him! I'll explain it all properly when I see you, but for now, I really need you to do this for me, please?'
'Yes, of course!'
'Thank you, Jenson. And will you call me back straight away, on this number when you get him. And if they're after us, then they're probably going to come after you as well. So be careful.'

'Okay. Thanks Ellie. I'll call you as soon as I warn him. Goodbye.'
'Everything okay?' Jenson's mother asked. She half turned her body around to face him. She could tell from the call that something was up.
'I don't know Mum, but we need to get to Ellie's house as soon as possible.'

~~~

Jenson's father drove as fast as he could, allowing some hesitation with all the rain.

As they approached Ellies street, they could see two of those Stem jeeps parked up outside her house.
Reaching the driveway and slowing down, Jenson began to wipe the inside of his window, cleaning the condensation to see a little clearer. Stem soldiers were now coming out of the bungalow.

Looking closely, he could see two of them holding onto Wardy as he was being escorted out of his home in a pair of handcuffs. The condensation beginning to fog up once more, Jenson decided to roll down his window.
Just then, he heard a man's roar from inside the house. Then suddenly, running out at full speed, 'Meatloaf' appeared, barking like mad. And in one quick instance, he was cut short.
A loud bang caused him to drop.

Jenson's whole body shot back in the seat. His eyes scoured the front lawn. He could see a soldier with his hand raised. A small mist of gunpowder smothered by the rain, quickly dissolving any trace except for the injured pet on the ground.

Jenson's mother screamed. She too had just witnessed this killing instinct.

'We need to get out of here now!' Jenson's father said. He had noticed some of the soldiers, who had turned around after hearing his wife's scream.

Jenson quickly rolled up his window.
'Dad! Quick, come on!'
But the car did not move.
Jenson turned to face forward. And just then, he noticed why his father had not driven off.

A Stem soldier was standing out in front. His hands were pressed and leaning on the bonnet. And as each second went by, more soldiers surrounded the car, the flicker of the window wipers revealing their images even clearer.

'What do we do?' Jenson's mother asked.
'I'm not sure?' Her husband replied.

The condensation began to suffocate the inside. And the claustrophobia of the advancing soldier's caused panic. A hysteria took hold of Jenson's mother as she began to shift uncomfortably in her seat.
'John? John? What are they going to do?'
'Everybody, stay calm. And act natural.' John said.

'GET OUT!' The soldier ordered. He pointed his gun towards John's window.
'John please be careful!' Sarah cautioned. She sat there watching her husband roll down his window.
'Yes?' John muttered, giving off a fooling composure.
'I said get out of the car!'
'But it's raining?'

The soldier pulled opened the car door and pointed his gun at John.
'I said get out!'
'But I didn't do anything wrong?'
'I won't tell you again, get out!'
'Please John, just do as he says,' Sarah uttered.

The trigger of the gun cocked back.

'Okay okay,' John said. His arms raising out in front. He cautiously stepped out of the car.
But the soldier had lost his patience. Without warning, he dragged John by the scruff of his collar and threw him onto a ground.
John landed in a puddle, his body pressing down, headfirst. His mouth regurgitating the unwanted filth.

'JOOOOHNNN?' Sarah screamed, as she opened her car door.
She too, had been manhandled as she emerged. She was dragged out and was thrown up against the car bonnet. Her face impaling against the wet hood.

'MUUUUM?' Jenson screamed, as he too followed his parents. But he jumped out of the car voluntarily.
And like his father, he was thrown onto the wet ground.
Pinned down on all fours, he turned his head sidewards. The rain drops pelting off his eyelids like tiny blocks of ice. He could see a stocky, bald man, walking towards him, his suit saturated from the rain, and his shoes squelching in the pool beside him. He had remembered this man's face. He had seen him before. He was one of Mr. White's men that had taken turns in following them over the last two weeks. But Jenson noticed he had a fresh cut on the side of his forehead. And waning stains of

blood began to slither down his face as every raindrop bounced onto his glaring bald head.

Where these cuts something to do with what Ellie was talking about? Jenson thought. *And if so, what kind of trouble did they get themselves into back at the church?*

'Well well, look what we have here?' George questioned, 'If it isn't little Jenson and his family.'

'Please let us go!' Sarah cried. 'We did nothing!'

'Well, if it was up to me, I would let you all go, with bullets in your head! But lucky for you all, Mr. White wants you alive, for now. We have another one of your gang members.'

Jenson looked up from the ground, beyond George. He could see Wardy being hauled into one of the Stem jeeps.

'We WILL catch the rest of you,' George continued. 'And as soon as we have that Drifter boy Davrin, we will stop him from doing any of that dream magic shit again. You'll be sorry you messed with Payton's family. He'll have no use for any of you after that.'

'You go around like hard men, hiding behind guns, and an army, killing innocent people.'

'What was that Mr Rose?' George asked, his attention now focusing on Jenson's dad.

'John please!' His wife called out. 'He didn't mean it.'

George walked around the front of the car and over towards John as two soldiers began to manhandle him into position. They placed him onto his knees.

Now upright and restrained, George approached. Without hesitation, he swung his arm, smacking the gun into John's face, sending him crashing back down into the puddle.

'DAAAAAD?' Jenson screamed as his mother also let out a loud cry.

'Just give me a reason,' George said, pointing the gun at his head.

'PLEASE JOHN! JUST LET THEM DO WHAT THEY WANT!'

'You should listen to your wife.' George insisted. 'Now get out of here before you regret saying anything else.'

George nodded his head at the soldiers. 'Escort them home.' He then stepped back over towards Jenson.

'Tell your friends to turn themselves in. They have 24 hours.'

'Your face John?' Sarah acknowledged as she got back into the car. She raised her hand up to examine his face.

'I'M OKAY!' John snapped. He pushed her hand away and slammed his door shut. 'How do they get away with it?'

'Are you alright Dad?'

'Yeah, I'll be fine. Are you two okay?'

'I'm sorry, I shouldn't have brought you here.' Jenson said.

'Don't ever apologise for any of those people son!'

'Can we please just get out of here.' Sarah interjected. Her plea proving how scared she was.

As they drove by the second jeep, Jenson glanced out of the window. One of the soldiers had just opened the back door. And there smuggled inside was another body. But it wasn't Wardy's. Jenson let out a gasp.

'What is it Jenson?' His mother asked.

'It's Callum.'

'What about him?'

But Jenson didn't reply. He immediately picked up his phone and began to search for the last received call.

Chapter 19

Robyn hadn't a notion where she was going. She just held onto Myral as tight as she could. And although she didn't know this fairy, for some strange reason she trusted her. Maybe it was because Myral had saved her life, or because she knew Jenson, but all the same, she trusted her as they flew across the peculiar land.

They hovered past fields of immense colour, bright and beautiful. And trees of all shapes and sizes, which were so creative, just like bonsai trees. It was as if they were individually sculptured and personally planted, one by one.
They passed by rivers and lakes, which looked so beautiful, the water seemed to flow with a fresh sparkle on every drop. And fish jumping out. The healthiest, and wildest of fish, again, with the brightest of patterns.
This world was something Robyn had never seen before. An enchantment she had never ever visualised in any story book.

'Are you okay?' Myral asked, looking down at Robyn.
Robyn nodded. She couldn't bring herself to say anything. Her eyes dipping as she took in the breath-taking views. A fraction of fear showing across her face, but this was the result of being suspended so high up. Truth be told, this was the first time she had felt safe since being here.

'We're nearly there,' Myral acknowledged.

Just then, Robyn diverted her attention away from Myral's big blue eyes. She looked ahead again. And there, in the distance, a beaming lemon haze, with sparks of light, glistening outwards. And as they moved closer, she realised the grasslands had merged into a chain of sandy banks.

She began to see objects below. The images, capturing a hazy blur, like tiny dots moving. But as they descended, these blurry dots forged into creatures, the same shaping's as Myral. They were fairies, just like her. And lots of them, buzzing along the water's edge.

Some of the younger fairies were fluttering around playing on the sandy shorelines, while others stopped to look up and stare at them.

A castle came into view, big enough to see the markings. It was nothing Robyn had ever imagined before, not even in any fairy-tale ever told to her. It looked like an enchanted castle jutting out from the side of a mountain, with tall turret structures so delicately carved out, and each one spiralling upwards.

It was beautifully arranged, all building up towards one giant peak. But what fascinated Robyn the most was that it looked as if it was all made from sand. Glittering sunlight on every grain carving a scene of a large sun-drenched beach. And a castle sketched as the edging centrepiece.

If this view wasn't spectacular enough, a foaming waterfall poured down alongside the mountain. Powdery water clouds evaporating from the chutes above as each wave crashed below. And unlike Robyn's experiences at the beach, building sandcastles with the rippling waves washing away every effort, this castle seemed to stay strong, withstanding every wrinkle of the tide.

It was utterly amazing. Robyn was held there, suspended in mid-air as they approached. Her mouth wide open. Her eye's captivated. Her breath taken. The warm gentle breeze blowing against her youthful face. The memories of the dark and chilling forest, the horrid retention of what had happened to her previously had been forgotten. She was nearly eaten by the Lost Forrest, but any memory had now, well and truly, disappeared. Each memory had buried itself into the soft and fluffy sand dunes.

Robyn suddenly spotted two larger fairies flying towards them as they got within landing distance of the castle. They looked like male adult fairies wearing only khaki ripped shorts, exposing their upper torsos, and showing their heavily muscled physiques.

They did look like Myral, with their long black hair, pointed ears and pale grey complexion. But the distinct difference was that they had much larger wings, wings that were not as colourful as Myrals, but expanded in greater length. They also looked like warriors, clutching their swords that were strapped in against their waists. But not the type of swords Robyn was used to seeing on T.V. These swords looked like they were carved from some sort of a stone substance. Little did she know that these weapons were made from teeth, children's teeth, stolen by tooth fairies. And blended, with other ingredients to make them the coarse tools, strong and sharp enough to slice through the toughest of components.

'Please don't say anything. I will handle this,' Myral instructed.
Robyn had no words to object.

The two fairy guards intercepted.
'Hello,' Myral greeted.
'Myral, is that a human?' One of the guards asked. His face conveying his anger.'
'But…'

'But nothing! You do know our kind are not supposed to interfere with human dreaming?'

Even though Robyn could tell that her being here was frowned upon, she still felt somewhat safe. And the fact these guards had not retrieved their weapons made it even more so.

'I do know this Carveld, but I can explain.' Myral answered.

'We cannot let you into the castle. You do know Fae are only allowed inside the walls?'

'Yes Carveld. I am well aware of this. But please, I really need to see my father. He will understand.'

'This human could be a demon in disguise, trying to penetrate the castle walls. I cannot allow it Myral. Even though you are my niece, it is against the rules!'

And with this Carveld raised his sword, only now causing a sudden panic inside of Robyn.

Myral could feel Robyn squeezing tighter.

'Please Carveld, she has been through enough. She is not here to hurt us. She is scared. And I would not endanger the lives of any Fae. Let me show you.'

Myral released one arm as Robyn held on tight. She then began to locate her pouch. And placing her hand inside, she retrieved some sparkling fairy dust. She immediately sprinkled it over Robyn without warning her.

Robyn's grip instantly relaxed and Myral held on tighter as she passed out.

'See…. she's no demon. A demon wouldn't let me put pixie dust on them. So please, I need to speak to my father.'

Chapter 20

Chloe could hear the cries from out in the hallway. She glanced over at Tessa who looked back at her. Davrin was seated next to her, his hands, gripping tightly around the groove of the backrest as he bit down hard on the wood. The needle came to a sudden pause, suspended in Tessa's hand as she put a halt to the stitching of his wound. Tessa nodded when Chloe stood up. She understood something bad must have happened. Something so bad, it was exposed during the phone call.

Chloe shifted out from the table. The other two watched on as she left the room.

She approached Ellie who was seated at the end of Tessa's stairs. She could see the distraught look on her face.

'What is it Ellie?'
Ellie didn't answer.
'Ellie? Is everything okay?' She asked again.

Not waiting on an invite, she squeezed in and sat down. She put her arm around her and waited. She didn't know how long it would take for Ellie to come round, so all she could do was wait.

Within seconds, Ellie tilted her head into Chloe's shoulder and wept even further.

'They took him,' she said.
'Took who?'

Ellie retracted her position to face Chloe. Her sniffling indicated a strengthening composure. Chloe knew the answer was about to land.

'I'm sorry Chloe. Look at me getting all upset.'

'What happened?'

'It's my dad. Stem took him.'

'Don't worry Ellie, we'll get him back, just like Jenson's family. We have the upper hand. We have Davrin. They won't do anything to your dad until they have him.'

After a pausing silence, Ellie spoke.

'And Meatloaf. Meatloaf tried to help him. They shot him. He was only protecting my dad. They didn't have to kill him.'

'Oh Ellie, I'm so sorry.'

'It's my fault. If I hadn't of left my bag. If I hadn't of waited...'

'You can't blame yourself.' Chloe declared. 'There was nothing we could have done differently. They would have taken us eventually. They were following us all the time. They know who we are. They're getting worse! They're dragging people out of their homes in broad daylight now. They don't care who's watching. They won't stop until they get what they need. When Callum and Jenson come here, we'll think of a way of getting your dad out of there. You have my word, okay?'

Ellie nodded with a regretted commitment in her face. She knew she had to tell her. But equally, she didn't want to be the bearer of bad news.

'Chloe?'

But that was as far as she could get before Chloe interrupted her.

'Did Jenson say where they took him? I presume it's to Stem Industries?'

'Chloe, I'm sorry but you need to hear this. Jenson did say something else.'

'What?'

'It's Callum.'

Chloe's heart sank.

'What about him?'

'He never made it out of the church.'
'Is he?'
'I'm not sure, but I don't think so. Jenson saw him. He was in the back of their jeep.'

Chloe stood up. But unlike Ellie, an angered mist flashed across her face.
'Chloe, hang on!' Ellie said. 'Try not to panic! Jenson did say he was in the backseat, so that must mean he's okay. I'm sure they didn't harm him. They probably want to question him so....'
'We have to get him!' Chloe interrupted. Her voice was raised. 'We have to get them both!'
'I know we do, but we have to be patient. We can't just walk right into Stem and demand them back.'
'So you don't want your dad back?' Chloe questioned. A harsh pitch in her bark.
Ellie's face dropped. She couldn't believe Chloe had said those words.

Chloe paused. She suddenly realised the sharpness in her tone.
'I'm sorry Ellie. I didn't mean that. I just…'
'It's okay Chloe. I understand. You're upset. We all are.'
'So what are we going to do?' Chloe asked.
'We might be in luck. Jenson think's he has a way of getting them out.'
'But how?'
'He did say he met that scientist from Stem, the one who experimented on Robyn. Jenson said he came to the hospital to try and help Robyn. He had to leave before Stem got suspicious. So that must mean he's willing to help us. He did say he'd meet Jenson back at the hospital tonight. Maybe he knows something. And maybe he can help us get them out of there?'

'You think we can trust him?' A weighing doubt plagued Chloe's mind.

'I'm not sure. Jenson did sound optimistic though. We must wait it out here until he meets up with him. And then we'll know more.'

'Yeah, that sounds like a plan.'

A sudden scream caused them both to turn. But neither one seemed too worried.

'Was that Davrin?' Ellie asked.

'Yeah. Tessa's stitching him up. If you ask me, she looks as if she's enjoying it a little too much.'

Ellie smiled.

'Come on, let's see how they're getting on. It'll give us a good distraction.'

Chapter 21

Tom turned around abruptly. A sudden startlement caused his elbow to hit against the mounted telescope and knock it off the table. He had been caught off guard as the silent lab transformed into a bustling commotion.

The laboratory doors burst opened, and George walked in with two soldiers trailing behind, each holding onto the corner of a wheely chair. They were all drenched from the rain. And a white covering, now transparent, revealing a body underneath.

Tom scurried round to pick up the fallen apparatus. He then stood to attention, as if saluting the oncoming troops. He noticed Georges blood-stained shirt as he got closer.

'Is he dead?' He asked, indicating towards the body in the chair.

'If I had my way, he would be.' George declared.
And as he got closer, Tom could see the graze on the side of his forehead.

'What happened? Are you okay? Is Davrin hurt?' He asked.

'This isn't Davrin. I nearly had him, until this little shit came out of nowhere and hit me over the head.'

Tom could sense the bitterness in George's reply.

'Do you want me to take a look at it?' He asked.

'What do you care anyway?'

'I was just asking….'

'Well don't. Where do you want the body?'

'If it's not Davrin, then who is it……Jenson?'

'No, it's not Jenson either. But I did have a run in with him and his parents.'

'Then who is it?'

'I don't know, some teenage boy we've been following. Couldn't find out who he is. He's been staying with that redhaired woman Ellie, and her father. We have him now. It won't be long until we have the rest of them. We won't let them slip away this time.'

'I didn't know there were others involved?' Tom questioned.

'And how is that my fault?'

'No, I didn't mean to….'

'I'm sure you didn't, but remember, we don't owe you any explanation. You work for us. We can make you disappear in the blink of an eye. You just do your job and keep your mouth shut.'

'I'm sorry.' Tom acknowledged. His inferior position showing.

'Where do you want him?' George probed.

'Is he alive?'

'No, we're bringing you a dead body to experiment on, of-course he's alive!'

'Should he not be in the interrogating room. Do you not have to question him to find out who he is?'

'Are you telling me how to do my job?'

'No, not at all! I just don't know what you want me to do with him. I'm assuming you need to question him to find out who he is?'

'What did I tell you? You do your job and I'll do mine. Mr. White told me to bring him in here. He's finishing up something. Perhaps you can explain to him why you're not co-operating.'

'No, oh no, I am co-operating. Please, put him over there.' Tom said, pointing over to the vacant area where Robyn had been tested on.

'Quick.' George instructed. 'Make sure he's strapped in. He looks to be coming round.'

A sudden twitch caused the saturated covers to move. George was right, the body did look as if it was regaining consciousness. And just as George had asked, the two soldiers made sure the body was secured before they made their exit.

'I'll be back in twenty.' George said. 'And whatever you do, do not take that cover off his head! Don't even go near him. No one is to touch him until Mr. White has spoken to him, you hear me?'

'Yes. But do you want me to look at that cut on your head?'

George chuckled.

'I've had bigger cuts shaving my bald head.'

The automated doors shut behind him. Tom was left in the room alone with the body. A curiosity grew inside him as he turned back round to watch the cover's twitch even more. But he had received strict instructions from George not to touch the body.

Tom continued over to his workstation. And with every passing minute, the urge increased. His body was trying to resist reaching for the wet covering. But his obedience was proving too tough for any retribution.

The body began to stir again.

Tom had waited long enough, and although George had given him clear instructions not to uncover the body, he couldn't help but wonder who it was and why they were here.

Is it Jenson? He thought. *Had George lied to him. Had this been the boy he had just spoken to at the hospital, the boy desperately seeking his help? But if it wasn't Jenson then who was it? And why were they brought in for questioning? Why were they fighting with the resistance?*

Tom's urge finally suffered defeat. He slowly walked over to the chair and cautiously began to lift the covering.

A darkened sack had been thrown over his face, concealing the identity.

Tom considered this to be a test. *But if it was, then why would they do this to him?*

He wasn't too sure if he should take off the added disguise. He could see this person's chest moving up and down, desperately trying to intake air through the weighted bag over his head.

'I'm sure they won't mind,' Tom whispered to himself. He figured George was due to return any moment now, but he could always excuse himself for thinking that the boy would have suffocated.

The body began to twitch again.

This startled Tom. He stepped back as the twitching increased. He paused for a moment, but then continued. And even though the body looked to be wakening, he figured it was safe as the boy was strapped in and couldn't do anything to hurt him.

He began to unravel the furrowed edge, lifting the face covering up past the boy's mouth. He noticed the start of a small marking on his left cheek.

More curious now, Tom lifted the bag up even further, revealing the whole scar.

He was speechless. He immediately tore off the rest of the bag and looked more closely at this boy's face, completely forgetting that George could return at any moment now.

Callum sluggishly began to wake. His eyes gently rotating, trying to remain open long enough to focus.

His pupil's eventually fixating in on Tom who was standing over him.

Callum could not believe it. He suddenly froze. *Was this a dream?*

He knew he wasn't dreaming, so this must have been his reality. *Was it some sort of a joke? How could this possibly be?* With all these questions floating around in his mind, he couldn't speak. But in this precise moment, and when the saliva returned to his dry mouth, he spoke. He knew he had to say something. He opened his mouth and blurted it out.

'Dad…..is that really you?'

Chapter 22

The door opened as George walked in, buttoning up the buttons of his new white shirt.

'Hello George,' Payton acknowledged, turning round, and revealing Miss Belshaw's body strapped into another experimental chair.

'Mr. White. Dr. Shafer,' George politely greeted both men, nodding at Payton and then to the other man, another scientist, a thin pale faced man who had the same hairless dome on top. He was a tall man. And looked even taller as he walked over to Stephanie's sedated body, with a needle in his hand.

'Is he downstairs?' Payton asked, not even looking up at George. His eyes were too busy scrutinising Stephanie's body.

'Yes. I left him in with Tom as directed. Tom has been acting strange. He's been asking all kinds of questions lately.'

'I know he has. It all started when he began to work on Jenson's sister, Robyn. That is why he doesn't know about any of this.'

Payton turned to watch Dr. Shafer jab the needle into Stephanie.

'I got word back that he went to the hospital to see Jenson's sister.'

'What?' George said. His distaste for Tom clearly showing.

'Yes, but don't worry, I'll deal with that matter in my own time.'

'I never did like him.' George declared. 'He always asks too many questions.'

'Well, we don't need him anymore now that Dr Shafer has come on board.'

Payton's eyes glared across at Stephanie's body. And a smile grew on his face.

'What do you want me to do with him?' George asked.

'I'll be down in a few moments. I will deal with Tom myself.'

'Okay.' George agreed. 'Oh, and before I forget, one of the soldiers just gave me this on my way here. They found it on the boy.'

Payton glanced over. It was the first time his eyesight had left Stephanie's body. There, sitting neatly in George's hand was a small brown wallet.

'And is there any identification in it that reveals who this boy is?' He asked.

'I'm not sure. I haven't looked at it yet.'

'Okay, I'll be with you shortly. Leave it over there on the table.'

George did what he was told and left Callum's wallet on top of the table just before leaving the room.

'So will you have this new drug ready for tomorrow's delivery?' Payton asked.

'Yes,' Dr. Shafer replied.

'Good.'

Payton's smug face radiated.

'Oh, and one more thing. How is it coming on with my son's cure?'

'Your son will walk again very soon.' The doctor answered.

'He'll be pleased to hear that Dr. Shafer. You have been a valuable asset to this company over the past few weeks.'

~~~

The automated doors opened. Both Callum and Tom looked over to see George stepping in.
'What's wrong Tom?' George asked. 'You look like you've just seen a ghost.'

Tom was terrified. He panicked, and quickly grabbed the tranquiliser needle beside Callum. He immediately stuck it into him and injected him unconscious. He knew what Callum was like, even after all these years. He knew his son was tough. And since they had only reunited seconds before George had entered, there had been no time to go through the formalities, or even to devise a plan.

'What's going on?' George demanded, storming over after seeing this reaction.
'I….I….I'm sorry.'
'What did you do that for?' George challenged.
'I didn't mean to, he was just….'
'I told you not to go near him.'
'I know, I'm sorry, I just reacted. He started spouting things about Stem. How much he hated us all. He was trying to get out. I just panicked.'
'Mr. White won't be amused.'
'I know. I'll take full responsibility.'

George laughed.
'Damn right you will,' he said. 'Mr. White is coming down to interrogate this boy. And when he finds out what you have done, he won't be happy.'

'I'll explain it to him. I'm sure he'll understand.'
'I think Mr. White is losing patience with you. We all are!'
Tom didn't know what to say.

'When will he wake up?' George demanded.
'I'm not too sure, but hopefully soon.'
'Right, well you better call us the minute he does. And don't let anything like this happen again, you hear me?'
'Yes of course,' Tom replied. 'I'm so sorry.'
'You are an idiot! I don't know why Mr White has you working for him.'

George was only a fraction away from letting the secret slip. The covert plan that Mr. White had deliberately brought in Tom's replacement a few weeks back. But he remained quiet. He turned and left the room.

Tom looked back around at his son's unconscious body. He didn't know why he had panicked. But he knew he had to do something to stop this reunion. This was not the time or place, especially in the company of George. He couldn't stop his mind wondering. *Why the hell was his son here, and mixed up in all of this? And if Callum was here, where was Chloe?'*

Chapter 23

Callum was slowly coming back around. The injection of adrenaline had worked, and Tom could see this from his lab chair. He immediately jumped up and hurried over to his son.

'Please stay calm Callum,' he whispered, hoping to reassure his son that everything would be okay. 'I'll explain it all, but please do not make a sound or they'll come in and take you away.'

Callum had managed to come round, but his speech was still a little slurred.

'I….don't….get it?' he asked. He was in complete shock. 'You… are….supposed….to be dead?'

'I know. And I am so sorry for what I have put you all through. I will try and make it up to you.'

'But….how are you here?' Callum asked. His voice becoming stronger and louder. 'I don't understand?'

'Callum please. I need you to be quiet. I know this probably won't make any sense to you now, and maybe you will never trust me again, but I had to leave. I just couldn't watch you and your sister and, well what happened to your mother and Carly. It was for the best, for all our sakes, especially mine. I just couldn't stay there. It would have killed me.'

Tom looked as if he was beginning to get upset now.

'What about us? Did you ever consider us?'
'I did Callum. I did it for you, and Chloe. I did it to keep you safe. I am so sorry Callum.'

'Those tears won't make a difference!' Callum broadcasted. His anger becoming visible now. 'Did you fake your own death? Why did you leave us? We were only kids. We needed you!'

'I know. I know Callum. You must have so many questions. But now is not the time. I do regret it, and still do. Every single day of my life. But I had no other choice. It was Stem Industries. I swore to myself I would stay here until I made it right. I've tried so long and hard to find a cure for you, and your sister. Where is she? Please tell me Chloe is okay?'

'Yes, she's fine. So was it you? Did you do the experimenting on Robyn?'

'What?' Tom questioned.

'Jenson's little sister? The little girl who is lying in a coma.'

'You don't understand,' Tom said. 'They made me do it.'

'And I suppose they made you kill those innocent people in that psych place, the one with the so-called cure a few weeks ago? We would have taken it only for Henry telling us about it.'

This revelation had taken Tom by surprise. He knew some patients had died as a result of taking the ineffective cure. But he wasn't aware that his own children could have taken it. He could have killed them.

'I am so sorry Callum, for everything. I truly am! I told them I didn't know the true effect it had on people. I hadn't fully tested it. I told Mr. White that we might never get a cure. They think I don't know, but I've heard rumours of another room in Stem. Another room with another doctor. A scientist. I think I've heard the name Doctor Shafer being used. I don't know what they've done with that failed cure, but I have a strong feeling they've added things to it. They're doing more experiments without me.'

'And you're telling me this, why?' Callum barked.

'I'm not sure. About two weeks ago they got a female patient in from St. Anita's. Miss Belshaw is her name. She was showing signs, very bad signs. They tried to do this behind my back, but I have friends in here. They've been telling me things.'

'Davrin's mother?' Callum stated.

'Yes, Miss Belshaw... you know her?'

'Yes, well no. I've read the stories about her hearing voices, and about the demons in her head. She's killed people. Chloe should be with her son now, Davrin.'

'So you and your sister are helping the resistance?' Callum began to chuckle.

'The resistance?' He rattled. 'I wouldn't call a few people and a dog, a resistance.'

'Callum, please be serious now!'

'I am serious. And you do not have the right to tell me what to do. Not after all this time.'

Callum's tone changed. He was angered that his father could still believe he had a hold on him, especially after ten years of not seeing him and the biggest lie ever.

Tom felt this beating. He knew he had let his children down. But he had no time to dwell on this right now. He needed to think fast.

He turned around. His eyes were scanning the room. He held his hands up to his temples, moving his fingers in a circular motion, trying to remain calm. He was thinking of a way to get his son out of Stem safely.

'What are you doing?' Callum questioned.

'Please Callum, I'm trying to think.'

'Well you can start by getting me out of this chair. I'm a sitting duck here.'

These words never hit Tom. His thinking had deflected them from ever entering his brain.

'How are you even mixed up in all of this?' He asked.

'What?' Callum answered.

'How are you involved in all of this?'

'We came to get answers. We wanted to find out why Stem killed you. That was a big mistake now.'

'So you're here because of me?'

Tom's face displayed the hurt he was feeling. The main reason his children were here was because they had come to search for answers, answers into the fake death he had plotted. His conspired plan was supposed to keep his children safe. But now, it had somehow managed to do a full three sixty and bite him in the backside.

'I'm so sorry Callum, I really am. I didn't mean for this to happen. I promise you. I will try my best to make it up to you both. But for now, we need to get you out of here.'

'What are you waiting for?' Callum asked, pulling at the straps. 'Get me out of these things.'

'Callum, it's not as simple as that. There are soldiers everywhere. Something bad is about to happen, I can feel it.'

'Like what?'

'As you now know, they have Stephanie Belshaw. And if you've read up on her, you must also know how insane she was, how insane she still is?'

'Yeah, but it was years ago. Davrin met up with her. Ellie said she was like a child.'

'What?'

'They met her. A few weeks ago. They went to St Anita's and met her. They said it was like talking to a baby.' Callum paused, and then continued. 'Wait a minute.' His thoughts began processing another bit of information. 'Jenson did say she freaked out when she saw him. I don't know if that's any help?'

'Well it doesn't sound like she's changed. When she came in to Stem two weeks ago, I heard that Mr. White began testing on her. He used my results, and together with Dr. Shafer, they've been experimenting on her. With these tests, they have to take her off any medication. I'm not too sure of the results as I'm not involved, but I've heard rumours that she still has some sort of a deep connection into the Dreaming World.'

'Is that not a good thing?' Callum asked. 'Maybe she'll be killed in there.'

'No Callum. This is different than you and I. She's been deteriorating, but perhaps deteriorating from our world. From what I am hearing, I believe she is changing. People are saying that voice she used to hear, it's back in her head again. It's like she's possessed again.'

'Possessed? Why don't you just get a priest in to do an exorcism?'

Callum's sarcasm had quickly returned. But Tom didn't entertain it. He continued.

'I didn't think it was a good idea to use her, but I was out of the loop. I have been trying to ask questions, trying to find answers without them knowing, but I feel they're catching onto me. They had to move her to another section of the building. A restricted section I believe. Sound-proof so we wouldn't hear her screams. Others, like me are still testing on her and whatever results they are getting, they're mixing it with our formula. I don't know what the repercussions will be. She's not stable, so please, we need to get you out of here. They'll start testing it on you too. And once they move you to the restricted area, I'll have no access. I won't be able to protect you. You need to leave.'

'Well hurry up and get me out of these.'

'I can't Callum. We can't just walk out of here.'

'But you can sneak me out.'

Tom hesitated.

'Ah, I have it!' He said, sticking his index finger into the sky. 'Jenson. You are in this with Jenson, yes?'

'Yes.' Callum replied.

'Well, I'm meeting him at the hospital later. I can tell him what I've told you and maybe I can get them inside Stem? Make it look as if they broke in to get you out?'

'But what do I do in the meantime?'

'You wait here while I go to the hospital.'

'But what will they do to me? What if they move me to the restricted area?'

'Don't worry. I'll reset the code for the door so that only I have access on my swipe card. They'll just have to wait outside 'til I get back. It will give us a little time. Just stay here and be quiet. And don't move. Pretend you're still unconscious.'

'I don't think I have a choice, do I?' Callum declared, as he watched his father hurry over to his chair and grab his coat.

'I'll be back soon. I'm so sorry for all of this, but I will make it right. I love you son, I always have.'

Chapter 24

Tom had just stepped outside, closing the electronic door behind him. He remained calm as he began to deactivate the lab door.

Suddenly, he heard a voice from down the hallway. His back was turned but he recognised the call.

'And where are you off to Tom?' Payton asked.
Tom turned around.

Mr. White and George were walking towards him. He could feel his hands beginning to shake. The sweat was beginning to evaporate from his pours. His calmness had quickly shifted to a blustery mess.

'Oh, I was just going to pop out for a while. I need some fresh air…and a bite to eat. I'm starving. You want anything brought back?'

'Are you going back to the hospital?' Payton asked. This question caused alarm bells to ring inside of Tom's head. He didn't answer. He didn't know how to respond.

'We know you were at the hospital talking to Robyn's family.' George said, butting in.

'I don't know what you are talking about.' Tom answered. He felt more comfortable answering George back than he would Mr. White. But his nerves were beginning to show.

'Is he awake yet?' Payton asked.
'Is who awake?'
'Your son! Is Callum awake?'
Payton held out Callum's I.D. from his wallet.
'Is Callum awake?'

Tom panicked. He was lost for words.

'Come on Tom don't play dumb,' Payton suggested.
'Did you think we wouldn't check his I.D?' George asked.

George was relishing this moment. And Tom could see it from the smug look on his face. He knew he never liked him. But Tom knew he had to try harder to convince them otherwise.

'Are you sure it's Callum?' He asked. 'I haven't seen him since he was a little boy. I wouldn't even recognise him now.'

He slowly turned back round to open the lab door again with his swipe card.

'Are you sure?' He asked again, taking one step inside. Maybe they were caught off guard with Tom's persistent questioning and denial, but just then, as the door opened, Tom swung round, and with one huge effort he pushed George as hard as he could in his chest.

Never expecting anything like this, George stumbled back and fell into Payton. They both crashed to the ground.

Tom scurried inside. He ran as fast as he could. He instantly punched the emergency switch with his palm. This action caused the doors to close immediately. He then began to type a sequence of numbers into the panel, overriding the system, and jamming the lock.

Payton walked calmly over to the small window panel of the door. And with a stern look, he directed it at Tom. He spoke.

'How foolish of you Tom. You will not get away with this. You could have had it all. Nobody betrays me and gets away with it.'

Tom could see George smashing at the key panel on the other side of the door.

'IT'S NO USE!' He shouted as he ran off behind Payton to get some help.

'What is it Dad?' Callum asked. He could see some sort of a commotion over by the door.

Tom turned around and scurried over to him. It was only a matter of time before they would open the doors.

'I'm so sorry son,' he said. 'They are on to me.'
Tom was aware that Callum had just called him Dad, but now was not the time to start being emotional. This rekindling reunion would have to wait. And Tom hoped they would get another chance.

'They know everything Callum.' He declared.
'How?'
'Your wallet.'
'Shit!'
'Don't be blaming yourself Callum. I am sorry. My plan won't work. I won't be able to get to Jenson at the hospital.'
'Get me out of these straps and I'll help you fight.'
Tom smiled. Even though his world had just come crumbling down, he smiled. This was the first time he had established just how grown up his son was.

'If I let you out, they'll kill us both, without any hesitation.'
'But we need to fight. They'll kill us anyway.'

Tom looked confused. His constipated stare alarmed Callum. But then Callum remembered how his father used to do this when he was a child.

He began to shift his body, motioning it around the room. He then revealed a plan that may work.

'Do you and your sister still see each other in your dreams, like you did the night Carly…'
He couldn't finish his sentence.

'Yes.' Callum answered. 'But I'm not going back to sleep. Get me out of these things and I'll help you fight.'

Callum began to struggle again. But it was no use. He couldn't free himself.

'I'm sorry Callum, that is not an option. You need to go find your sister. Tell her what's going on. Tell her something bad is going to happen.'

'But she won't be asleep. I won't be able to find her. She won't sleep without me.'

'Callum please.'

'A demon found her last time. She was on her own. We don't sleep without each other. We're stronger together.'

'You still see demons?' Tom asked. A concern now growing on his face.

But not waiting to hear Callum's answer, he quickly ran over to what looked like a fridge, a cooler, with different types of medicines inside. He opened the door and retrieved a blue vile. He then quickly grabbed a syringe and stuck the needle into the vile, suctioning the liquid out.

'What are you doing?' Callum questioned.

'This should help you if anything bad is after you.'

'What is it?'

Tom didn't answer. The door behind him had just opened. He had no time left. He stabbed Callum with the syringe, injecting the liquid into him.

'DAD?' Callum called out.

And with a confident surge, Tom quickly grabbed another needle.

Just then Callum heard a shot. He screamed as his father fell on top of him.

'DAAAAD!!!' He called out again.

But as soon as he did, Callum felt a sharp pain in his stomach. It was the needle from a tranquiliser. Tom had managed to stick it into him. But before his senses had faded, his father spoke.

'Go find your sister.' He sluggishly demanded. 'Please warn her!'

Chapter 25

Jenson was lying on his bed, listening to music, when his bedroom door creaked opened. It was his mother.

She walked in, dressed in a black frock, indicating through sign language for him to take the earphones out of his ears.

'We're heading off now,' she said. 'Will you be okay?'

'Of-course mum, I'll be fine. You two enjoy yourselves.'

'Are you sure you're okay?'

'Yes, I'm okay. You said it yourself. We were escorted home by Stem. That'll tell you they don't want to hurt us. They just wanted to scare us.'

His mother came walking over. She leaned in and kissed her son on the forehead.

'I can't believe how grown-up you are sometimes.'

Jenson's father then stuck his head in through the gap in the door.

'Are you ready?' He asked, referring to his wife.

'Yes…. How do I look?'

'Beautiful!' He answered.

And as Sarah looked over at her husband, she noticed the cut on his face.

'Are you sure you're up for this? I can't stop thinking about what happened earlier. Are we doing the right thing by going out tonight?'

'Mum!' Jenson exclaimed. 'You need a night out, you both do. Ever since Robyn went into hospital, you have been back and forth. Hospital. Then home. Then back to the hospital again. Just try and forget about what happened. We're all safe, aren't we?'

'For once, listen to your son,' Jenson's father said. His smile from the doorway motioned an agreeance with Jenson.

'Yeah…. you're probably right. I just can't help but feel sorry for poor Meatloaf. And what about Wardy and Callum?'

Jenson was starting to regret telling his mother everything. But there was one thing he had left out. He still hadn't told them about meeting up with Tom from Stem industries tonight. He just needed them out of the picture.

'Go on,' he instructed. 'Get out of here! And make sure you bring me back some cake.'

His mother laughed as she walked back over to the bedroom door.

'It still looks sore,' she said, taking another glance at her husbands damaged face.

'It's only a cut,' John said. 'It'll be a good story for tonight. And sure, isn't that why you married me, for my rugged tough guy image?'
Sarah began to chuckle.

'Goodnight Jenson,' his father said as he slapped his wife's bum, coaxing her out of the room.

'Yes, goodnight honey,' his mother said from out on the landing. 'And if you need anything at all, just ring us.'

'Yeah, yeah, I know.' Jenson retorted. 'Have a good night.'

As soon as the car drove out of the driveway. Jenson looked over at his alarm clock. It read 8:16pm.

'Right Jenson, let's go,' he whispered to himself, pressing up from the bed. 'You've to be at the hospital by 9pm.'

The toilet chain flushed as Jenson stepped out of the bathroom. And just then, the doorbell suddenly rang.

Had his parents forgotten something? But they had keys. Could it be Ellie and the others? He thought. *But the plan was for them all to stay putt until he got information from Tom at the hospital. It couldn't have been Stem, for they had already used force to gain access before. Surely, they were not going to be polite and knock this time, especially considering what had happened today.*

The doorbell rang again, which alerted him once more. He stepped out of his bedroom and slowly began to descend. He was half expecting the front door to smash in again with a handful of Stem soldiers, just like last time. But everything remained calm.

As he got to the end of the stairs he waited, hoping whoever it was, had gone. He looked at his watch which read 8:25pm. And just then, suddenly another noise at the front door alerted his attention. But this time it was a rap at the door followed by an older male voice.

'Hello?' The voice called out.

'Hello?' Jenson replied. 'Who's there?'
He then heard some whispering.
'Oh….Hi. My name is Sterling, Sterling Harper. We met earlier. Yourself, and your parents were at my shop today. I'm sorry to disturb you but we really need to talk to you.'
'We?' Jenson asked.
'Oh yes, sorry. My daughter is here too. Her name is Grace. You met her earlier as well.'

Jenson was a little relieved when opening the front door. He figured it was something related to the medicine he had just received earlier that day.

'Hey,' he said, unlocking the front door and pulling it back a fraction. 'My parents aren't here.'

'Yes, we know that. We saw them leave.' Sterling explained.

This confused Jenson.

'So you don't need to speak to them?'

'No. It's you we came to see. May we come in?'

This alarmed Jenson even further. He was hesitant to allow them access. And with everything that had happened, he was only seconds away from closing the door in their face.

'I'm sorry, I don't have time.' he acknowledged, securing one foothold behind the door. 'I have to go out, I'm late.'

He began to close the door when another voice called out, causing him to stop.

'Please!' The young girl said, holding her hand out to try and stop him from closing the door. 'It's important. I've seen you in my dreams.'

'Your dreams?' Jenson asked.

'Yes. Please, just give us a few minutes to explain,' Sterling interrupted. 'My car is just across the road. We can drop wherever you need to go.'

Chapter 26

'So let me get this straight, your dad helps non-dreamers and you've seen me in your dreams, even though I cannot dream. You say you've dreamt about me dying, but I'm not dead? And you think it could be in the future or something, but it's soon?'

Jenson summed up Grace's explanation. He was now seated in the back seat of Sterling's car, and on the way to the hospital.

'I know it sounds crazy.' Grace acknowledged, turning around to face him from the passenger seat.

'So how long have you been able to see the future in your dreams? Have you seen anybody else die?'

'You are the first,' Grace answered. 'You see, I got this necklace for my birthday. I had it on when I fell asleep. And for some strange reason, it did something, it made my dreams feel different.'

'Are you a Drifter?'

'No. I have no abilities. I am a normal dreamer. My father said the necklace is supposed to enhance someone's powers or ability, so I'm not quite sure what happened. I think I can see the future in my dreams or something?'

Grace suddenly felt a surge of self-importance. Perhaps she was a Drifter, but her powers had not yet manifested, until now. Or this necklace had helped find an inner power, a new ability to combat this Dream-death disease. But her sudden surge declined as she realised Jenson had died in her dream. If this new ability was true, then there was a chance it would lead to a devastating truth.

'I'm sorry,' she continued. 'But maybe now that you know, we can change what happens?'

Jenson looked dumbstruck. He was trying to understand. He was trying to comprehend the truth behind this, the truth he could die.

'So where did this happen?' He asked.

'I'm not sure. I've never seen the place before. It was like we were inside some sort of an experiment lab. As I've said, I've only dreamt of it once. I thought it was a normal dream with a boy dying, but then when I saw you in my father's shop, I knew it must mean something else?'

'And there was me thinking you both came over to talk to me about my medication.'

'Have you taken it yet?' Sterling asked.

'No. It's been a crazy day. I'll take one when I get home. My headaches don't seem to be as bad now. Maybe my body is getting used to them.'

'I've tried to check back on my notes,' Sterling began, to find out why you started taking the tablets, but I can't find anything. You'll have to excuse me. I don't keep things like that lying around just in case Stem search the place.'

'It's okay. My parents told me why. They said I was seeing things, like fairies. I know it sounds strange, but...'

'WHAT?' Sterling asked. His car suddenly skidded across the lane.

'DAD!' Grace called out.

'Sorry guys.' Sterling said, pulling the car back into the lane. 'You said you've been seeing fairies?'

'Well not for a long time. I don't know what's going on. The morning after I got Robyn back, I started to get visions of a butterfly. It was so real looking. It was blue, a bright blue colour with purple blood vessels running through the wings. It was gorgeous. I've spent hours looking up butterflies. And the nearest thing I can get to it is the Morpho butterfly. I don't know what it's supposed to mean. But the visions, they keep coming and going. My mum said I used to see these fairies when I was younger, before the tablets. Maybe it's something from a distant memory?'

Even though Sterling and Grace were intrigued by what was going on. Now, Jenson's truth, the reveal of his hidden past, it had just added more interest. And even though Jenson didn't know these two strangers well, for some instinctual reason, he felt he could trust them. Perhaps it was the fact that Sterling had been helping 'Non-dreamers' like himself for years, hiding anything that would lead them to Stem. But now, with Wardy and Callum captured, maybe he needed more allies to help him take down Stem.

'Can you remember any of the fairies you saw as a child?' Sterling asked.
'No. It's strange though. Anytime I try to remember, I feel a migraine coming on. Have you ever treated anybody like this before?'
'No. But my grandmother spoke of such beings all her life. She told me a story about a boy, a 'Non-dreamer'. It was before this ever became a thing, long before the Dream-deaths. She was only a child herself. She said a boy began to speak of nights when a tooth fairy from another world would come to visit him. He said they stole our teeth from under our pillows and they would leave replicates behind.'
'And I suppose they left the money under the pillows as well?' Jenson responded.

This reply seemed out of character for Jenson. A cheeky comment, quite often conditioned by Callum. He didn't intend to be disrespectful, it's just that he was finding everything so overwhelming.
'I know you're probably finding it difficult to believe us right now,' Sterling suggested. 'But please do try and have an open mind.'

'I'm sorry. You're right. After what I've experienced in the last few weeks, anything is possible.'

'But that's the thing, it's all still new to us,' Sterling confirmed. 'And new abilities are happening every so often. I believe our two worlds are more connected than we believe. And this boy, the one who spoke of seeing a tooth fairy. When he was a teenager, he said he fell in love with her. He said he was going to marry her. People began to believe he was mad. He did eventually go crazy, searching for this so-called fairy. He said, she just vanished one night and never came back to him. And because of this, he eventually took his own life.'

Grace let out a sigh. She believed every word her father had said. She also felt as if it was a sad love story, corrupted with a sealed fate just like 'Romeo and Juliet'. She felt sorry for this boy and his lost love.

Jenson, on the other hand, wasn't too sure what to believe. He wanted to believe it, but something inside hm just couldn't grasp the concept of it ever being true.

'So why do they collect our teeth?' Grace asked.
'I'm not sure. Your grandmother, bless her soul, she believed that our world and the dream world are more connected than we could ever imagine. She believed this boy was special. She believed the stories to be true.'

Something shook inside of Jenson. It had caused a tremor from within. And whatever it was, it had fallen out onto the floor of his consciousness. It was a voice inside him. A voice he had somehow manifested from the back cupboard of his mind. He didn't quite know where it had come from. But it was there now, opening itself up to him.

'What is it Jenson?' Grace asked. She could sense something was wrong.
'I can hear her. It's a girl's voice.'

'And what is she saying?'

'She's saying the stories are true.'

'What stories?'

'Stories about me. Her voice. I can hear her clearly now. It's like a memory. She's talking to me. She's telling me the stories are true.'

Jenson was confused as to how he even conjured this sentence. But the voice inside his head, it was telling him something. It was as if he had heard these words before.

'Do you know who said this to you?' Sterling asked.

'No. I can't remember. I have no vision, just a voice. And then there it was, a vision of wings, fluttering inside his mind. Jenson fell back into the seat as an oncoming migraine began to strike.

'Jenson, are you okay?' Sterling asked.

'I just need a minute.'

And with that, Jenson retrieved a sachet of tablets from his pocket.

'STOP!' Sterling demanded.

Jenson flinched.

'The tablets. Don't take them.'

'Why?'

'They have a suppressant in them. They could be blocking out your memories. You said you haven't taken any yet?'

'Yes. I've been waiting for my next migraine to take one.'

'Well don't. This could mean something.'

'But you gave them to me?'

'I know I did. But they must do something to your mind. They might stop you seeing. Maybe you need to see.'

'Huh?' Jenson mouthed. 'But I'm getting these headaches. They're not as bad now, but they're still happening. It's as if they are waiting in the back of my brain.'

'It could be withdrawal symptoms. A side effect of your mind not having them?' Sterling said, pulling the car over.

The screeching breaks signalled a sudden stop. They had arrived outside the hospital.

Jenson looked in at the car dashboard clock. It read 8:52pm. He then looked up at the hospital lights shining into the car.

'I'm sorry, I have to go,' he said, 'it's really important. I need to meet somebody here.'

'But Jenson....' Grace muttered.

'I have to go. Thank you for the lift, but I really do need to go.'

Jenson climbed out of the car and shut the door. Even after all the revelations inside this vehicle, the only thing on his mind was to get the help he needed. The help to awaken Robyn from her coma.

Chapter 27

Robyn could hear voices in the background, even before she opened her eyes. It was like one of those moments when you are not fully awake, but somehow you know a conversation is happening around you in the distance. Her mind had not yet gained consciousness. But for some reason she knew people were talking about her.

'Mother, Father, come quick, she's waking up.'
Myral hung her head over Robyn's body. Her big blue eyes staring in at Robyn as she desperately tried to regain her composure.

Robyn's swift twinge made it look as if she was frightened. She was. And with her sudden jerk, she could feel herself sway. Only then did she realise she was in fact lying inside a large hammock, made from a huge leaf.

'No, please don't be scared, my mother and father are here. They will know what to do.'
'Where am I?' Robyn asked.
She looked around at the gold encrusted room. It was busy. It looked cluttered, all crammed full of plant life. Wonderful leafage of all sizes and colour, bright, dazzling creations. It looked more like an outdoor garden, tastefully transformed into some sort of living quarters. And inside the potted plants appeared to be the most colourful of soil. Unbeknownst to Robyn it was pixie dust.

Robyn looked over to the window where the radiant light was entering. It had filled up the whole room, allowing each exotic creation to seize enough light to grow. She then realised it wasn't quite a window, but more of an archway. An archway which looked to be the only way in, or out of this room. And decorated with heavily draped climbing plants either side. And where the radiant light entered, there came two figures walking over towards her, with gold crowns on their heads.

'Robyn, this is my father, Layorn, and my mother, Priel.' Myral said, introducing her parents. 'They are the King and Queen here in our land.'

'Why am I here?' Robyn asked. Her body shifting inside the unsteadied hammock. She was trying to fix herself into a more upright position, but her body was unable to sway comfortably inside.

'That, we are not sure of my dear,' Myral's mother answered.

Priel was very pretty. She had the same long black hair as her daughter. And the deep big blue eyes, just as identical. She too wore a long frock, but hers, the milkiest of white, the most elegant of taste. The flowing material created a refined vitality, with long sleeves enhancing the flow. She too, just like her daughter, had a subtle but distinct pale grey complexion of similar colour. And her wings, slightly larger than Myral's, but equally as harmonious to her body. Her beautiful blue wings jutted out from her shoulder blades, producing a lavender complexion as they glistened behind.

'Hello Robyn, please do not be afraid of us,' she added, gently holding out her hand and placing it on top of Robyn's wrist. 'We mean you no harm.'

'How do you know my name?' Robyn asked.

Priel began to smile. This sudden distrust seemed amusing.

'My daughter, Myral, told us your name. She brought you here. I assure you we have no hidden agendas.'

Myral stood there beside her mother. She was unsure of how this scenario would play out, but one thing she was certain of, she knew Robyn was safe, for now.

Just then, a shadow loomed overhead. Another figure came into view. It was Myral's father. He had just joined his Queen, standing by her side. He looked different. He too had long black hair and bigger than normal eyes, but his eyes were green, an emerald green. He also had the same grey skin but his, a slightly darker shade. And unlike the fairy guards that they encountered earlier he was wearing some sort of a white tunic with a brown belt. Robyn did notice the big, long, thick sword he had attached to his belt, identical to the swords the guards had. But what intrigued her the most was that he had enormous wings, much bigger than his Queen, and daughter. His looked more like the wings of a dragon, rather than those of a butterfly.

Layorn's expression was opposite to the friendly one Robyn had received from Priel and Myral. His strained stare brought with it a more curious disapproval. He was yet to accept a human in his chambers.

This frightened Robyn. But her attention withdrew. She moved her focus back to Priel as she spoke.

'Robyn, can you tell me how you ended up in the Lost Forest?'

'I….I'm not too sure,' Robyn replied, now glancing at all three of them. She was trying to think back. 'The last thing I remember is going to sleep beside Jenson. And then I woke up in that horrible place.'

'Yes…my daughter's told me all about your brother, which makes sense now.'

Priel glanced towards her daughter. And Myral's face had quickly turned to an apologetic narrative.

'Is Jenson in trouble?' Robyn asked.

'I'm not sure.' Priel answered. 'You see, Myral here, has been keeping a secret from us. We do not like secrets, do we Myral?'

'No mother.'

'Myral told us she has seen your brother.'

'WHAT DID YOU DO TO HIM?' Robyn shouted as she tried to sit upright in the hammock. But her whole body fell backwards again. Her sudden bravery had reversed its charge.

Priel chuckled as she held out her arm.

'Let me help you out of there,' she said.

As Robyn took her hand and got to her feet, she saw this as a sudden opportunity, and snatched it. She ran as fast as she could over towards the archway.

Layorn's reaction was fast, but Priel's was even faster. She held her arm out, restricting her King from moving. She suspended it up against his chest before he could do anything. She had restrained him from going after her.

'Mother...she is going to...,' but before Myral could finish her panicked sentence, Priel explained.

'Maybe she will trust us after this.'

Priel remained calm. And just as she said those words, Robyn came to the archway. She didn't stop. She ran straight through it. And as soon as she passed the climbing plants she began to fall away from the archway.

This was not an archway into another room, or a doorway leading out into a beautiful garden. This was the opening of a room, a room that was situated on the highest peak of the castle. It led out onto an edgeway; a ledge Robyn had just fallen from. It didn't matter to these fairies. In fact, this was how they had built their castle. After all, they had wings. A strategy to defend themselves against any intruder.

The faint cries dissolved into the air as Robyn fell even further. But Priel just stood there, her hand rigidly connecting with Layorn's strong chest.

'Okay, now!' She insisted, taking her hand away and allowing her King to go after Robyn.

Layorn's speed was that of an athlete. He sprinted quickly, over to the hanging vines. And as he reached the archway, he gracefully jumped off the ledge, without a second thought.
He leaped into a downward spiral, his large wings retracting into his body.

Robyn was petrified. Her screams had faded into a buffering delay as the air began to suck the life out of her. She was so high up, and with such a force, all she could do was frantically flap her limbs.
After a few moments drop, she began to feel the splashes of water from the waves below. But before she crashed to her doom, Layorn swooped in and grabbed her.

Robyn didn't say a word. For just as Priel had pre-empted, she had finally realised these fairies had meant her no harm. She had in fact now been saved twice.
Again, she was in awe. After never being able to dream, she was somehow transported to a world full of magic and wonder. This was something she had always regretted not being able to do, but now, the true reality of it had left her in an undecided predicament.

Having already seen the views earlier with Myral, Robyn should have been used to the suspension, but this time it was different. Lying there in Layorn's arms, Robyn could feel his secured grip. She felt safer. His huge frame, his enhanced speed, the vibrations from his wings, it released a toxin inside her, something she had never felt before. She lay back, as if half drifting into an ecstasy of comfort. She had never felt so alive, yet she was dreaming. She remained in Layorn's arms, her stare gazing out, and admiring his extensive power. His wings, each flap emitting a rumbling sound. Layorns wings were not like the Queen or Princess. They were not like the two fairy guards she had met earlier. His wings were even bigger and looked stronger. They must have spanned nearly six feet each in diameter. They were not as colourful as the others. They looked faded, as if somebody had stretched them out to make them bigger. And causing them to lose their vibrant colours, resulting in a smudging canvas. But still, just as incredible. And the clamour they made. The swooshing flaps, like a slow propeller sweeping up all the wind, buffering the noise and creating an induction of sound. It was truly the most mesmerising experience Robyn had felt in her life.

Layorn reached the ledge and propped Robyn onto it. He remained there, suspended in the air, waiting in case she attempted another foolish escape.

Robyn stood there in the archway. She then slowly took a few steps back inside, like a bold dog, crawling back to their owner, its tail nestled in between their legs. She stepped closer.

'Robyn, if you want us to help you, then you will have to trust us, do you understand?' Priel asked, putting her arm around Myral's shoulders.

This affection allowed Robyn a snippet into their existence. She nodded, now fully understanding.

'Good!' Priel acknowledged. 'So you say you woke up in the Lost Forest?'

'Yes.'

'And are you sure you were not taken there by something in your dream?'

'No, I wasn't.'

'Okay. So if you are here and still alive, well then that means you are still sleeping in your world.'

'Sleeping? I don't understand?' Robyn requested.

'Robyn, our world is the world in which dreams are made of. Co-existing alongside your world. As you dream at night, your spirit is transported here and remains here until you waken. It gives us our Sun, the spirits of Dreamers.'

'So I'm not really here?' Robyn asked.

'You are! In fact, the most important part of you is here. Your soul. Only your body remains in your world, like an empty casket. That is why things happen to you in your real world, consequences of being here. Anything bad will result in your body being altered. Do you understand Robyn?'

Robyn nodded her head. She remained silent.

Priel turned towards her daughter and continued.

'Myral, you said you saw her brother. And he could see you also?'

'Yes. He spoke to me. He could see me.'

'Hmmm, this has only ever happened once, and look how that turned out.'

'But mother, Jenson said he had never dreamt before. He could see me in his world, not in ours.'

Priel pondered. She shifted her look at Layorn, who now stood in the archway.

'Layorn, will you please go fetch my mother,' she asked. 'This is bigger than we imagined.'

And without hesitation, listening in on the whole conversation, Layorn flew off.

'It's true,' Robyn said. Her first proper sentence since returning. 'Jenson has never dreamt before. I was the same until the men took me.'

'What men?' Priel asked.

'The men who did tests on me.'
'Tests?'
'Yes. To help us. To stop the nightmares so people don't hurt anymore, to stop the dreaming.'
'Stop dreaming?' Priel emphasised. 'But if your world stops dreaming then our world will crumble. It will have no reason to exist.'
Robyn could see Priel turning her face. She could sense a disheartened sadness.

'What's this all about? Layorn is telling me we have a human inside the castle.'
Priel's mother was speechless. She stood there with the sun's ray glimmering around her body. She was another fairy, an older fairy. She looked like she could have been as old as Robyn's late grandmother, with her wrinkled face and shrunken body. But she, unlike the others had white hair, long, thin, flowing white locks.
She slowly walked over to Robyn and pulled up the sleeves of her yellow fairy dress.
'How has a human reached so far into our world?' She asked.
Without any apprehension, she took hold of Robyn's hair and began to sniff, her hands feeling the texture of it.

Robyn felt awkward, but she did not fear her.

'Robyn, this is my mother Soreen. Mother this is our new guest, Robyn.' Priel introduced.
'I just can't believe it.' Soreen explained. 'It's been so long since I've seen a human.'
'Myral said this boy, Robyn's brother, Jenson, he is a Non-dreamer, yet he was able to see her,' Priel explained.
'A GATEWAY?' Soreen echoed.
'A Gateway?' Myral asked.

'Yes, a Gateway between our two worlds. He cannot dream, therefore he holds the balance of both worlds. The earthquakes we've been experiencing, they're a sign of the Gateway. A sign that the Gateway could open. Where is he?' Soreen asked. A worried expression now forming on her face.

'He's back in his own reality,' Priel answered.

'He could be the last Gateway. If anything happens to him before he passes the gene on, the Gateway will open, and demons of our world could cross over.'

'We have no time to waste!' Layorn scolded as he approached. 'We have to get her back before anybody finds out. You know what those demons are like when it comes to humans. They can smell them for miles.'

'Yes you're right,' Priel agreed. She then turned to Myral.

'Myral, we're going to need you to go back and talk to Jenson. You will need to find out what is happening. Why his sister Robyn is here? Find out what is happening with people who dream? Can you do that for us?'

'Yes, of course.' Myral replied.

'And mother,' Priel continued. 'I will need you to fetch some extra pixie dust for Myral. She may be needing it.'

'Is that why she used all of it before?'

'I had to use it,' Myral pleaded. 'I didn't know what to do. He saw me!'

'Its fine, we just need to know what's going on. We need to try and stop this before it's too late.'

Chapter 28

Jenson sat there. His hands were resting in his lap. His phone, now placed out on one thigh as he continued to count down the minutes. The hospital lights were displaying a faint night mode. He looked over at his sister, her outline just about visible with the subtle lamp light from her bedside table. He was wondering if Tom was ever going to show. *He said he would be here at 9pm, so why wasn't he here yet?*

He looked down at his phone. He pressed the main circular button. The whole front panel illuminated. It read 9.26pm. *'Where is he?'* He thought. *'Did something go wrong? Or did he ever intend on coming back?'*

He wondered if this a waste of time. And if it was, then how long would he have to wait before finally giving up hope?

Then, suddenly, the door opened slightly. Jenson's heart bounced all over the place. His chair gave off a low squeak as he turned to observe who was entering. He was nervous. He was excited.

The white panel with a sheet of obscure glass made it difficult to see who it was. And the light outside gave no shadow through the stained glass.

It had to be Tom. The door handle pulled down and the door opened. But nobody entered. Somebody was on the other side. But they hesitated with caution. It was as if they had opened the door slightly and then stopped. It couldn't have been a nurse. They would have entered. Nobody had spoken. No sign of any introduction. And no sound from beyond the partition. Whoever it was, they had completely stopped in their tracks, but why?

It had to be Tom. He probably hesitated when Jenson turned round making the noise in his chair. Jenson figured he would just take charge. He couldn't let a change of heart collapse all hope. After all, his sister's life depended on this.

'WAIT!' He called out. The silence in the room had taken his cry louder than expected. His dwindling hope had now been recuperated.

He quickly stood up and dashed over to the door. He pulled it back. But nobody stood on the other side. *Did the door open all by itself? Maybe the wind caused it to open? But there was no wind. Was his mind playing tricks on him? Did he see the door handle twist open?*

Leaning forward, he stuck his head out onto the hospital corridor. He looked to the right. Nothing. He then peered round to the left. He saw somebody in a wheelchair coasting down the corridor.

'HELLO?' He called out, cautiously marching after them.

'Hello?' He said again, meeting up with the chair as it stopped by the elevator.

Whoever it was seemed to be ignoring him. And they pressed the elevator button to try get further away.

Jenson had enough of this game. This was not Tom, and by the look of things, Tom was never going to show. Something inside him snapped.

'Didn't you hear me?' He said, his hand reaching out and grabbing hold of the stranger's shoulder.

But as soon as he had made this hostile approach, his hand was whipped away.

The wheelchair spun around aggressively.

Jenson was completely taken aback. This was the last person he had expected to see.

'Ethan?' He uttered. 'I had no idea. What happened?'

Ethan just stared back at Jenson. He didn't respond. And Jenson could see the rage in his eyes.

'Ethan what happened to you?' Jenson asked again, staring at the wheelchair in detail.

Ethan's mouth opened with a pausing breath. He was trying to articulate the correct response. He had been waiting for this reunion for weeks now. Then suddenly, he spoke.

'You and your stupid new friends... that's what happened.'

'Did Davrin do this to you?'
Jenson was none the wiser. He had only heard something bad went down in the 'White' household, and that an ambulance was called for. True, the receptionist had told Chloe that an 'Ethan White' was admitted, but after everything that had happened with Robyn, Ethan was the last thing on Jenson's mind. And even though Jenson had become a regular visitor to the hospital, he had never once cared to think about his so-called best friend. Why would he? His poor sister was lying in a coma. And Ethan had betrayed his trust.

'Yeah, Davrin did this to me. Are you happy?' Ethan questioned as the elevator door opened.

Both boys looked inside.

A nurse stood still. There were no words exchanged. And by the disregarded stare back, the nurse pretty much knew they were not taking the elevator. She rolled her eyes and held her arm out to re-press the button. She then leaned back, resting in against the mirrored screen. And one last quick glance, she watched them in an awkward silence as the doors shut again.

'Was that you who opened Robyn's door?' Jenson asked. His mind now clearer.

'What if it was? You gonna get Davrin after me again?' This snapback had come as a surprise.

'Ethan, I don't know what you think I did, but I had nothing to do with that? And the only reason why Robyn is lying in there is because of your father!'

Jenson's feelings quickly changed. He had immediately felt sorry for Ethan. But now, an angered reaction washed over him.

'So you weren't looking for Davrin to help you?' Ethan asked.

'No. I mean yes, I was. But not for this. I never asked him to do this to you. How could you think I would do such a thing?'

'I don't know what to think anymore.'

'Can I help you two?' A voice called down towards the two boys.

Jenson had his back to her, but when he turned around, the nurse recognised his face. She nodded and walked back to the nurse's station. Visiting times were long over, but as an exception, Jenson and his parents were given permission. Robyn was an exception to the rules.

'I remember you saying his eyes lit up when he caused Joey's nose-bleed.' Ethan stated, reminiscing about that day in class. 'But I never knew he was capable of this.'

'I didn't either. What happened to you?' I haven't seen Davrin since that night. I don't know what happened.'

Just then an elderly man distracted the boys as he came walking out of his room wearing a navy dressing gown. He stood there in the doorway, a disgruntled look on his face.

'Maybe we should go somewhere else to talk?' Jenson suggested. 'Do you want to come back and see Robyn?'

Ethan dropped his head. He propped his arms up, resting both hands on the wheels of his wheelchair. It was an indication he was ready to follow.

Jenson held the door open as Ethan manoeuvred in. He then closed the door behind him.

'I'm not some freak who comes in here late at night to watch over your sister,' Ethan explained. 'I do care.'

'Why would I think that.'

'Well just so we're clear.'

Ethan wheeled his chair right up to the side of Robyn's bed. Jenson waited for him to talk again. He knew he wasn't finished.

'I know my father had something to do with this,' he said. His eyes were fixated on Robyn. He was watching her chest move by the air filling her lungs. 'He did eventually tell me he had done some tests on her, something he said he was not proud of. But he was only trying to help her.'

Jenson's forehead creased. And any commiseration he had for Ethan was swallowed up by the sound of the machine keeping his sister alive. The rasp suckling of air made his blood boil. Jenson knew that Ethan's father was the cause of Robyn lying here in this state.

'She doesn't deserve this you know,' Ethan continued. An admission that made Jenson's anger ease. 'Maybe that's why I've been coming here late at night when everyone is gone. I suppose I look at her and feel we have something in common. Neither one of us deserves to be here.'

'I'm sorry Ethan, I really am. If I could have prevented any of this from happening, I would have....'

'Would have what?' Ethan interrupted. He slapped the top of his wheels.

The room went silent. A wave of remorse took over Ethan.

'Forgive me Jenson, I don't mean to snap. It's just, being stuck in here and not having the use of my legs has just made me feel useless. I'm on anti-depressants. I don't think they're helping.'

'You need to give them time to work.'

'Time,' Ethan repeated. 'I have lots of that in here. And look at this,' he added, taking hold of his stomach, and squeezing it as if trying to pop all the fat. 'I've put on even more weight. All I do is eat and sleep.'

But Jenson couldn't see the humour.

'Ethan, I honestly had no idea,' he said. The carousel of emotion swinging back around. He felt sorry for him again. 'I would have visited you, only for Robyn being like this. And blaming your father, I just never thought.'

The room went silent again.

'I can see your pitying eyes watching me.' Ethan declared. 'Don't worry. I will be walking soon enough. My father's new scientist, Dr. Shafer, is working on a cure.'

'Another cure?' Jenson asked. 'You do know what happened with the last one?'

'Yes, but this is different. This cure will help me walk again.'

'Are you certain of that?'

'Davrin did this to me when I was sleeping. He did it in my dreams. There is no other option.'
Ethan paused.

'You don't know where he is, do you? Davrin? He might be able to fix me again.'

Jenson knew where Davrin was. Ellie had given him information on their new safe house in Tessa's. But he was never going to hand this information over to Ethan, no matter how much he pressed. Yes, he felt sorry for him and yes, he was right, maybe he didn't deserve to be in this state. But considering what had happened in the past, he was sure of one thing. He was never going to trust Ethan again.

'I'm sorry Ethan, I don't know where he is.' He replied.

'Are you expecting somebody?' Ethan asked.

'No, why do you ask?'

'I've noticed you looking at your phone a few times.'

'I'm just checking the time. It's getting late. I should probably go.'

Jenson pretty much realised that Tom was never coming. Maybe he never was. Maybe he had just arranged this meeting to get him off his back?

'Is anybody collecting you?' Ethan asked.

Jenson suddenly thought back to when Chloe had told him how she felt. She figured something wasn't right with Ethan. How he was asking all kinds of questions. Jenson had to now choose his words carefully, as saying something to Ethan could lead to serious consequences.

'Nope, I'm all alone tonight. My mum and dad are out. I'll grab a taxi.'

'Oh. Well let me walk out with you, or wheel you out in my case.'

'You're fine. I'll be okay.'

'It's not for you,' Ethan said. 'It's for me. I could do with some fresh air. I need my best friend back.'

Chapter 29

'So how long do you have to stay here?' Jenson asked.

Both boys had just come out through the revolving doors of the hospital.

Ethan took a big deep breath, taking in as much fresh air as he could. 'Hopefully soon,' he answered. 'My dad says the cure is nearly complete. Any day now, and I will be walking out of here. I told them I'm not going home in this.'

He banged down on the wheels again. But this illusion was more of a determined promise rather than anger.

'Well, I hope it works out for you.' Jenson acknowledged.

Even though Ethan did have an involvement into how things had turned out, Jenson did have a history with him, a history that could not be undone.

'I am sorry about Robyn,' Ethan said. 'If my dad had more time, he could have helped her.'

'Help her?' Jenson snapped 'Do you believe that? Do you know what your father is doing?'

The carousel had done another full circle and had brought so much anger back with it. This revolving ride was never going to end amicably. Jenson knew he had to leave.

'Of course I do,' Ethan responded. 'He's looking for a cure. We won't have to dream anymore. And then no more people will die in their sleep. Is that not what this is all about?'

'And how do you suppose he's finding this cure? It's not a few random tests anymore.'

'What do you mean?'

'What do I mean? Have you forgotten how Robyn ended up in here?'

'Yes. Your parents went to my father and asked for his help.'

'If you really believe that then why do you think I came to you, looking for your help that night?'

'My dad said you didn't trust Stem. He said you freaked out and ran away. You were acting crazy that night anyway. You had lost your mind, and it showed when you called at my house. You didn't even have shoes on.'

'That night, I came to your house after being chased from my own home. My family were drugged and taken. I came to look for your help. But you betrayed me.'

And there it was. The harsh reality they were both waiting for. The truth had now surfaced. And Jenson's voice was increasingly louder this time.

'My dad said you wouldn't listen.' Ethan retaliated.

Jenson began to chuckle. But he didn't find any humour in what Ethan was saying. He was laughing at how ridiculous his answers were. He knew Ethan's father was fabricating the truth. He was somehow brainwashing his own son.

'Where are you going?' Ethan called out as Jenson began to walk away.

And there it was. His questioning again. Would there be no end to his betrayal?

'I don't have to tell you anything.' Jenson answered. 'But I will say one thing. I really do hope you're not around when I bring Stem down to its knees.'

And with that, Jenson crossed the road.

'Come on, get in.' A voice said as the car pulled in beside Jenson. It was Sterling and Grace.

Jenson figured they must have waited on him. And for some reason, his enhanced rage somehow eased. He needed familiar faces. He needed to be in the company of people he could trust.

'Thank you, but I need to walk for a while. I need to clear my head.'

Grace could see the frustration on his face, plus she also saw the heated argument he had had with the boy in the wheelchair.

'Please,' she said. 'Let us give you a lift. We'll drop you anywhere you want. You don't have to go home.'

Jenson thought for a moment.

'There is a place I need to go if you could bring me?'

'Of course, Jenson.' Sterling replied.

'I'm not quite sure where it is though. I'll just have to make a phone call to get the address, is that okay?'

'Sure. Take as much time as you like.'

Jenson then stepped towards the back of the car. And as he opened the door, he took one glance back to see Ethan, who was still in his wheelchair by the hospital entrance. His eyes were following Jenson.

Jenson nodded his head at him as he got into the car. He shut the door. And in that precise moment, he knew he had lost his friend forever. He knew it was the last time he would ever speak to Ethan.

He then took out his phone and began to dial.

'Hey Ellie,' he said. 'Yes, I'm fine. I'll fill you all in when I get there. What's the address?'

Chapter 30

The car pulled up towards the building. The headlights shone across the front, revealing the outlook of a farmhouse. Jenson could see the front door opening.

Ellie and Chloe appeared and ran out to greet him. Chloe reached him first, giving him a big hug.

'What did he say?' She asked, hugging him. 'Do they have Callum? Is he okay?'

Jenson was bowled over by her questioning. And why wouldn't she be asking these questions? She was worried about her brother.

'I'm sorry Chloe, but he never showed up.'

'What? Why?'

'I don't know.'

Jenson then turned to greet Ellie.

'I am really sorry for everything Ellie, your father, and Meatloaf.'

With that, Ellie took hold of Jenson and hugged him tighter than ever before.

'I will get my father out of there and make sure Mr. White pays for what he's done!'

Jenson understood the quiver in her voice. And by the sound of how emotional she was, he knew she had meant every word of it.

Unlocking his grip with Ellie, he could see Chloe standing there. She was trying to be inconspicuous, but her skimming glances gave her intention away. Jenson smiled. This was amusing. He then spoke.

'Guys, there are two people I'd like you to meet. A father and daughter. They drove me here. And you are not gonna believe what they have to say.'

Jenson walked back to the car and ushered for Sterling and Grace to follow. He then turned back to the house and saw another figure emerge.

'YOU!' He shouted, noticing Davrin coming out of the house. 'I saw what you did to Ethan.'

He immediately ran toward the house and grabbed Davrin by the scruff.

'JENSON? What are you doing?' Ellie called out as she and Chloe headed back to the house.

'You're hurting me,' Davrin said. His free hand trying to prize Jenson away.

'They're after us because of you!' Jenson scolded.

'Me?'

'Yes you! Ethan is in a wheelchair because of you. Did you not think his dad would come after us?'

Davrin watched everyone approach. His eyes flickered from person to person. A remorseful plea in them as he stared back. He knew he had thrown Ethan down the stairs, but he never heard the severity of his actions.

'I didn't mean it. It was an accident.'

'Jenson!' Ellie pleaded. 'Stop this! Davrin is the reason Stem gave your family back. Mr. White is scared of what he can do.'

'Yeah, we know about what happened.' Chloe added. 'He didn't mean it. He told us everything. Let him go! He was shot earlier, helping us at his own grandmother's funeral.'

Jenson removed his hands from Davrin's throat. He then noticed the sling he was wearing. He suddenly felt a bit foolish. Chloe was right. Davrin's actions had forced Stem's hand. And Payton White needed to return his family, for the safety of his own. There was nothing he could have done to change Robyn's fate. And today was the day his grandmother had been cremated. In fact, the more he thought about it, the more he realised that Davrin had lost out the most.

'So are you all gonna make a scene out here in my garden, or are you gonna come inside?' Tessa remarked. Her stance as calm as you like, leisurely standing at her front door with a cup of tea in her hand.

'Jenson, this is Tessa,' Ellie said. 'Tessa, this is Jenson.'

'So you're the boy who started all of this? Well come on in while I get a good look at you.'

Chapter 31

'So basically what you're saying is If we all go marching into Stem Industries, Jenson is dead, and well, the rest of us might follow?'

Chloe's questioning made everybody feel a little uncomfortable. But the realisation that this was a possibility had already imbedded itself.

Now seated at Tessa's rather large, old, country style kitchen table, they were all observing Grace, waiting for her to answer.

'Thank you,' Grace said as Tessa handed her the glass of water she had politely requested.

Her father raised his hand and softly took hold of hers.

'It's okay. Take your time,' he said, knowing his daughter was nervous at all the faces staring back at her.

Grace picked up the glass and began to gulp it down.

'I'm not sure,' she said, after a quick gulp and placing the glass out in front. 'I can only remember the end of my dream. I saw you Jenson. I remember screaming your name. You were….you were dead. And you where beside another dead body.'

'Another dead body?' Jenson questioned. 'Was it anyone here?'

Grace timidly scoured the room. She was trying to recognise the faces. Everybody began to panic. Their heads bobbing like a cat and mouse game, each one secretly praying it wasn't them. But this Russian Roulette star-off was not needed. Grace nodded her head.

'So nobody here?' Jenson asked again.

'I'm not sure. I couldn't see a face. It was like the head was missing. And you had a hole in yours.'

Jenson's intense eyes locked onto Grace. She couldn't avoid his stare. He had hoped this intimidation would cause her to fold. But she didn't. This was the first time he found out how his fate was sealed. But before he could say anything, Chloe spoke.

'So it was a gun shot?' She recalled. 'And what did this man look like, the one who shot him?'

'I'm sorry. I don't really remember my dream. I just remember standing over Jenson's body and calling his name. I remembered your face Jenson. And then the next thing I know is that you show up in my father's shop.'

'Is this the first time you've had these visions?' Ellie asked.

'Yes.'

'And you think some sort of power from your necklace gave you the ability to see into the future?'

Grace looked at her father, waiting on him to reply. This was his cue.

'It was given to me by my mother,' he said. 'She got it from her mother and so on. It has been worn by our ancestors, who were very spiritual people. It has been passed down through the generations. The amber moonstone is said to enhance one's magical potential. I don't know. I never believed it and neither did my mother. But my grandmother did. I think as it was passed down along the line, the belief in it just seemed to fade away, well, until now.'

The room filled with silence as everybody processed what had just been said. Then a voice at the kitchen table disrupted the stillness.

'If I tried to contact my mother in my dreams and I had the necklace on me, would it help my ability?' Davrin asked.

'I'm not sure,' Grace answered. 'But you have it too? You can see the future in your dreams?'

Her face looked excited, as if she had just found somebody who was like her, somebody who really understood.

'No, my ability is different, I'm a Dream-drifter. I can drift in and out of people's dreams.'

'Oh,' Grace said.

'What about your mother?' Jenson asked. 'Have you tried to look for her again?'

'I have been trying. Ever since I met her in St Anita's I've tried to link up with her in my dreams. But every time I feel I'm getting close to her, it's like a black cloud comes over me and I wake up. It's like she doesn't want to be found.'

Davrin grunted as he jerked back from the table. He had momentarily forgotten about his wounded shoulder. A sharp throbbing pain greeted him as he moved.

'Those pain killers must be wearing off,' Tessa stated. 'I'll go get some more, hang on.'

But before Tessa exited the room, Sterling spoke.

'Can I ask what involvement your mother has in all of this?'

'I'm not too sure yet. I never knew she existed until two weeks ago.'

Tessa stopped herself in the doorway. She couldn't continue with the lie she held onto so tight.

'This is where I need to tell you the whole truth Davrin,' she said. 'I think it's time I come clean.'

Davrin turned to face her. He didn't know why she had said this. He sat there, watching her, waiting for her to continue.

'There's something I haven't told you Davrin. I did know about your mother, but before you freak out, I only found out a few weeks ago myself. Margaret rang me late one night. She told me about it. I never knew either. And she only told me because she wanted my opinion. She was in two minds if she should tell you.'

'So it was you who rang late that night?' Davrin asked, only now sticking the pieces together and finally completing the jigsaw. 'It was the night Jenson and Chloe came knocking at my door.'

'Yes. Margaret asked me if I could look at the cards.'

'What cards?'

Tessa stepped back and slowly approached the table.

'I do Tarot card readings. Nothing fancy or magical, I just do them in my spare time, for spirits, and people's fortunes. Margaret rang me and told me that a boy from your class came around asking for your help. She wanted to know if it was a good idea to help him. I said I would read the cards and call her back. These cards can symbolize an event, an emotion, or even a situation in somebody's life. The pictures are interpreted according to their meaning. They predict something related to the individual pulling the cards.'

'But I never pulled any cards. I don't know anything about this.' Davrin said.

'I know, I know. I got Margaret to pull them for you. It goes against her religious beliefs, but she wanted to know. We couldn't do it properly, seeing as you were unable to pull out the cards yourself. But when we did it, the weirdest thing happened. They all came out as Major Arcana.'

'What does that mean?' Jenson asked.

'You see, in a deck of 78 cards, 22 belong to Major Arcana and the rest are Minor. And when I pulled the cards, all three were Major, but what struck me the most was that it was "The Chariot", then "Strength" and then the "Wheel of fortune".'

Everybody remained quiet. Nobody knew the meaning behind this. They all continued to gaze on in silence as Tessa continued.

'The Chariot means embarking on a journey, hurried decisions with vengeance, turmoil, perseverance. Strength is courage, energy, heroism. And the last one, the Wheel of fortune, this brings luck, fortune. Destiny. Progress.'

'This a good thing, no?' Chloe asked.

'I thought so too,' Tessa answered. 'Until I found out what happened to Margaret. I feel it is somehow my fault. When I never heard from her, and she never turned up for our Prayer meeting, I should have known something was wrong, but, I mean, I never even called her. I figured she needed time with just the two of you Davrin, so she could explain to you about your mother. I'm so sorry. I really am.'

Tessa had a look on her face, a look as if she really believed she was to blame for Margaret's death. And this was the first time she had seemed serious about anything.

Davrin sat there opposite her. He didn't say a word.

'But you couldn't have known any of this was going to happen.' Ellie interrupted. She could see Tessa trying to own the blame.

'Yeah, it's not your fault,' Jenson added.
Reflecting and looking around the room, Jenson did not want to start playing the blame game. Because if he did, he would probably feel the worst. After all, everybody in this room had made it here through some connection of his. And whatever loss they had all experienced, it was all because of their involvement with him.

'Are you okay Chloe?' Ellie asked.
Everybody looked over at Chloe who had suddenly appeared dejected. It seemed as if everything had gotten to her.

'I'm sorry, I just hope nothing bad has happened to Callum.'

The room went silent again. Ellie wrapped her arm around her. Then suddenly a voice spoke.

'I have been practicing my dreams,' Davrin said. 'I think I'm a lot stronger now. I can even move things with my mind. We can try to find him, just like we tried in the church. Maybe he can help us.'

'I'm not sure.' Chloe replied. A sudden shiver crawled up her back and circled around the scar on her shoulder blade. It was taunting her from the last time they tried this in the old church. Her thoughts began to provoke the memory of what happened in that dream. She was scared. And Davrin knew it.

'I know I can do it now Chloe.' Davrin insisted. 'I know I wasn't able to help before, but things are different now. Ever since I saw my mother. And then what I did to Ethan, I just know I can help.'

Davrin glanced over at Jenson. He hadn't meant this to sound boastful. He was ashamed of what happened to Ethan. But he had been practicing. He knew he had gotten better. He was sure his ability had improved.

'We don't even know if Callum is asleep.' Chloe confirmed.

'Maybe Stem have knocked him out for testing?'

'But look what happened last time, with that demon?' Ellie questioned. She didn't want anybody to get hurt again, or worse.

Sterling and Grace both looked at each other even more amazed now. What kind of a mess had they gotten themselves into?

'Please let me help,' Davrin suggested. 'Please, just give me another chance.'

Jenson looked surprised by his offer. He hadn't seen Davrin since his disappearance. This shy boy had somehow changed. He seemed different. He seemed braver. But Jenson knew he had to say something.

'But you couldn't find her the last time? And she was hurt. A demon sliced her shoulder open.'

'I know Jenson, but please give me this chance to prove it to you all.'

Jenson hesitated. He knew there was substance behind his offering. He had just seen the result of it with Ethan.

'But how do we fall asleep?' Chloe asked. 'It's not like we have the tranquiliser gun this time. My mind is in overdrive right now and I've just had a cup of coffee, I don't think I'll be able to sleep……'

But then a notion flickered across her mind. 'OH GOD, what if Callum is already looking for me? What if he needs me?'

She began to panic.

'You need Tranquilisers?' Tessa interrupted.

'Yes. It helps them sleep straight away so they can dream,' Ellie explained.

'Well why didn't you just say so.'

Tessa quickly stepped out of the kitchen.

She had been gone for a few minutes. And in her absence, the room filled with a mysterious cloud overhead. But before anybody could say anything, she walked back into the kitchen, holding a rusty old looking rifle in one hand, and a dusty box of bullets in the other.

'I told you, if you need anything at all, you just have to ask.'

Faces changed from a curious wonder to disbelief.

'I don't know why some of you look so shocked.' Tessa retaliated. 'We did have a farm when Terry was alive. Let's just say this rusty old thing became my best friend. It came in handy a few times, and not just for the animals.'

She smirked, knowing she had used it on her drunken husband before.

'So who wants a shot?'

Chapter 32

'Are you sure you want to do this? Remember what happened last time when you went to sleep without Callum?' Ellie asked, her worry beginning to show.

'I'm sure!' Chloe replied. 'We've no other choice. And what if he's looking for me already?'

Ellie nodded. She understood. But this time she would stay and watch over her.

Chloe lay down on Tessa's couch as Jenson brushed past Ellie to give some encouragement.

'Good luck Chloe. We'll be right here if anything happens. Just call out my name if you feel something isn't right. I'll try to wake you straight away.'

Chloe nodded.

'Thanks Jenson.'

'What if Callum isn't asleep and you end up on your own?' Ellie asked. A nervousness had truly taken over. She still seemed unsure of this idea.

'I'll be okay,' Chloe said, squeezing her hand. 'It's Callum. He would do the same for me. This is our only way to find out what's going on. I have to try. We need to rescue him and your father. He could already be looking for me.'

'Okay,' Ellie agreed. She squeezed Chloe's hand one last time. 'SLEEP SAFE.'

She then stepped out of the room whilst they prepared. She had grown fond of Chloe. It was hard to watch. The anticipation of a worst-case scenario had started to weigh in on her mind. She needed a few minutes alone to shift these negative thoughts.

'I'll go first this time,' Davrin said.

His active approach sent a positivity throughout the room, something he lacked first time round. He had so much fight in him this time. Losing somebody so dear to him had changed him in ways he never knew.

Jenson admired this new trait. He took one glance back at Chloe and then looked over at Grace and Sterling, who both watched on from the sitting room door. They were eager to see how this would play out.

Tessa approached. Without any hesitation, she shot Davrin in the leg. She figured his upper body had taken enough damage. She then turned round, and taking a few steps towards Chloe, she shot her in the arm.

The wait had now begun for Jenson and the others.

~~~

'Where is he?' Chloe muttered to herself.
She had arrived back in the church and was seated on the dusty altar step. It was the same church as before, their previous sanctuary. They had both agreed before being knocked out that this would be their meeting point.

Chloe suddenly heard a noise from the end of the church. Fear set in, for last time things did not prove well in her favour.

The church was dark with only a subtle moonlit glow looming in from the night sky. And bringing with it, was the same darkness through the stain glass windows. It felt the same as before, the time when Davrin never showed. Had she made the same mistake?

She nervously homed in on the big wooden doors as they gently shifted. The wind outside was howling. It's force proving strong as it rattled the structure. One side suddenly opened, and just like before, she could sense a presence. Something had just entered the church.

'DAVRIN….IS THAT YOU?' She called out, the panic inside her increasing.

'Chloe?' A voice called out. It was familiar. It was Davrin.

His reply was faint, but swept in like a mild sedative, brushing away any unease.

He stepped out from the dark shadows, his body in full view as he continued to walk up the aisle. He looked different in here. His arm was not bandaged up. His walk had more confidence. But as he got closer, Chloe could tell it was still him.

Davrin wasn't good with words, so when his approach came to an end, he stood there hesitantly. His awkward silence reassured Chloe.

'You made it,' she said. A sarcastic enamel painted her remark.

'Sorry, I woke up in my own bed first. I think I wasn't ready when Tessa shot me.'

'Yeah, she didn't give me much notice either. I think she enjoyed it. How come you don't have your sling?'

'I'm not sure,' he replied, a slight movement as he waved his arm in the air. 'It doesn't seem to hurt anymore.'

'Maybe it's because we only use our minds in the dream world?'

'I suppose. So where to now?' Davrin asked.

Chloe could see a fight in him. She had sensed it from the moment he entered the church. Maybe he was right. Maybe he had been practicing. And maybe now, he was stronger.

'Myself and Callum, we always meet up at our grandparents house. It's our safe place. Nobody knows about it.'

'And how do we get there?'

'Hold on to me.'

Chloe reached out her hand.

Davrin stepped forward and took hers. He looked uncomfortable as he did it, but Chloe closed her eyes.

She needed to concentrate. She needed to imagine her grandparent's house.

'Okay, now close your eyes and I'll take us there.' She instructed.

Davrin closed his eyes. He didn't know where she was taking him. His mind collapsing into a void. He had blocked out any visions, losing all form of consciousness within this dream. He allowed Chloe to take over.

'Okay, you can open your eyes now,' Chloe said.

Even before Davrin had opened them, he could feel the gentle warm breeze on his face. He preserved this feeling by keeping his eyes shut a little more, longer than he needed to. He stood there retaining the sensation. It was a luxury he had not been given in weeks. Freedom! He could smell it. And then he opened his eyes.

They both stood there, still holding hands. Davrin looked on in amazement as they were now positioned outside a two-story detached house. It was surrounded by an old picket fence, and a narrow walkway, fusing it's end to an open porch deck.

'This is your grandparent's house?' He asked. His hand touching the bordering fence. Its dazzling white contrasting with the flowerbeds inside. And beyond the house stood a meadow. With stalks waving in the breeze, and visible as far as the naked eye could take you. A purity emanating a great love that resided inside. And the smell of pollen, the aromatic microspores, forming like a fine dust, and setting flight for any nasal passage nearby.

'Welcome to our home,' Chloe replied. A proudness resonated within her voice.

'Is this your real house?'

'Not quite. You could say we've done some adjustments. It's amazing where your imagination can take you. Come on, let's go inside. I hope Callum's in there.'

Chapter 33

Chloe ran up the steps. Her eager anticipation left Davrin in her wake. She opened the door and rushed in.

'CALLUM?' She shouted.

A chill lingered from within. And a deafening silence greeted her from the hallway. The sweet-smelling flowers from outside wafted in, filling the cold room with a warm scent, and bringing with it, a sedated substitute. But the family home felt empty.

Just then, a voice called out.

'CHLOE IS THAT YOU?'

Chloe instantly recognised his call. It was Callum.

She took to the stairs, leaving Davrin at the doorstep. Her ecstatic climb confirmed her excitement.

'Oh Callum, I can't believe it's you.' She said, meeting him at the top of the stairs and swinging her arms around him. 'I didn't know if you'd be here.'

'What kept you so long?' Callum said as he held on tight.

Chloe slapped his arm.

Then suddenly, a loud bang startled them.

'Quick Chloe, they've found us!'

'It's okay, it's just Davrin.' Chloe explained.

She released her grip and turned round. She stood there watching Davrin approach the staircase.

'Sorry, I didn't mean to shut it so hard.'

'How?' Callum asked.

'Come on, we've some catching up to do.'

Chloe recounted their steps since the last time she saw Callum. She had told him about Meatloaf's death, how Davrin was shot, and that Wardy was taken too. She also told him about the added two new members of the resistance, a father and daughter duo, who, in the midst of things, are trying to warn them. She explained how they are all in Tessa's house and how they were shot with a rusty tranquiliser gun. But Callum's reaction was not as great as she had imagined. Even though he looked comfortable, sprawled out on the beanbag, she knew his mind was elsewhere.

'Is everything okay Callum?' She questioned.

Callum nodded. He knew he had to tell her about their father. But he wanted her to go first, for he believed his news would knock her for six.

'So now you know we're all fine,' she continued. 'How are you? Where did they take you? Are you somewhere in Stem?'

'Yes.'

'And do you know how you got there? Did they drug you?'

'Yes.'

'Was it Payton White?'

'Yes.'

'Are you sure everything's okay?' She questioned again. 'I don't think you're taking this serious Callum. We need as much information, so we have the best chance of getting you out.'

Chloe knew something was a little off. Callum was not the kind of person to give one-word answers, especially with no substance behind them.

'Chloe?' Callum said, 'I've something to tell you. And I don't know how you're going to react.'

'Just spit it out Callum, what is it?'

'It's dad!'

'Okay. Did you find out anything? I knew they had something to do with his death.'

'No Chloe. He said something bad is going to happen with the cure.'

'Who said?'

'Chloe please. It's not what you think, but I need to tell you.'

'Tell me what Callum? You're not making any sense.'

'It's Dad.'

'What about him?'

'He's alive!'

Chloe paused.

'Callum, if this is some sort of a joke, it's not very funny.'

'It's not Chloe. I promise you this is not a joke. I saw him with my own two eyes.'

Chloe's blank expression said it all. She slowly raised her hand, securing it towards her lips, emphasising the shock she was feeling.

Callum got to his feet and walked over to sit beside her. He put his arm around her, tucking her in tight.

'I know Chloe, I couldn't believe it either, but I saw him. I spoke to him.'

'Are you sure it wasn't a dream?'

'No Chloe. He helped me get here.'

Even though Chloe did not cry out loud, she began to shed a few tears. They were tears for the family that was once broken. And more tears for the family that were torn apart because of the so-called death of their father.

But within seconds, her sadness suddenly lost all of its charm. An anger set in. She shoved Callum away.

'After all this time. How?'

'I know Chloe. I'm not quite sure how. We didn't have much time to talk. He did say it was for our own good. He said he had to do it.'

'For our own good?!'

Davrin could hear the anger in Chloe's reply. He got to his feet. He knew this revelation was a hard one to take, after all, he had been in the same position. He placed his hand gently on top of her shoulder just before leaving the room.

He closed the door behind him. He knew he needed to give them some space. And even though he had quite some time to focus on his own thoughts, spending the past few weeks hidden away in Tessa's home, he couldn't help but wonder where his own life was heading, and if he would ever get to see his mother again. He knew they were all on an emotional rollercoaster, each compartment spinning on its own, spiralling out of control. He didn't know whose compartment was spinning the fastest, or even if this ride would ever stop.

He got to the bottom of the stairs and walked straight into the living room. He needed to sit down again. His thoughts were flowing fast, faster even for him to catch up with. *Where was his mother? What did Stem want from her? Will he ever see her again? Could he even help her, or was it too late? Did they even stand a chance at getting them all out of Stem?*

He glanced out of the window to look at the summer sky. The real-life Autumn sky was too dismal. He wanted to watch the flowerbeds, their colourful glow emitting a happiness, a happiness he felt had left him a long time ago. It seemed so long since he had seen the summer sky.

He got up and stepped out onto the front porch, gently closing the door this time. He sat down and tucked his knees into his chest. He slowly began to inhale the warm summer breeze.

After a few minutes, he leaned back and extended his arms onto the porch deck. He stretched his legs down onto the steps. He tilted his head back, sweeping his mid length black hair out of his face. He wanted his mind to revert to the summer, to go back a few months when everything was normal. The sun's ray began to descend upon his pastel skin. He closed his eyes again and relaxed for the first time since it all began.

Then suddenly, without warning, a shiver crawled down his back. He opened his eyes and looked up.

Nothing. The sky was still as unclouded as before. The sun's ray, still shining down. He looked around at the blooming garden and beyond the white picketed fence. But nothing unusual caught his eye.

A continual flicker beaconed in the distance. He spotted some sort of a light, but a darker light, diverging from its surroundings. His eyes now squinting, seeking affirmation, but he couldn't make out what it was.

He stood up, trying to look at it more intently. But whatever it was, it seemed to be getting closer. It looked as if it was coming towards him.

This image somehow caused a stir inside him. He turned round and retreated cautiously.

Reaching for the door, he pulled down on the handle. But it didn't budge. It was locked. He couldn't open it. For some strange reason it was jammed.

He began to rap on the door. He was desperate for Callum and Chloe's attention. But this brought an air of confusion with it. Every time he went to bang on the door, he was prevented from hitting it. He even tried to shout out their names, but nothing would come out. His mouth was speechless. It was as if something stronger within this dream was preventing him from doing these things.

Helpless, he turned back towards the dark light. This time, it was much closer. He could now make out that it was some sort of a figure flowing towards him. It looked like a female with some sort of a dark flowy dress.

Then, to his astonishment, he realised who it was. It was Stephanie Belshaw. It was his mother. And she was coming for him!

Chapter 34

Jenson stepped outside, leaving Tessa to watch over the bodies. He continued into the kitchen where Sterling and Grace had been seated at the table.

'Have any of you seen Ellie?' He asked.

'No.' Sterling replied.
Grace too shook her head.

When Jenson walked back out into the hallway, he heard a noise near the front door. He walked down, approaching the bottom of the stairs. There, he could see Ellie sitting at the base, crouched into a ball with her knees tucked into her chest. But she didn't seem upset.

'Are you okay?' He asked.
Ellie nodded. But even though she had given him a signal of reassurance, Jenson knew she was lying. He didn't mean to intrude, but he felt she could use a friend right now. He sat down on the floor beside her feet. He waited. He didn't say anything. He just waited.

There was a calm silence between the pair until Ellie eventually spoke.

'Oh Jenson, I don't know how I'd cope if anything was to happen to my dad.'

'We will get them out of there,' Jenson insisted. 'We have to. We've come this far.'

It was Jenson's turn to give the pep talk. He remembered back to the time Ellie had intrusted her words of encouragement. The time when they were back in the church, when Jenson was ready to throw in the towel.

'What about them?' Ellie asked, referring to Sterling and Grace who were waiting in the kitchen.

'We can't involve them, it's too risky. At least they can turn back now before it's too late.'

'But what about what Grace said?'

'About me dying?'

'Yes.'

'I appreciate their help, but we don't know if it's true. I mean yes, she said she saw me in her dream, but she doesn't know who killed me. She doesn't know where. I was at their shop earlier. Maybe it's some sort of déjà vu? Maybe she thinks she saw me, or somebody that looked like me?'

'But she knew your name?'

'I know. But I can't let that be the reason to give up. I don't even know if Robyn will ever wake up. I need to try and find this guy Tom. He could be the key to helping her. And if there's a possibility of getting hurt... even worse... then I'm willing to do it. I just can't sit around and do nothing. No one is safe. Stem Industries are so powerful now, any one of us could be taken out in the blink of an eye.'

'What are you going to say to them?'

'If Grace saw it happen to me, that means she was there. So, if they go home now, she won't be anywhere near me. And nothing will happen to her, or me.'

Ellie softly nodded her head. She knew he had a valid point. She agreed with him. There had already been enough loss and suffering.

'I'm gonna go in and say it to them now.' Jenson affirmed. 'Are you sure you're okay?'

'Yes. I'm fine. Don't worry about me. You go on and do what you need to. I'll go in and check on Chloe and Davrin.'

Jenson got back up on his feet and began to walk towards the kitchen.

But just as he reached the kitchen door, Tessa came bustling out of the sitting room.

'Ellie, Jenson, come quick……it's Chloe!' She cautioned.

Jenson didn't pause. He changed his direction and darted for the sitting room. Recollections of Chloe being dragged across the altar floor had come flooding back.

As he stepped in past the door, he immediately looked over at Chloe. She seemed to be murmuring something.

He got closer. He still couldn't make out what she was saying.

'What is it?' Tessa asked.

'I'm not sure?'

'It looks like she's crying,' Ellie commented, now arriving at the scene, and reaching over Jenson's shoulder.

'She doesn't look to be in any danger. Do you think she found Callum?' Jenson asked.

'I hope so,' Ellie replied. 'I really do hope so.'

They all stood there momentarily. Each one looking at the sleeping bodies, allowing the false alarm to restore any undoing. Tessa had never seen this before. Jenson and Ellie's experience had given them an added advantage.

'I'm going to send Grace and Sterling home.' Jenson said. 'They have a young family. They can't risk getting involved.'

This statement triggered something within Ellie.

'Tessa?' She questioned. 'Would I be able to use your phone again please?'

'Of course you can. And what did I tell you. A friend of Dav's is a friend of mine. You can use anything.'

Ellie immediately rushed past Jenson. She hurried out into the hallway to use the phone. She remembered she was supposed to call Henry and update him when Jenson had arrived. Henry told her he might have a plan up his sleeve. A trump card if ever they needed one.

Chapter 35

'Come on, let's go get Davrin so we can get back to the other's and get you out of Stem.' Chloe said, wiping the few tears she had shed from her cheeks. 'It's so good to see you Callum. Please don't do anything stupid.'

They both hugged one last time before leaving the bedroom and heading out onto the landing. But as soon as they reached the top of the stairs, they both noticed the dark skies outside.

'Something's wrong?' Callum suggested, taking a glimpse out through the window. He watched the leaves blow outside. He had seen this before, back when Chloe was in trouble, back when he was in the bedroom. A dark grey cloud causing an overcast shadow to dim his light.

Without a reaction from Chloe, they both immediately ran down the stairs.

Callum, got to the front door first. He was trying to open it, but it wouldn't budge.

'What's going on Callum?' Chloe asked. She was surprised to see him struggle.

'I don't know....it seems to be jammed.'

'DAVRIN?' Chloe shouted, running from the hallway into the front room.

She immediately looked out the window. And there he was, standing at the end of the garden by the white picket fence. But he wasn't alone. She saw something with him. He looked to be talking to some sort of a shadow, a dark hazy shadow.

'CALLUM?' She screamed.
Without delay, Callum ran over.

'What is it?' He said. He could see it too.

They both began to bang on the window, both calling Davrin's name, and prompting him to return.

~~~

'...but what about my friends?' Davrin asked.

'They will be fine honey,' his mother replied.

Davrin was contemplating on whether to go with his mother as she had requested. After all, this was what he had been searching for over the last two weeks. And as Chloe had mentioned, this was their safe house. *They would be fine without him, wouldn't they?* He thought.

He looked at his mother, a loving sincerity in her reaction. He then glanced back at the house. And just as he did, he saw Callum and Chloe in the downstairs window. He couldn't quite make them out. They looked to be banging on the window. But he confused their warning to be an innocent greeting. He smiled.

Callum and Chloe were shocked when they saw Davrin smiling. He seemed to be waving back at them.

'What is he doing?' Chloe rasped.

Callum stopped banging at the window.

'I don't know. But we need to get out of here. This isn't good.'

'We can't just leave him out there.'

'But he's talking to a demon. Why is he doing that? Why isn't the demon trying to hurt him?'

'IT'S OKAY GUYS, IT'S MY MUM,' Davrin called out. His hand pointing toward her at the picket fence.

'What is he saying?' Chloe asked.

Callum began to point towards the front door, his index finger accentuating the urgency. Chloe began to imitate this action.

'Mum, they're pointing to the front door. I think they want us to come back. Come on, I'll introduce you. They're good guys.'

But just as Davrin was about to return to the house, his hand was pulled back. He immediately froze.

His mother's hand was cold. For some reason it didn't feel like a warm touch. And the hand suddenly began to take hold, squeezing his with great strength, a strength that certainly didn't feel like a mother's reuniting touch.

Davrin turned around and looked up. His mother's face had somehow just mutated. Fragments of her soft skin had just been ripped away and replaced by a hard exoskeleton. A demonic figure stood in front of him.

He jumped back. But he couldn't move. He was still being held by the hand of the demon.

'YOU'RE NOT MY MOTHER!' He yelled.

The shapeshifter had just lost all recognisable features. Davrin had never seen it before. A dark face, and skin stretched so tightly, it looked like a bone structure bulging underneath. Its eyes were larger than normal but looked disturbingly deep. A boundless matter of black. And its body was thin, very frail. And just like its face, every bone seemed to be visibly clear, protruding out through its shallow dark covering.

Davrin screamed. He tried to rip himself free from its grasp, but it was of no use.

'GET OFF ME.... WHAT DO YOU WANT? WHERE'S MY MOTHER?'

'I'm here to take you to her.' The demon answered. Its voice was deep and coarse, just like it's touch.

'Let me talk to my friends. Get off me! You're hurting me!'

Davrin continued to tug himself away from the demon. But again, it was of no use. Its grip had become even tighter. He could feel the sting.

He glanced down and could see a trail of blood oozing. The demon had embedded its prickly fingers in so tight. It felt like sharp nails indenting their bony fingers into him, scoring his wrist.

'GET OFF ME!!!' He demanded again. And another attempt to wrangle himself free.

'I need you,' the demon said, pulling Davrin away from the picket fence. 'Your mother needs you.'

Davrin's feet began to scuff. He was being dragged out further. The waving stalks from the flower beds were now grappling at his feet to help pull him further. He turned round to call out for help, but this time the blooming flowerbeds had all decayed. They had changed into a weeded infestation. And the house looked as old and rundown as if it had not been lived in for centuries.

'What's happening?' Chloe called out. She too could see this sudden change.

'It's the demon. It's doing all of this.' Callum answered. But he didn't stay. He was already running for the front door again. He needed to prise it open.

Suddenly the inside of the house began to wither. Crumbling cement began to drop from the ceiling. And inside, the walls began to crack, all merging with the decomposing exterior.

'CHLOE, SOMETHING'S HAPPENING? WE NEED TO LEAVE!'

Callum roared from out in the hallway. But Chloe continued to bang hard on the window. She continued to call out for Davrin.

Davrin's body was arched over, his weight leaning forward as he was being pulled away from the house. His feet were sliding, but he managed to grab hold of a now ruined and broken fence.
His grip loosened, and a large chunk of fence snapped off. He immediately fell to the ground.
The demon quickly leaned in to grab a better hold of him. It's claw reaching in to take hold of him once more.
Davrin raised his hand to lash out in retaliation. And just then, the demon flew beyond the wilted fields. It immediately let out a roar as it was catapulted into the air by Davrin's push.
'QUICK, CALLUM LOOK!' Chloe demanded. She had seen the whole thing unfold.
Callum ran back into the room. He turned to face Chloe's direction.

Davrin had now picked himself up off the ground. He was sprinting back to the house. He had never moved so fast. His feet were gripping to the decaying soil beneath, but he kept running. He didn't want to turn around. He watched his friends in the window, their movement, encouraging him to continue. He knew he needed to get back into the house.
Callum and Chloe were both watching on and searching for the demon's body.
'There, look!' Chloe cautioned.
Callum could see it too. The demon's body had just risen through the weeded grassland beyond the picket fence.
Just as Davrin had reached the front door, he held out his hand again, determined to push it in. He never touched the door. But it slammed open.

Chloe and Callum had just reached the hallway, startled by the sudden crash.

'COME ON DAVRIN, GET IN!' Callum yelled, closing the door behind him.

Davrin hurried inside.

'What happened?' Chloe asked.

'It was my mother, but then it wasn't. She was gone. I'm not sure. I just wanted to get it away from me. It tried to grab me, but I pushed it away. I didn't even touch it.'

'Is that what you meant about moving things in your dreams?'

'Yes, but not like that. It happened when I went to Ethan's house.'

'You're a Drifter, Davrin. You must have some sort of ability. Maybe your powers have increased?'

'Guys I think you need to see this.' Callum insisted. He stood in front of the window again.

Chloe and Davrin could see him inching away. They both ran over to see what was wrong.

All three of them stood there watching on as the demon slowly raised its long underweight arms, both elevating a few feet off the ground. It looked like it had been lifted from the ground by small bony stumps, a poor excuse for a set of wings, now flapping from the back of its shoulders.

'GUUUYS!' Callum called out. He spotted a patch of weed immerging together, clumping into a ball of soil. And then another patch submerging, followed by another.

Then, suddenly the three patches of shrubbery transformed into three large-sculptured weed creatures, each one, easily ten feet tall.

The demon then directed its arms towards the house. And the newly forged monsters began to trudge in their direction.

'What do we do?' Chloe called out.

'RUN!' Callum screamed. 'WE RUN!'

Chapter 36

'I really do appreciate you both coming to find me, to help me, but I don't want more people getting hurt. I can't have you involved.'
Jenson sat back at the kitchen table, allowing his instruction to sink in.

'I know I've never met you before, but I saw you,' Grace replied. 'You died. And I was there. It was so real.'

'I know, but that's exactly it. You said you were there. If you leave now, you won't be involved. You won't be there. Your vision won't happen.'

Grace had no answer for this. She paused for a moment, allowing Jenson's words to penetrate. What he was saying did make sense. *How come she had never thought of this before? Where was she when she saw this happen, one of Stem's labs? Why would she have even been there? How had she allowed this vision to corrupt her?*

Sterling put his arm around his daughter.

'He has a point, Gracie. There's no reason why you would be in Stem Industries? If we go now, then maybe your dream will never happen. Maybe us leaving now will somehow change Jenson's fate?'

Grace stood up from the table. Something had imploded inside her. She knew what she saw. She knew how it felt. But this truth did seem to wipe any heroism.

'I'm sorry to have wasted your time,' she said.
Grace wasn't one for huffing, but the tone in her remark caused a wave of offence to follow her as she removed herself from the table.

'Don't be sorry. You do not need to apologise at all,' Jenson replied.

But Grace didn't respond. She continued out of the kitchen while her father shook Jenson's hand.

'Thank you for taking the time to listen,' he said. His tone seemed calm, unlike his daughters. 'I don't know what it all means for Grace. But I will try my best to help her. Good luck with everything Jenson.'

Jenson smiled. A short, but genuine appreciation.

'Thank you,' he replied, watching Sterling leave the room.

The front door closed just as Jenson sat back down at the kitchen table. He blew out a gust of air. The built-up tension had suddenly been released. It was as if he had just escaped death. But this was short lived.

'JENSON?' A voice called out from the living room. It was Ellie.

Jenson ran into the living room again. He could see Tessa kneeling over Davrin's body. She had his arm held out, showing him the blood emerging from his wrist. It looked like trails of blood oozing out, as if from a freshly deep cut.

'What is happening?' Tessa begged.

'Something's wrong!' Jenson quickly answered. 'We have to wake them, NOW!'

~~~

All three of them had only reached the end of the hallway when the front room window came crashing in. A weeded monster had just entered the house.

'COME ON!' Callum shouted, now standing inside the kitchen, waiting for Chloe and Davrin to meet him.

He was trying to open the back door. But just like the front door previously, it was jammed shut.

'Davrin, you try,' Chloe suggested.

Callum turned and stepped out of the way.

And just like before, Davrin raised his hand and pushed it out, aiming towards the back. And with one quick exertion, he blew the door off its hinges.

The smashing noises behind them grew louder. So, without any hesitation, they all immediately ran out into the back garden.

Outside, the garden was just as dilapidated as the front, with weeds everywhere. And amongst the weeds, there was a worn out shed which stood to one side, and a larger beaten-up barn on the other.

'OVER THERE!' Callum instructed.
He pointed over to the barn after a quick scan. And instantly, the three of them began to surge towards it.

They had not even reached a stone's throw from beyond the house when one of the weeded monsters came crashing out through the back door, taking half of the wall with it.

Chloe screamed. She was trailing behind Callum and Davrin in the race for the barn. She could feel the debris from the wall land around her, with one chunk hitting her leg. She fell to the ground.

The two boys turned. They could see the monster hot on Chloe's tail.

They both stopped in their tracks watching the monster lifting its twined arm and swooping it into Chloe. It smashed against Chloe, sweeping her across the garden like a twig.

'CHLOEEEE?' Callum screamed as Chloe was sent flying through the air.

The creature didn't hesitate. It was as if it had swatted Chloe out of the way to get to Callum and Davrin. Perhaps its instructions were to get Davrin, and crush anything in its way.

Davrin didn't have time to think. The weeded Monster approached. It lifted its trunk up again and smashed down on top of him.

An air of silence encased Davrin. It was as if a void of emptiness had surrounded him. Davrin suddenly realised he had not been hit. The Monster had not struck.

Davrin moved his arm away from his face. It was as if some sort of an invisible shield had been suspended over him and Callum.

Low muffled sounds emitted from within the enchanted protection. But outside this forcefield, loud smashing thumps bellowed. The monster didn't stop. It knew its strikes were not landing. But it continued to smash down, hitting the blanket of strong air.

It was Davrin. His powers, now protecting them from the attack.

Both boys, secured from within this fortified bubble, but suddenly the ground began to quake. Another weeded monster came crashing out of the house.

They watched it advance. But Callum's stomach dropped. He quickly realised where it was going.

'CHLOEEE?' He screamed.

Chloe began to pick herself up. Like a fawn taking its first steps, she was unsteady. The knock had taken the wind out of her sail. She quickly glanced over at them.

'DAVRIN?' Callum called out. 'ITS GOING AFTER CHLOE!'

Davrin looked over to see the monster. It had reached Chloe just when she started to run again. And as it swept its large tree trunk arm down at her, Davrin shifted one of his hands, slapping it towards the monster. His other hand remained suspended, maintaining their own protection.

The monster's body snapped in half. Its top half fell to the ground as the bottom collapsed into a pile of undergrowth, emptying itself all over the mouldering ground.

An internal combustion took over Davrin's body. A green light emitted from his eyes. A confidence grew from within. He then brought his two arms together, slapping his hands as the vibrations shattered the force field and exploded towards the weeded monster.

The monster, just like the other one, dispersed its limbs all over the ground, spraying itself against them like a whirlwind of decaying leaves.

Davrin had just destroyed two of the creatures in an instance. And in that moment, before all the weeded remains had fallen, the last monster came crashing out of the house.

Davrin raised his hand. A further confidence growing from within. He instinctively knew what to do.

Callum's concerns had eased. He knew Davrin was different. He knew he was a force to be reckoned with within this Dream world.

But suddenly, Darvin's green light adopted a misty fog. His vision went blurry.

~~~

It only took a few seconds, but Davrin's vision had returned. Something was wrong. Everything had changed.

'Oh thank god you're okay Dav,' Tessa said, leaning in over his body with the tranquiliser dart in her hand.

'What have you done?' Davrin urged.
Tessa looked surprised.

'I was only trying to help. You were bleeding. We saw blood on your wrist.'

Davrin's voice became louder. He looked over at Chloe's twitching body, lying there on the couch across from him.

'NO!! You Fools!! What have you done? It's coming for them.'

Chapter 37

Callum stepped outside of the blinding mist. He sprinted towards his sister.

'Are you okay?' he asked, swatting the leaves from her body.

'What happened?' Chloe questioned.

'It was Davrin. He's different. He's stronger now.'

Callum turned around to see the dissolving mist disappear. And only then did he realise that Davrin too had disappeared.

'Where is he?'

But before they had time to think, Chloe took hold.

'Callum, there's another one!' She said, pulling at his sleeve and urging him to move.

But they were too late. The last weeded monster sliced its arm across and swept them both away.

Callum landed hard onto the ground, but the weeds beneath had broken his fall. He straightened his body and glanced up. He could see his sister, whose body remained on the ground, motionless. In that moment Calum could tell she wasn't going to run. The fall had been too much.

Callum was too far away to help. The monster had reached her again. It was standing over her now.

Callum began to scream. He was desperately trying to draw its attention away from Chloe, but his efforts were in vain. The monster wasn't listening.

Chloe managed to roll over on the ground. She looked up and saw the elevated trunk come crashing down. It was too late. She couldn't move. She turned to face Callum.

'I love you,' she mouthed, without a single word being spoken.

It was all she could do before the arm came smashing down on top of her.

'NOOOOO!!!' Callum roared as he watched his sister's final moment.

He held his hand out, stretching it like Davrin had. He wanted to do what he had. But he couldn't move the monster. Its giant fist smashed down right on top of Chloe, crushing her body.

'CHLOEEEEE?!!'

Callum was distraught. He had just watched his sister being crushed to death. But he didn't have time to grieve. The monster turned towards him.

Callum began to run, but the monster was bigger and faster. It reached him within seconds. It then swiped him up, sending him flying across the weeded plantation, and crashing into the shabby barn.

He smashed through the barn and came toppling down onto the concreted floor. He could feel his back cracking off the ground, but for some strange reason it wasn't sore. His back didn't break.

He got up with ease. He could feel a tightening sensation around his chest. He looked down to see some sort of strapping. He then turned his neck and saw a broken shield covering his back. It must have been the shield that cracked. But how was a shield even on him?

He was sent in the air by the monster and all he could think of was how his body would have been broken as it smashed into the barn wall. He had been forced through metal scaffolding and had landed onto a cold concreted floor. How could he have survived this unhinged?

He didn't have long to contemplate this, because within seconds, the monster had smashed through the side wall of the barn. It began to thump at the contents, to clear a way in to get at Callum.

Callum's eyes scanned the barn, but before he could search for a weapon, he felt something in his hand. He looked down. It was a sword. He had imagined something sharp, a weapon of some description to hack away at this weeded creature. And there it was, sitting neatly in his hand, a sword.

The monster had now reached inside. It was furiously swinging its branched arms at him.

Callum didn't hesitate. He dodged out of the first attack. And with one swoop, he sliced down and chopped one of its arms off.

A conviction took hold and he charged towards it.

He began to slice down in a frenzied attack. He didn't stop until there was nothing left, each slice producing a venom. A retaliation for his sister's death.

Standing there, breathing heavily, he eventually stopped as the last weed fell.

~~~

Chloe's eyes opened. Everything had changed.

'What? How am I here?' She asked, now focusing in on the dated interior of Tessa's living room. A reassurance invaded her whole body. She knew she had just managed to escape death.

'We had to wake you,' Jenson answered, standing over her body. 'Davrin said you were in trouble.'

'Callum?' She called out. 'I need to go back and help him.'

Jenson didn't hesitate, especially considering what happened last time they had done this. He picked up the tranquiliser gun and shot her in the shoulder again. He knew she needed to go back.

'What did you do that for?' Ellie shouted. She knew Davrin and Chloe were both awake. All they needed was for Callum to wake.

'I don't know what's going on.' Jenson answered. 'But they need each other.'

~~~

Callum fled the barn to find his sister's body. As he reached the condensed undergrowth, he couldn't find it anywhere. He was confused. He then looked around to see if he had remembered where she had been crushed.

A dark shadow revealed itself from the rubble remains of the back door. It was the demon who had summoned the monsters.

Callum was enraged. He immediately charged toward it, screaming, and holding out his sword.

'You're going to pay for what you did to my sister, even if it's the last thing I do!'

The demon pressed forward, reacting to Callum's charge. It had just accepted his challenge, knowing it would win.

But then, suddenly it flinched as if hearing something in the distance.

'You are lucky,' it rasped. 'We will meet again!'
And with that, it disappeared into a black haze.

Callum's reluctance returned, but it wasn't because he had missed out on this final battle. It was because he had suddenly heard a familiar voice, a faint cry in the distance. It was Chloe.

'CALLUM?' she shouted as she appeared from the side of the house, running towards him.

'Chloe…..you're….alive?' He said, dropping his sword and reaching out. 'But how?'

'They woke me,' she said, falling into his arms. 'Jenson woke me. They knew something was wrong.' Callum began to cry.

'I thought I lost you, just like I lost Carly.'

'Oh Callum, It'll take more than that to get rid of me.' Chloe's masked sarcasm had been overlooked. It was something Callum would have been proud of, but he was too upset to even notice. He stood there crying into her shoulder.

'We better wake up Callum. Before any more of those creatures come back. And where did you get that sword, and the shield?'

'I'm not too sure,' he replied. He simply leaned his forehead into hers. 'I'm just so glad you are alive. I don't know what I would have done?'

'Me too,' Chloe said. A smile on her face. 'I know I won't see you after this, but we'll find a way to get you out of Stem. Please just hold on tight. And cooperate. Do anything you need to for them to keep you alive. Promise me?'

'Yeah sure.'

'Callum? Please promise me you will cooperate?'

'Yes, okay Chloe. I promise!'

'Good. We're going to get you out of there. Just hold tight.'

Chapter 38

Chloe's eyes opened. Everybody gathered round her, waiting for her to speak.

'Where's Davrin?' She asked. She was trying to sit up and brush them out of her way.

Davrin was unconscious and sitting on the armchair.

'We need to wake him,' she said.

'We did Chloe,' Jenson replied. 'But he insisted on going back for you.'

Chloe's face dropped.

'No…we need to wake him now. Something was after him. I brought him into my dream. He won't know how to find me.'

Ellie, who was standing nearest to Davrin, ran over and instantly yanked the tranquiliser dart out of his arm.

'Davrin….Davrin….wake up!' She called out, shaking him profusely.

Davrin's groggy murmurs elated Chloe. To her delight he was wakening up. She let out a sigh of relief.

'What happened Chloe?' Jenson asked.

'I'm never sleeping again,' she said, taking a few deep breaths. 'Where do you want me to begin?'

~~~

Callum's eyes opened. He was back where he had started. He was back in Stem Industries.

He was relieved the dream was over, but mostly, relieved that his sister was still alive.

Looking around him at all the scientific equipment and all the coloured solutions in the test tubes, he suddenly remembered what had happened to him earlier. His father had given him a phial of blue liquid. He had injected him with it and told him it would help him in his dream. But he never got the chance to explain what it did. Callum was shot with a tranquiliser bullet, leaving him to figure it all out for himself.

Was this the reason he was still alive? Had this potion given him the ability to manifest things in his dream, to make them appear instantly? It had to be the only explanation. He thought.

The lab doors opened. Mr. White walked in.

'Ah, you're awake,' he declared. 'Seems like we have a lot of catching up to do.'

'Where's my father?' Callum asked, yanking at the straps.

'You are in no position to be demanding answers Callum? That is your name isn't it, Callum?' Callum didn't acknowledge this statement.

'Don't blame yourself' Mr White added. 'Your father wasn't much help ever since we had Jenson's sister here. He said she reminded him of his daughter, the one that died, what was her name again? Ah yes, Carly wasn't it?'

'Don't you dare speak her name!'

'Very protective I see. I'm sure your father would be proud.'

'Where is he? He better be alive!'

'Oh don't worry, he is alive…..for now. He never did like my ways. So let's just say I don't have much use for him anymore.'

Payton's smug gestures made Callum even more angry.

'WHAT DO YOU WANT?' Callum shouted.

'A bit of fight in you I see. Something your father lacks.'

'What do you want, I said?'

'Well we did want Jenson and his sister, at first. Then it was his friend Davrin. But now, as it turns out, we don't need any of you. We have what we want.'

'Davrin's mum?' Callum questioned. He had remembered Davrin saying he saw his mother in the dream. The mother that turned into the demon.

'Aaaaah, you know of Miss Belshaw? Tough, and smart. Maybe I will find some use for you after all.'

'I would never help you!'

'I don't think you have a choice.' Payton responded.

Callum suddenly remembered what Chloe had said, about cooperating.

'Ok, well maybe we can make a deal?'

Payton began to snigger.

'You think you can make a deal with me?'

'Yes. I know where Davrin is. I saw him in my dream. I can help you find him.'

Callum knew he would never help Payton White. He hoped his ploy could buy him some time.

'And you think I believe you?' Payton suggested.

'Well as you said, I'm not in a position to demand. Maybe I can earn your trust?'

The room filled with silence. Payton White had somehow began to consider Callum's offer.

'What do you want with Davrin and his mother anyway?' Callum asked.

'It's Stephanie.' Payton answered. 'I believe she is the key to all of this. She came to us many years ago. She could hear voices in her head. We did some testing on her, but your father said she was too unstable. She was of no use. We shipped her off to that nut house, St. Anita's. But now after enhanced technology, and all the years of sedation, she is proving very useful.'

'Useful for what?' Callum questioned.

'She is so far involved in the realisation of her dreams. If we stabilise her, I believe she can help us reach the minds of society. We can use her to be the link, for when people sleep. And all we need is the finalisation of Fusion four.'

'Fusion four? What's that?'

'It's the cure that will help every dreamer out there. And put an end to the nightmares once and for all.'

'More like a drug that warps their mind, so you can control them.'

Payton laughed again.

'You are quite smart. That's the only thing you and your father have in common I suppose.'

'So I'm right?'

'Not quite. We don't want to warp their mind. I look at it as a mutual understanding. If they scratch our backs, we'll scratch theirs.'

'And how does that work?'

'Well Stephanie will be the hub, the heart of the project. If we get her connected correctly, she'll be the link that will keep everyone together as they sleep, a protector as such.'

'And what if it doesn't work, like last time?'

'That cure didn't work last time because of your father. He is too emotionally involved. We have Dr. Shafter now. He believes Stephanie is nearly ready for the transition. And with a little tweaking, and Stephanie on board, we will be unstoppable.'

Callum was speechless. *Could this be true? Could Miss Belshaw somehow protect civilians in their sleep, control their every move? But if so, what would these people be used for?*

'If that's true,' he said, 'then why do you still want us?'

Mr. White smirked.

'You keep getting in the way.'

'We won't say anything. Just let us go. If this new cure works, then you'll be happy.'

'I don't want anybody to stand in our way. You kids keep showing up, like a decaying rot. We need to eliminate you all.'

'What if this cure doesn't work, like your last attempt? And what if Stephanie can't help you?'

'It will work Callum. We've found a better Scientist. Dr Shafer is so eager for this. He assures me it will work.'

'And you can trust him, like you trusted my father?'

'He can speak to Stephanie. For some reason, he wanted to be a test subject. That's how dedicated he is. He put himself forward to be tested on. I've seen it with my own eyes. They can communicate, and he does what she wants him to do in his dreams. So yes, the new drug does work. We just need people to start taking it now.'

'That's not a cure! That's controlling people like robots as they sleep. You want them to do your dirty work for you.'

'They won't know that will they? And I will destroy this so-called Resistance before anyone finds out.'

Chapter 39

'We have a plan,' Ellie confidently said, stepping into the kitchen. The bounce in her step brought with it an air of enthusiasm. She scanned the room to see Jenson, Chloe, Davrin, and Tessa, all sitting around the kitchen table.

'What is it?' Jenson asked.

'Henry is going to help us get into Stem Industries.' She said, rushing her words. Her rambling tone confirmed her consent to this plan.

'But how?'

'We leave in the morning. My advice is to get a good night's sleep.'

'But how is he going to get us in?' Jenson asked.

'Well, you see…..'

Ellie pulled out a chair and sat down before it steadied itself. Her arms stretching out in front, her hands flexing in preparation to give the eager gestures.

'…..Stem have a delivery in the morning. It's a new drug. Henry said he'll sort it out. He's going to look for a way to sneak us in. He said he'll have something more concrete tomorrow.'

'Will he be able to get us all in?' Chloe asked.

'I'm not too sure. We'll know more in the morning.'

'I don't think Dav is in any fit state to go,' Tessa exclaimed. She looked across the table as Davrin sat there, subdued, with one hand holding onto his injured arm.

'No. Oh no,' Ellie replied. 'Davrin has just been shot. I think he'll have to sit this one out.'

'So it will be myself, you, Jenson and Henry?' Chloe questioned.

Ellie hesitated. She glanced over at Jenson, but Jenson didn't notice this delay. He stood up from the table, showing his interest.

'So what time do we need to be ready for?' He asked.

Again, Ellie delayed her response. This time Jenson caught her action. An uncertain silence took over him. And Ellie's bounce had taken a tumble. She no longer held onto that enthusiastic lead.

'Ellie?' Jenson questioned.

'Yes?'

'What time do we leave at?'

A silence took hold. And then Ellie spoke.

'Jenson. Both myself and Henry, we think it's not a good idea if you come with us. After everything that has happened, we just can't take that chance.'

'What do you mean?'

'Your family barely escaped last time. It's my father and Callum in there. We think Chloe and I should go with Henry.'

'But I'm still part of this.' Jenson barked. A temper now forming inside him as he slammed the table with his fist.

'I know you want to help. But you need to be there for Robyn and your parents.'

'Don't tell me what I need. I got you all into this mess. And even though my sister escaped, she still might as well be in there. She's lying in a coma because of what Stem did to her. I'm going. This is the only way to get answers. I need to find Tom.'

Jenson's eyeline slide across the table to Chloe. She had told him that her father was alive, and he was the man who was trying to help.

'But Jenson, that girl Grace, she's never met you before and she saw you die. What if she's right? What if, by chance, it was some sort of a vision?'

'You don't think I've thought about that Ellie? And if it's true then she would have to be there. She's not coming. I've sent them home. She won't be anywhere near Stem. She's gone.'

'I don't know,' Ellie responded. 'Up until a week ago, I didn't think such things could ever happen. But now? I feel anything is possible.'

'I don't care. I'm going, whether you like it or not. I need to finish this. So what time are we leaving at?'

Ellie hesitated. She looked across at the others. But nobody had anything to say. At the end of the day, they all knew it was Jenson's decision. And it seemed no matter what she said, he was determined to go.

'But Jenson, are you sure you want to risk everything?' Ellie asked, one last time for him to change his mind.

'It's too late to be worrying about risks. What time do we leave?'

'Seven o'clock.'

'Okay, I'll be back in the morning, before seven. I need to say goodbye to my parents just in case we don't come back.'

～～～

The taxi pulled up outside Jenson's home. Looking at his watch he noticed it was 11:42pm

'Shit,' he muttered under his breath. He could immediately see that his parent's car stood still in the driveway. He knew they were back. He knew he was going to have to explain himself.

The front door opened just as the taxi pulled off. Jenson could see his mother standing in the doorway.

'Where have you been?' She asked.
'I got bored, so I went to meet the others.'
'Are they okay?'
'Yes, they're all fine. Ellie is still upset about Meatloaf.'
'I'm sure she is. Come on, let's get you inside. It's getting cold, plus there's a nice slice of cake in on the kitchen table for you.'
'Hey Jenson,' his father said, greeting him as he came inside.
'Hey dad, how was your night? You're home early?'
'Ah it was okay. Your mother couldn't wait to get home. We made an excuse to leave early. We're not that long in before you.'
'It just didn't feel right,' his mother declared. 'Especially considering what happened today.'
'I understand,' Jenson said. 'I'm wrecked, so I'm gonna go to bed.'
'What about your cake?'
'I'm not hungry. But thanks.'
'Are you okay Jenson? You seem quiet.' His father asked.
'It's just been a long day.'
'It sure has. We're going up to the hospital in the morning to see your sister. You wanna come?'
'Yeah sure.'
But Jenson knew he had no intention in doing this.
'Okay well get some rest.'
'I will. Good night dad.'
Jenson stepped over toward his father. He threw his arms around him, giving him the biggest hug ever. 'I love you. I love you both.' He added.
His father was taken aback. He let out a chuckling sound and looked over at his wife.
'What's this all about?' He asked Jenson as he began to return the squeeze.

Jenson had just about held it together in his answer.

'Just with everything that has happened, I want to tell you both how much I love you because you never know what could happen.'

'That's so true Jenson,' his mother agreed, as she too embraced the cuddle. 'And we love you too honey.'

'Yeah Jenson,' his father added. 'I don't know what your mother and I would have done these past few weeks without you.'

He kissed Jenson on the top of his head. This sort of affection was rare from his father. Maybe what happened to Robyn had changed him, maybe it had changed them all. And perhaps better things were to come. But Jenson knew he mightn't be here to experience it. If this was his last chance to say goodbye, then he wanted them both to know how much he loved them. For tomorrow, he was going to help the others. They were going to break into Stem and free his friends. Tomorrow, he was going to find the answers he was looking for. And tomorrow, Jenson was going to make sure Stem would pay for everything they have done.

Chapter 40

Jenson opened his eyes. His bedroom was in total darkness. Looking around the room, he realised he had fallen asleep prematurely, lying on top of his covers.

He turned his head over towards the alien alarm clock Robyn had bought him. The luminous digital time was displaying bright enough to see. It read 2:53am.

He reached over and began to set the alarm for 6:00am. He figured that would give him enough time to sneak out of the house and meet up with the others before they left for Stem.

Just as he lay back down, he noticed a sudden flash of light in the corner of his eye. A silhouette of a child emerged from the darkness. But within seconds it was gone. *Had he imagined it? Could it have been a vision of Robyn? Somehow, her soul visiting him, to warn him.*

He rested his head on the pillow and looked up to the blank ceiling. A blurred flashback popped into his head. A vision he had seen before but didn't know where. It was like a déjà vu moment. *Had this happened to him before? Or was it a memory, resurfacing from his childhood, a memory of the fairies?*

'Please don't be afraid,' a girl's voice called out from the darkness.

Jenson shifted in the bed. His arms pressed out in front as if protecting himself. The room revealed a darkness. But within this darkness, something was watching him.

He reached over and immediately turned on his bedside light. He wanted to unveil the shadow from within the room. His whole body ceased. The image, now visible.

The light revealed a fairy of some kind, standing at the bottom of his bed. It looked like an elf child. A girl. With blue eyes that were big, bigger than the average human. Her face was a pale grey, and Jenson noticed her whole body balancing this anaemic shade. She had long black hair with pointed ears. They were small ears, protruding out through her locks. She looked like something from an enchanted place. Chalky brown material clung to her body with lace bodices draped all over. Unsuitably matched, but aesthetically pleasing. And her wings. Jenson could see wings attached to her back. They were jutting out over her shoulders. And even though they were small, he could see the vibrant blue of the morpho butterfly in them. The richest of blues with a purple shimmer throughout.

Déjà vu hit him again. *This butterfly, the morpho butterfly. Had he seen this fairy before? The stories of fairies, the headaches, everything that Sterling had said, was it all true?*

This vision had reignited an image he had seen before. It was the very same fairy he had seen that night, the night when Robyn had come home from Stem Industries. He had now suddenly remembered.

'I've seen you before,' he said.

'Yes, you have. My name is Myral. I hoped you would forget.'

'I did, until now.'

'Please forgive me. It was Pixie dust, only a little bit.' Myral rolled her thumb against the inside of her index finger. She was emphasising how small the sprinkling was.

'I have been getting these flashbacks,' Jenson said. 'Flashbacks of butterfly wings. I thought I had imagined it because of what my mother had said. The stories when I was younger.'

'I'm sorry.' Myral pleaded. 'I panicked. I've never met a human who could see me before. We've only read stories about it.'

'We? There are more of you?'

'Yes,' Myral answered.

'Where do you come from?'

'We come from the 'Realm of the Fae'. You know it as the Dream World.'

'And what do you want?'

'We mean no harm to you in your world. We collect your teeth.'

A huge grin revealed her own sparkling white teeth. A cheeky hilarity linked by her response.

'What?' Jenson questioned. He realised how ridiculous this sounded but he was too curious to see the humour in it. 'Tooth fairies exist, and they really do come to take our teeth?'

Myral nodded.

'So it's true?' Jenson asked.

Myral approved his question again with another nod.

'When I was a kid,' Jenson continued, 'my mother said I believed in tooth fairies. But as I got older, I was told there was no such thing. But how? We just gave our parents our teeth. My mum still has them in a little box in her room.'

'Yes. It is a little more difficult to find the teeth when they are not under your pillow.' Myral replied.

'But how? Why?'

Myral dipped her hand into a fold in her dress. It disappeared inside a concealed pocket. She then lifted it back out. Grains of colourful dust sifted between her fingers. It looked as if it was moving, but not a single drop fell from her palm.

'This is our magical pixie dust. It helps us travel to your world. With the help of children's imagination.'

'The monsters, those demons who kill people in their sleep, they are like you?'

'Oh no,' Myral answered. Her tone deepened as her brow flexed. She seemed offended. 'We collect human teeth because they are of magical value in our world. We make our weapons with your teeth. Your teeth are strong and help us fight against demons.'

Jenson couldn't help but wonder how old this fairy child was. She seemed ahead of her years talking to him like this. But looking at her, she was only a child.

'A war between fairies and demons?' he asked. His mind was trying to imagine such a notion. 'Do you fight as well?'

'Not me,' Myral replied, emptying the contents of her hand back into her pouch. 'My father's army does. I am only a child.....well not for long.'

'Not for long?' Jenson asked.

'Yes, I will be bigger soon. We don't grow like humans. And when I change, I will not be able to enter your world.'

'Why?'

'It is only the children Fae that can enter your world. They are smaller and do not need as much magic. We are not made the way you humans are made. We are made by the magic of the Elder Fae, and the magic from our parent's wings.'

'Why are you here then, with me?'

A chill drew its mark along Jenson's back, like a chalk scraping down against a blackboard. *Had this fairy child come to speak to him directly? If so, then what did she want with him?*

'I need to talk to you Jenson.'

And there it was. His name being used. This was the first time she had mentioned him by name. *If she was here to see him, and she knew his name, then what did she want?*

'How do you know my name, and what do you want from me?'

If this was the last time Jenson would see her, he needed answers.

'We are all in great danger. We believe you can help.'

'Me? But I can't dream. I can't help you fight those demons.'

'Our Elders, the most powerful Fae in our land, they've told us stories of a human who will save us all. We believe that is you.'

'How can I save you all? I told you. I can't dream.'

'I'm not sure. My grandmother, she is an Elder, she believes you are special. She believes you are a Gateway between our worlds, the last Gateway. And if something happens to you, the portal will open.'

'What Gateway? I don't know what you mean. I have no powers. My friend Davrin has powers. He can dream. Maybe its him?' A frustration took hold. 'How can I save you all? I couldn't even save my sister.'

'But you can Jenson. Robyn can be saved.'

'Robyn? You know about Robyn?'

'Yes! That is why I am here. I have spoken to her.'

'How?'

Suddenly the room light switched on. Its bright glare overtook Jenson's side lamp. His pupils dilated. He was trying to block out the overwhelming glow, his hand, covering his eyeline. He looked over to where the light had been ignited. His mother stood there in the doorway.

'Are you okay Jenson? Who are you talking to?' She asked, now stepping into his room. Her night shorts and t-shirt indicating she had been woken up.

'She said she has spoken to Robyn,' Jenson explained, pointing over to the end of his bed.

'Are you sure you're okay Jenson?' His mother asked. She followed his finger to see the void between his bed and his wardrobe. A confusion painted her face, and Jenson could see this.

'She's just there. She's standing at the end of my bed.'

'Only a Gateway can see us Jenson,' Myral explained. She stood firmly at the end of his bed. A self-assured composure strengthening her explanation. She remained there, looking at him

'But?'

'Jenson have you taken that medicine we got you earlier?' His mother asked.

'Not yet.'

'Don't you think you should start taking them?'

'Yes,' Jenson answered. But he knew this was a lie.

'Are you imagining those fairies again, like when you were younger?'

'No.'

Jenson knew his mother would never believe him. She always refused to see what was not in her hand.

'Okay, well at least that's a good sign. You must have been talking in your sleep.'

Jenson was quiet now. He looked over at Myral who stood there looking back at him. He then looked over at his mother.

'You go back to bed mum. I'll take a tablet now. Sorry for waking you.'

'It's okay honey. Maybe take two of them, just to be sure. Goodnight.'

And with that, the bright light faded. His mother left the room.

Jenson got up from his bed and closed the door after her. He reached for his tablets on the table. He picked them up and momentarily questioned his actions. He then opened a chest drawer and threw them inside, locking them away. He remembered what Sterling had said, about not taking them because they would flood his mind, and close it off from any supernatural ability.

He went back over and sat down on the side of his bed.

'How many people can see fairies?' He asked.

'Only people who possess the Gateway magic. They cannot dream or enter our world. They are the balance, preventing both worlds from collapsing into one. But if all Gateways are gone....'

'Gone? How many Gateways are there?'

'We believe you are the last Gateway Jenson!'

'Is Robyn not a Gateway? She can't dream either.'

'She was a Gateway. But her link has been severed ever since she entered our world.'

'Robyn is in your world?'

'Yes. She has been there for a while. I found her in the Lost Forest. Nobody makes it to the lost forest alive.'

'Is she...?'

'Oh no, she is safe now.'

'But she's in a coma. If she is in your world, then she must be in some sort of a dream?'

'We don't quite understand what has happened to her. Something has corrupted her mind. These Gateways, they pass on through the generations, sometimes skipping a generation or two. But now that she has entered our world, she no longer possesses the magic. So that only leaves you.'

'How am I the last one left?' Jenson questioned.

'The Elder's cast a spell. They believe there is only one Gateway left. The last Gateway standing in the way. All the others must have somehow lost their magic.'

'But if I'm the last one, what happened to the rest of them?'

'They have either passed on from this world, or else the same thing that happened to Robyn.'

'STEM!'

'What is Stem?'

'Stem have been testing on everyone. They must have got to all the non-dreamers over the years.'

'We have to stop this Stem.'

'Yes. I'm going to try and stop them tomorrow.' Jenson stated.

'Is it dangerous?' Myral asked. An apprehension in her response.

'Yes, but we have to do it. We know somebody on the inside. He's a scientist. His name is Tom. He says he can help Robyn. Maybe he can help her come back? She could become a Gateway again?'

'It doesn't work like that Jenson. Once you cross over, the Gateway magic you once possess is gone.'

'We have to try. A lot of people have died. Stem must have broken all the links. They were supposed to be finding a cure, but Callum said something else is happening. He told Chloe that they are using Stephanie, to somehow get inside minds. Can you help us? We need to get my friends out of Stem. You could use your magic.'

'I cannot intervene with matters in your world.'

'But something bad is about to happen. We're going to Stem tomorrow, to get everyone out. It will be dangerous. We could do with your help.'

'Why are you going if it's dangerous?' Myral asked.

'I have to. I have to take a chance. They have all helped me. And now I have to help them.' And then Jenson suddenly remembered what Grace had seen. 'Can you see visions in your world?'

'Visions?'

'Yes. There is a girl. Her name is Grace Harper. She said she can see future dreams, with a moon goddess necklace or something.'

'The goddess holding the amber moonstone?'

'Yes, that's it. Have you heard of it?'

'Yes, it's a token from our world, brought over to yours many years ago.'

'Okay, good. So you know what it does? Grace had a vision. She saw me die.'

Myral flinched. For the first time she had lost her composure. Something inside her grew afraid. And even though Jenson had heard it so many times now, Myral's reaction suddenly caused him to see some truth in it.

'If the amber moonstone has revealed this vision, then something terrible is about to happen. And if you die Jenson, the Last Gateway will open. You will not be able to save us!'

'Save you from what? I don't have magic abilities like the others. I can't even dream. I told Grace to go home. They won't be there, in Stem. Her vision won't come true.'

'The Elders say if all Gateways are open, great evil could be unleashed upon us.'

'But that is why I am asking for your help. Can you not help us? Can we have some of that magic dust you have?'

'I'm sorry, but it doesn't work like that.'

'But I remembered you. I remember you using the dust on me.'

'Yes Jenson. That is because you can see us. It will not work on those who do not see.'

This was not the answer Jenson was looking for.

'What will happen to Robyn now?' He asked. 'Can she come back to our world? Will you tell her that I love her just in case I don't make it.'

Myral tilted her head. She knew the harsh consequences of this statement.

'But you cannot go if it puts you in danger. You are our only hope!'

'I have to help my friends. They just want to get their loved ones back. I want to put a stop to this once and for all. I'm going to take down Stem tomorrow. And I think Tom will help me.'

'No Jenson. You must stop. You cannot put yourself in danger.'

'It's too late. Stem will keep coming for us all if I don't. Can you come back tomorrow? And if we make it out alive, I'll have them here with me and we can try to help each other?'

'I cannot. I am changing tomorrow.'

'Changing?' Jenson asked.

'It's like when you grow in this world. We change.'

'Do you change into something?'

Jenson's mind wondered. His imagination had run away from any normality, and Myral could see this.

'We don't change into something else.' Myral answered. 'We grow, just like you do, but in a different way. It's at every cycle of our moon, the amber moon.'

'Will you be back after that?' Jenson asked.

'No, I'm afraid not. I cannot return once I have changed.'

'But if we get out alive tomorrow, we might need you. I'll need you to talk to my sister for me.'

'Jenson, you have to survive!' Myral declared. 'The worlds fate depends upon it. This is bad. I have to tell my parents. I am sorry but I have to go now.'

'Will I see you again?'

'I hope so!' Myral answered.

And with one sprinkle of pixie dust over her head, she vanished into thin air.

Chapter 41

Jenson woke up. He felt drained when his alarm clock went off. But this time he could remember the fairy. This time she didn't sprinkle the pixie dust over him to forget. This time he knew he was not imagining it. And this time, he was more determined than ever to get into Stem and get them all out alive.

Myral had given him the encouragement he needed. She had told him that Robyn could be saved. And going into Stem to get Callum and Chloe's father out, along with Wardy, this was the hope he needed to get his sister back to normal.

Having gotten dressed, he cautiously opened his bedroom door. He quietly tip-toed out onto the landing. He knew he had to thread carefully for he didn't want to wake his parents.

The skies had not yet pulled back their blanket of night. The house was still. The darkness had given Jenson the right elements to sneak out unnoticed.

As he got to the staircase, he began to descend. Halfway down, his footstep caused a creaking sound. The panel below called out. It had created an alert. Perhaps attracting attention to prevent Jenson from going any further. The universe was sending out a satellite call. But Jenson was the only one listening. His parents were still fast asleep.

His sudden apprehension caused him to stop. He remained there, statuesque, and waiting for any movement. The house reacted in silence. A false alarm. He continued.

But just as he got to the end of the stairs, he heard a voice. It was his mother from the top of the landing. She must have woken and answered the call.

'Where are you off to at this hour of the morning?'

'I just need some fresh air.' Jenson whispered.

'You can't be walking around so early. Go back to bed and open a window '

Jenson had been caught. His Mother was oblivious to any plan. But he knew he had to mask his intentions and excuse his absence.

'I'll be fine mum. I just really need some fresh air. I've taken those tablets like you said, but I still have a headache.' It was a lie, but a good lie all the same.

'Okay then.' His mother retaliated. 'I'll come with you, just hang on.'

Jenson's insides churned. His plan had not worked. His mother was now going to tag along. But he couldn't have this.

'It's okay Mum. I'm sure you've a lot of things to get done. Don't worry, I'll be back soon.'

'You're right I do have things to do. But a nice fresh walk with my son will help start my day.'

Again, Jenson's hopes were fading. And then he remembered her coming in last night.

'I think it's best I go alone. I just need some time to think. Those visions of fairies. And the headaches. I just need to understand what it all means.'

A pause brought the house to a silence once more. And now the convincing ploy had worked.

'Well don't be beating yourself up too much. It might take a few days for those tablets to kick in. I'm sure the visions and headaches will fade, just like they did before. Oh, and make sure you bring your coat with you. These mornings are getting colder. I'll have some breakfast ready for you for when you get home.'

Jenson continued without saying another word. He had escaped, but the guilt began to plague him. He had lied to his mother, and he knew he would not be back for this breakfast. He would perhaps never be back.

~~~

The blanket of night was drawing back, slowly revealing the morning sky. Jenson looked down at his watch. He had just reached Tessa's house. It was 6:32am. He was early. He had 28 minutes to spare before they would set off on this dangerous mission.

Suddenly, reaching for the front door, the noise of a car coming up the driveway alerted him.

Turning round, he saw Henry.

He waved, but Henry never returned this gesture. He looked rather surprised to see Jenson standing there. Then, the noise of the front door opening startled him.
Ellie appeared.

'Jenson?' She mouthed. The door drew back and revealed her shock even more so.

'Well good morning to you too,' Jenson replied.

'Jenson?' Chloe muttered, having followed Ellie out the front door. She too looked confused to see him.

'What's going on?' Jenson asked. A hint of suspicion had spurred him on. He quickly realised something was up.

'I'm sorry Jenson, we just didn't expect you this early.' Ellie explained.

But this made no sense to Jenson. He was here so they could all go to Stem together.

The continuing hum behind him resonated. It didn't seem like it would be stopping anytime soon.

Jenson looked around. He could see Henry sitting comfortably in the car. He then knew Henry was never going to leave the car. He suddenly realised what was happening.

'You were leaving without me? You never did intend to wait on me, did you?'

A wall of silence hit Jenson just as Tessa and Davrin appeared in the doorway. Jenson didn't say another word They were all in on it. He turned and walked away.

'Jenson please! We can explain.' Chloe said, jogging down the driveway after him.

'No. I don't care,' he replied, shrugging her arm off.

'Please Jenson. It was for your own good. We didn't want you to come. What if Grace's dream comes true?'

'And what if anything happens to any of you? Do you think I won't care? I brought you all into this. And now I'm supposed to sit back and do nothing?'

'Jenson please don't do this.' Ellie begged.

'You both have guns,' Jenson declared.

He spotted a handgun lodged in Chloe's trousers, and now Ellie, who was holding onto a tranquiliser gun as she approached him.

'Please Jenson,' Ellie repeated.

'Where's the other one?' He asked. 'The other gun? Where is it?'

Jenson had remembered the two guns they took from the men in the church. But Chloe and Ellie were hesitant. He both looked back in the doorway. And there it was, nestled neatly on top of Davrin's sling.

'Why does he need a gun?' Jenson barked. 'He's been shot. I'll stand a better chance.'

'It's not for him,' Chloe said, glancing over at the car.

'It's for Henry, isn't it?' Jenson questioned.

Again, another wall of silence.

'Was that your plan all along? To leave me behind?'

'Jenson, we just…..'

But that was as far as Chloe could get.

'Just give me the gun.' Jenson demanded.

He began his approach. He marched on past Ellie and Chloe, over towards Davrin who now stood nervously in the doorway beside Tessa. Davrin flinched back as Tessa stood out in front, as if shielding him. This was not the brave Davrin in his dreams. For in the real world, Davrin was wounded. He had no powers. He was helpless.

'Davrin, just give me the gun!' Jenson repeated. His hand holding out for his friend to give it to him.

But the short silence was replaced by the clocking of a trigger.

'Jenson, stop!' The voice said. It was Ellie.

Jenson turned round. He could see the raised tranquiliser gun in her hand. It was pointed directly at him.

'I'm sorry Jenson, but we can't let you do this. It's for your own safety.'

'Ok then.' Jenson said. He knew he was outnumbered. He felt his ranking would prevent her from shooting. 'I won't take the gun then. You can give it to your boyfriend, I don't care. But I am going to Stem Industries, with or without you all.'

He began to march back down the garden.

'Jenson you don't understand.' Chloe said. 'We had a vote and we all agreed that you shouldn't go just in case…..'

'….in case what? Do you all believe Grace, a girl we only met yesterday? You think her vision will come true? I sent them home. Grace is gone. She's not here. They are no longer apart of this. Her dream can't come true. I'm still going. I don't care what any of you say.'

Jenson continued to push away. He was just about to pass Henry's car when a voice called after him.

'I'm sorry Jenson.'

It was Ellie. She had quietly followed him. And with one short rasp, the noise of the tranquilizer stunned the silence.

Jenson felt a sharp needle in his back. He fell to his knees.

'JENSON?' Chloe called out.

And that was the last thing Jenson heard before he lay on the ground unconscious.

'I'm sorry Chloe, but it had to be done.' Ellie said. She was now standing over his body.

'I know.' Chloe agreed.

'Ya need a hand,' the Irish voice sounded, as both girls looked up.

'Yes please.' Ellie replied.

'Quick, put him inside on the couch before any of my neighbours see,' Tessa sarcastically ordered. 'I don't want them thinking I've gone mad.'

This seemed inappropriate. A joke at this vital moment. They all knew Tessa's house stood alone, exposed by the surrounding pastures. And nobody around for miles. They also knew this statement had come from Tessa, for they wouldn't have expected anything less. In fact, they were getting used to her odd sense of humour.

'What if he wakes up?' Chloe questioned as Henry placed Jenson's body out onto the couch.

'Those darts have knocked out horses for hours,' Tessa remarked. 'If he wakes up, he deserves to go to Stem. I'll even drive him myself.'

'So there is a chance he could wake?' Chloe hadn't quite got Tessa's sarcasm.

'It was a joke,' Tessa exclaimed. 'Don't worry. He'll still be fast asleep by the time you get back. We'll keep an eye on him, won't we Dav?'

Davrin didn't say a word. He had just handed the gun to Henry as he walked past him and out of the sitting room.

'We better get goin,' Henry instructed. He began to walk down the hallway towards the front door.

'Be careful,' Tessa encouraged as she and Davrin had made their way out to wave them goodbye.

'WE'LL GET YOUR MUM OUT AS WELL,' Chloe shouted back to Davrin just before she sealed her fate and stepped into the car.

~~~

'So how are we going to do this?' Chloe asked. They were all now seated in the car. 'Myself and Callum, we used to scope out Stem before we met Jenson. I think I know a way we could try to get in.'

'We're not going to Stem right now,' Ellie explained.

'What? Why?'

'We need to go somewhere first.'

'Where?'

'St. Anita's.'

'The mental place? The one where you met Davrin's mum?'

'Yep,' Henry answered. 'It's where I wurk. Stem are bringin in a shipment of dat new cure.'

'And how does that help us?' Chloe questioned.

'It's ar ticket in. We're goin ta steal der jeep an go ta Stem.'

Ellie placed her hand on Henry's knee. A reluctance in her gaze.

Henry looked back. Neither one knowing what would happen, but each one understanding what they had to do.

'We're goin ta get yur da out of der.' Henry said. 'We're goin ta get dem all out.'

Chapter 42

The guard lifted the barrier and waved as he saw Henry's car pull up to St. Anita's. Ellie could see how nervous Chloe looked. She was sitting in the back seat, her legs rattling with a nervous twitch.

'It'll be okay,' she said, stretching her hand back and resting it on Chloe's knee.

'I know.' Chloe replied. 'I just remember having an argument when I was younger, with a girl in my school. Jane Freeman was her name. I'll never forget her. She told me that my sister died because she was weird, and that she would have ended up here anyway.'

'Wat did ya do?' Henry asked.
Chloe smiled.

'I punched her in the face.'

'I bet she never said anytin to ya after dat.'

'Nope, never even looked at me again.'

'Well let's hope we all have that same courage today,' Ellie said.
Being a teacher herself, she had come across this type of behaviour before. And her un-told secret was that she obtained a kind of pleasure when the bullies got what they deserved. Just like in Chloe's story.

'Righ, der it is,' Henry said, directing their attention over to the blackened-out jeep. It was parked right outside the main entrance. 'Der's always two of dem,' he added. 'One dat stays by da boot, an de udder one brings in all da boxes.'

Ellie could see a uniformed Stem soldier at the back of the jeep. He looked to be standing guard. And just as

Henry had explained, another one came emerging out of the reception area, ready to collect another box.

Henry pulled up opposite the main building.

'Ya ready?' He asked, just as the engine cut out.

'What do I do with this?' Ellie asked, holding onto the tranquiliser gun.

'Jus leave it down der. We don't want dem seein ya wit it. We'll come back for it after we've gotten rid of da guards.

Ellie wasn't too sure where Henry had gotten this covertness from. He was like some stealthy army man. Perhaps there was a past she knew nothing about. After all, she had only known him for a few weeks now.

Chloe let out one big deep breath and nodded her head. She indicated she was ready.

'Now just act normal an follow me lead.' Henry directed.

They all got out of the car and began to walk over towards the main building. Chloe glanced over as the uniformed man returned her stare. He stood at the back of the Stem jeep. Even though he was wearing a helmet that blocked his face, Chloe could see it move. It had pivoted to the side, turning in their direction, and looking straight at them.

'Did ya bring dat ting ya were talkin abou? De ting ta show your grandfawder?' Henry asked.
Chloe looked up at him, reacting to his cue.

'Yeah, I hope he remembers it. It's been a while,' she replied.

Feeling somewhat distracted now with this chit chat, she continued calmly. 'Hello', she said, looking right at the soldier.

The soldier didn't say a word. He remained still, observing the newcomers.

'Oh sorry,' Henry said.
He had opened the main door, and nearly walked straight into the offloading soldier as he came out.

'Watch where you're going,' the soldier retaliated. His tone, muffled from the covering of his helmet.

Henry stepped to the side and held his arm back, indicating to the others to do the same. They all stepped out of the way.

'I think they own everyone,' Chloe whispered. But this whisper was louder than expected.

'What did you say?' The soldier barked.

'She didn't say anything,' Ellie answered.

'I wasn't talking to you,' the soldier barked again. His helmet, directing straight at Ellie and then turning back to Chloe. 'Have you something you want to say to me?'

Henry was halfway through the doorway now. He could see the other soldier coming towards them to investigate.

'You're not mouthy now, are you?' The soldier asked. He hesitated, but then removed his helmet. 'I've seen you before?'

Chloe recognised him instantly. He was the Stem soldier she had met outside Jenson's home, the day she went back to retrieve his tablets. She didn't know what to do. She could feel the gun nestled around her waist. *What if he tries to frisk me?* She thought.

Ellie immediately inched her way in past Henry. She needed to avoid his gaze, for she had been talking to him also. This detail would have only led him to suspicion. She felt guilty that she was unable to help Chloe, but she knew she had to get out of there.

'Aren't you friends with that Jenson fella?' The soldier asked.

'I'm sorry,' Henry said. 'Apologise to dat man an get in here now.'

'Sorry,' Chloe said.

But before she could step inside, the soldier held out his arm, preventing her from entering.

'What was your name again?' He asked.

'Jennifer.'

'And what are you doing here Jennifer?'

'I'm here to see my grandfather.'

The soldier looked at her. His eyes squinting with suspicion.

'And who do we have here with you?' He asked, only noticing Henry at the doorstep.

'Hi, me name is Henry, an I am a close friend of da family. I work here.'

Henry rooted inside his pocket to retrieve his identity card. He handed it to the soldier.

'There was somebody else who went inside,' the soldier declared. 'Who was that?'

And with this, something triggered inside of Chloe.

'That was my mum,' she replied. 'She rushed in needing to use the toilet. She's pregnant. She only found out a while ago. It was a shock to us all, but we've managed to...'

'Oh yes, I remember you.' The soldier said. 'I forgot how annoying you were. You're the nosy next-door neighbour who doesn't shut up.'

He handed Henry back his I.D.

'Keep a leash on this one,' he continued. 'She'll get you into a lot of trouble with that mouth.'

This comment made Ellie furious. She could hear him from inside. These people took her father. They killed Meatloaf. And now they are demanding respect. Chloe was right. They think they own everyone. This made her blood boil. And this bubbling scorch had just scalded any nervousness. She grew more determined to do this.

'An you keep up da good wurk,' Henry declared. A sarcasm hidden deeply within his reply.

The soldier retreated as Chloe stepped inside.

The cold marble floor greeted them.

Henry eagerly continued past Ellie, and over to talk to the receptionist. Ellie recognised her instantly. It was the nurse she had spoken to the last time she was here. The woman she had lied to in order to see Stephanie Belshaw. She remembered her name. It was Gail.

Ellie smiled. It was a weak smile. But she knew Gail was in on this. She had hoped this would wipe the slate clean. It didn't. Gail did not return this friendly gesture. She looked over Henry's shoulder with not even the faintest of grins. Her bold eyes stared blankly.

She then stood up from the desk, picked up her swipe card, and disappeared through the door behind her.

'She doesn't like me, does she?' Ellie questioned, as Henry returned.

'Not really,' he replied, taking her by the arm. 'She doesn't like wat we're doin, but she's not gonna stop us. Come on, we don't have much time. Dey nearly have all da boxes in. Follow me!'

He began to hurry over to the already opened door, which led down a narrow corridor and into the storage room.

The storage room was big, with enough room to hold all the supplies for the whole complex. It had plenty of containers and shelving. A playground for any child to enjoy a game of hide and seek. But this was no playground. And there were no games to be had.

'You two hide over der behind dose boxes. Wait for me signal,'

Ellie and Chloe immediately ran over to where the boxes had been stacked. They crouched in behind.

'What's the signal?' Ellie whispered.

'Jus don't move til I tell ya ta,' he said.

And off he went leaving them alone inside.

Chapter 43

'That's everything,' the soldier said as he appeared in through the storage door.

He dropped the last box down. It was placed right in front of Ellie and Chloe, but they were concealed behind the other stacked boxes. They could see him through a small opening in the erected structure.

He then retrieved some papers and tossed them towards Henry. His forgotten decency had caused the papers to scatter on top of the last box he had produced.

'Sign this!' He instructed, in yet another impolite tone.

'Sure,' Henry said, scooping the papers up. 'So ya tink dis new drug will wurk better dan da udder one?' He asked. It was his attempt to distract the soldier.

And just as he had asked the question, he pulled out his handgun.

In one quick motion, he had even managed to distract Ellie and Chloe. For a moment, they too had forgotten what they were here for. And they were both intrigued to hear the soldier's response.

'Get over der!' Henry demanded, still pointing his gun at the soldier.

'What's this? The soldier questioned.

'It's where ya cooperate wit us or ya get shot.'

Ellie was gob smacked. She had never seen this side to Henry before. Maybe he had watched too many movies and fancied himself to be a hero? But this wasn't how she had imagined this to go. In fact, she wasn't too sure what way his plan into Stem would unfold. She figured maybe the guns were the last call of action. But this was not the case. She stood there watching on with sheer uncertainty. She then looked down to watch Chloe retrieve her gun.

'Now wait, you don't have to do this,' the soldier said. His hands were placed out in front of him. He was pleading for Henry to put down his weapon.

'GET BACK!' Henry demanded, as the soldier began to inch forward.

'Okay okay. But don't shoot.'

'Put your hands up in da air.'

The soldier's posture changed. It looked as if he was lowering his hands. But he dropped one arm around to reach behind his back.

'I said put your hands up where I can see dem!' Henry's tone was stronger now. He knew what the Soldier was attempting, but he didn't really want to use the gun.

Concealed behind the boxes, Ellie and Chloe could see the soldier. They had just enough visibility to notice the button illuminate from his belt. It looked as if he had just pressed a panic button. The silent red light began to flash, and Ellie instinctively knew it was a beacon for help.

'HENRY?' She shouted, rushing out from behind the boxes. 'He just pressed a button on his belt.'

The soldier turned round. He was startled to see other people in the room.

Distracted from Ellie's warning, Henry had lowered his gun. And taking his chance, the soldier lunged for him. He immediately knew this was his time to engage.

He pushed Henry back against the wall. Both men, now grappling to take hold of the gun.

Ellie stood there in sheer fright. She didn't know what to do. She watched on as the gun bounced around, the nozzle shifting from Henry, then back to the soldier. Each man attempting to get the upper hand.

The soldier seemed to be stronger. His grip suddenly screening most of the gun. And only moments from ripping it out of Henry's hands.

Henry managed to spin the soldier round, smashing him into another steady stack of boxes.

By this stage Chloe was out from behind her enclosure. Her gun, pivoting from Henry and back to the soldier. She didn't have the aim for a clean shot.

'STOP OR I'LL SHOOT!' She called out.
But both Henry and the soldier were too eager to seize full control of the gun. They were oblivious to Chloe's demand.

Ellie picked up a box. And seeing her chance, she smashed it into the back of the soldier's head.

His helmet fell off. He stumbled slightly. But he managed to keep hold of the gun. And in one swipe, he smacked Henry in the side of the head.

This sent Henry flying over some of the stacked boxes, crashing heavily to the ground.

The soldier then secured the gun, immediately pointing it at Henry.

A shot fired. The loud torrents sliced the air in two. It was a deafening bang followed by a numbing silence. But it wasn't the soldier. Before he could manipulate the trigger, Chloe had taken her chance. And just like back beside the campervan, she had pulled the trigger without any uncertainty.

The soldier stumbled forward. He hadn't time to pull his own trigger. The gun dwindled from his hand. Chloe didn't hesitate. She shot her gun for a second time. The second bullet, now sending the soldier crashing into the shelving.

Ellie could see that even this second bullet had not taken him down. He had staggered into the shelving, and even though he had lost grip of the gun, he remained on his feet.

This was her cue. The bullet proof uniform must have taken the brunt. So, without any hesitation, Ellie picked up another heavier box and bashed it over his head.

The soldier, having lost his helmet to her first attack, had no chance this time. His whole body plummeted to the ground like a dead weight. And the blood began to seep from his head.

Ellie felt elated as the panic seemed to be over. The blood began to surge towards her footing. She stepped back. And even though she was uncertain of the damage caused, she had no regret. She had remembered how horrible this soldier was to them when they arrived. So, unconscious, or dead, it didn't matter. She knew she had done the right thing.

'Are you okay Chloe?' She asked.
'Yes. I never liked him anyway.'
Disparity shone. Unlike the campervan incident, Chloe seemed to have no guilt. She knew they needed to do this. There was no going back now.

'What was that button,' she added.
'I'm not too sure,' Ellie said. 'Maybe it was a distress button to alert the other soldier. We have to hurry.'
And with that, Ellie shuffled past the unconscious soldier. She headed towards Henry. She could see he was dazed. His body was spread across the jumbled boxes on the ground. The smack he received must have uprooted him badly.

Just then, as Ellie had reached over to check on him, she heard another gunshot. She immediately turned round.

Chloe was standing there with a dazed look on her face. But Ellie knew there was somebody else in the room.

In the doorway, there stood the other soldier. Ellie watched him, his gun still pointing over at Chloe.

Ellie looked back at Chloe who suddenly dropped her gun. She was holding onto her stomach.

Ellie could see the blood coming from her gut. It was seeping out through her fingers. She had been shot. And in that moment, Chloe fell to the ground.

'CHLOEEEE?' Ellie shouted.

'Don't move or I'll shoot,' the soldier threatened. His gun, now pointing at Ellie. The smoke, still fresh from the shot.

Chapter 44

Jenson suddenly woke. He took a deep breath and instantly sprung up from the couch.

'What happened?' He asked. A panic suddenly washed over him.

Davrin sat there by his legs. His dumbstruck gaze gave nothing away. He didn't say a word.

'WHAT HAPPENED DAVRIN?' Jenson asked again. 'WHERE ARE THEY?'

Jenson was hysterical, but he was too weak to move. He had just about managed to swing his head from side to side. His eyes, scouring the room. Davrin's bemused expression led him to believe something awful had happened.

'Ah…you're awake!' Tessa acknowledged, now stepping into the living room with a glass of water in her hand.

Jenson was becoming more impatient now.

'WILL SOMEBODY TELL ME WHAT HAPPENED?'

Tessa's hand shook. The water spilled. And then Davrin spoke.

'It just didn't feel right.'

Jenson noticed he was holding a tranquiliser dart. It was the one they had shot him with. He was staring at it, fidgeting with it, just like a rubik's cube, scanning it and rotating it as if trying to solve the equation.

'Are they okay? Please, somebody tell me they are okay!'

Jenson looked up at Tessa. His attention homed in on her, waiting for her to respond. He knew Davrin was somehow caught up in a trance. His wilted desperation had caused his mind to wither elsewhere.

'It's okay, I'm sure they're fine. They're gone about twenty minutes or so.'

Tessa's reply was a little uncertain.

'I better go,' Jenson said, swinging his legs over onto the ground. But as he began to lift himself up from the couch, his body stumbled backwards.

'Give yourself a few minutes.' Tessa said, handing him the glass of water.

Jenson began to drink. He suddenly felt thirsty.

'What about Grace, her vision?' Davrin whispered. His mindset had returned.

Jenson nodded. He felt a tinge of discouragement, but he leaned forward. He placed his hand on Davrin's shoulder.

'Thank you for waking me. You did the right thing. I got you all into this mess. I'd rather take my chances and do something about it. I can't sit here and let you all risk your lives for me.'

'Wait there!' Tessa demanded.

Jenson watched her flurry from the room. He then steadily got to his feet and followed. He knew he had to hurry. Time was running out.

He had reached as far as the internal garage doorway when he heard Tessa rummaging around inside. She seemed to be searching for something. A moment later, she returned.

'Oh,' she said, nearly bumping into him. She didn't know he had followed her out. 'You don't take orders well, do you? I could have sworn I told you to wait there.'

'I'm sorry, I can't just sit around and wait. I need to find them.'

'That's where I can help,' Tessa explained, handing him what looked like a wooden pocket-knife.

'What's this?' Jenson asked.

'The others took the guns, but you'll need something. It flicks up, watch…'

Tessa effortlessly flicked up the shank to reveal the sharp blade.

'…It was Terry's. He never went anywhere without it. Always said it would come in handy. And he was forever sharpening it. He loved making them. This was his favourite, so promise me you'll bring it back to me.'

Jenson could feel the warmth in her request. For the first time he could see a sincerity in her face. Her jesting remarks had faded. She, like the rest of them knew how high the stakes were. It was serious now. And she wanted them all to return safely.

'Thank you,' Jenson answered. 'I promise I will bring it back to you.'

Jenson slipped the knife into his back pocket and made his way towards the front door.

'Hang on,' Tessa ordered.

Jenson turned back round. He watched her walking towards him. She had picked up a set of keys from the hall table.

'Well you won't get far on foot,' she said, passing him out into the doorway. She opened the front door.

'I can't let you do this, please, it's too dangerous. I heard about your camper van. I'm sure they'll be on the lookout for it.'

Tessa sniggered.

'I have one more trick up my sleeve,' she said. 'They haven't seen this.'

She opened the front door. And there, sitting in the driveway was a white 1960's Chevrolet nova.

'Now this was Terry's real baby. He preferred it more than me.'

'I can't let you do this,' Jenson said. 'What if they….'

'Don't worry, I'll just drop you wherever you need to go. That's all.'

'Are you sure?'

'Of course. Girl scouts promise and all that jazz. I can't afford to get any bullet holes in this baby. I swear, Terry would come back from the grave and haunt me for eternity.'

They both smiled at one another.

'You ready?' Tessa asked.

'Ready as I'll ever be!'

Chapter 45

Ellie was face down on the ground. Her arms were placed out in front. She could see Chloe's body on the floor, blood oozing from her gut. Only a few feet away, she knew she needed help.

'Please help her, she's only a child.' She begged.
The solider didn't say a word.

Chloe was huddled over against the boxes they had previously hidden behind. She lay sprawled against them, holding onto her stomach. Her short sporadic breaths alarmed Ellie. There seemed to be a lot of blood coming from her wound. Ellie could see the life draining from her face. This time it wasn't as simple as patching her up like before in the abandoned church.

'Please. I promise to do anything if you just get her help!'

'Shut your face or I'll do the same to you,' the soldier barked. He didn't seem to care that he had just shot a teenager. He reached over to his partner's body and began to check his pulse. 'You're lucky he's still alive.'

'Well then nobody got hurt,' Ellie retorted. 'So please, can you just help her. She needs a doctor before she bleeds to death?'

'I said shut your face,' the soldier shouted. He stepped over towards her. 'What were you all trying to do?'

Ellie didn't answer. She wasn't too sure what to tell him.

This lack of response triggered an anger in the soldier. He abruptly slid his leg back and quickly let it fly forward, kicking Ellie in her ribcage.

'I won't ask you again?'

Ellie let out a squeal. Her arms retracted into her torso.

'Now, are you going to tell me what you are doing here?' The soldier asked again. His gun digging into the back of Ellie's head.

'Please, don't shoot!'

'You have two seconds to tell me what you are doing here, or else you'll end up just like your friend.'

'Please,' Ellie begged again.

She was trying to think of what to say, but she knew a few seconds wasn't enough. She didn't know if the truth would even help her in this situation. Everything went silent. It was all over, and she knew it.

'We were just trying to help a friend. We didn't want to hurt anyone.'

Then suddenly, Ellie heard a thump. It was as if something big had dropped to the ground. Her tears began to drip. Her chin pressed hard against the cold flooring.

'Get up!' A voice called out. But it wasn't the solider.

Ellie slowly lifted her chin. There on the ground beside her was the soldier's body. She then noticed another pair of legs standing right beside the soldier.

She cautiously looked up. It was the female nurse, 'Gail', the receptionist from outside.

'Where's Henry?' Gail asked, revealing a needle in her hand. It was the same needle she had just stuck into the soldier's neck to sedate him.

'He's over there,' Ellie said, pointing over to the boxes.

Ellie immediately got to her feet and ran straight to Chloe. Chloe was barely conscious.

'Please! We need to get her to a hospital?' She called out.

She got no response. She looked up. Gail was stepping over the fallen boxes. She was trying to help Henry to his feet.

'Please?' Ellie called out again. 'She needs a hospital!'
'And where do you think we are?' Gail snapped.
Ellie could hear the sarcasm in her tone.

Gail scurried over as Henry stirred. She quickly began to examine Chloe's wound. She then stood up.
'Keep pressure on it while I get some help.'
'We can't,' Henry said. 'Nobody else knows.'
'I think it's too late for that, don't you?' Gail scowled before hurrying out of the room.
A woman who had lived her whole life solely by the rules, now reduced to helping the resistance. And all because Stem had forced a drug on them, the same drug that killed her beloved patients two weeks ago. She never asked for any involvement into this. She had respected Henry so much to throw a blind eye. But now, she had somehow managed to get herself mixed up in it all.
'She can't die Henry. We can't let her die.' Ellie cried as her blood-stained hands maintained the pressure against Chloe's stomach.
Chloe seemed to be falling in and out of consciousness. Her eyes were desperately trying to remain open. And the blood seemed to be everywhere.
'Please Chloe. You need to hang on.' Ellie demanded.
'Ellie?' Henry said. 'We need ta go.'
'We can't just leave her here to die.'
Henry felt a shroud of guilt. But they needed to go before it was too late.

'Tilt her over,' a sudden voice called out. It came crashing in with authority.
They turned round to see Gail scurrying back in with another man. Henry knew this man. He was the consulting doctor on shift.
'I'm really sorry,' Henry acknowledged. 'I didn't mean for eider of you ta get involved.

'I think the bullet went through.' The doctor said, ignoring any apology.

'What does that mean?' Ellie asked.

'It means she has a chance.' Gail declared.

Ellie could tell that this woman did not like her. For she knew none of this would have happened if they had not come here. The blame was well and truly designated.

'Thank you for this! Please just help her. I'll do anything.' Ellie begged.

'Just go!' Gail said.

'What?'

'Just go!' Gail demanded again.

'But we can't just leave her.'

'We'll take it from here, NOW GO!'

'Come on!' Henry said, getting to his feet and grabbing Ellie's arm.

'But we can't just leave her now.' Ellie said.

Gail had no patience at this point.

'It's too late now,' she scolded. 'You've got us all into this mess, so you might as well see it through. Do you not think Stem will notice when their soldiers don't return? You need to fix this, otherwise we are all going down.'

Ellie was speechless. She watched Gail scurry over to a shelf, pulling out some bandaging.

'What are you waiting for?' Gail continued. She stopped searching for a moment and turned round. 'I'll sort the soldiers and Dr. Conway will help your friend. You need to go now. You're of no help to us here.'

'Come on, let's go.' Henry said, grabbing hold of Ellie's arm again.

But Ellie wouldn't budge.

'ELLIE? We need ta go now! Dey'll be lookin for dem soon.'

Chapter 46

Jenson was hiding in the grassy bank. Tessa had just dropped him off. He was peering out over the dune, looking all around the fenced perimeter. He was searching for the best way into Stem. He needed to get in undetected.

There were several guards patrolling the area inside. And Jenson quickly realised there was absolutely no way he was getting in without being noticed.

Just then, with a bit of sheer luck, he spotted his chance. It was the clattering noise of a vehicle approaching.

He sunk down, hiding behind the lengthy foliage. And looking out through the grass, he spotted a Stem jeep coming towards him.

This was his only way in, and he knew it. *Could he unarm the soldiers inside the jeep? Or would he have to surrender? Either way, he knew he had to cease this opportunity.*

He jumped to his feet and instantly ran out onto the road surface, waving his arms frantically above his head.

The jeep's speed declined as Jenson's signal produced caution.

It stopped just yards in front of him. The engine stayed ticking over, hesitation it seemed, from both sides.

Jenson was about to make his move, when suddenly, the passenger door of the jeep opened. A uniformed soldier came stepping out from behind the door.

Jenson dropped one of his hands, moving it round to his back pocket. He retrieved the knife Tessa had given him.

The soldier began to step forward, approaching him. They had a gun in their hand.

Jenson flicked the knife open. Still concealed behind his back, he began to push forward.

He didn't know how many other soldiers were in the jeep, or what was going to happen? But this was it. He needed to do this. He needed to get into Stem.

Just a few feet from the soldier now, Jenson took his chance. He immediately lunged forward, revealing the knife. He grabbed the soldier, manoeuvring him around and shifting his body to stand behind him. Even though the soldier had a blackened-out helmet, Jenson made sure the knife was accurately placed just below it, edging against his neck.

'Stop!' The soldier said. A panic in their cry as the knife began to draw blood.

The driver's door immediately opened. Another soldier jumped out waving their hands in a frenziedly display.

'Stop Jenson!' The voice said.

Jenson was taken aback. He recognised the voice.

'Henry? Is that you?'

'Yes. An dat's Ellie!'

Jenson immediately released his grip. Easing off, he lowered the knife.

'I'm so sorry Ellie. I didn't know it was you.'

He then remembered her cry. It had sounded familiar. But he was too roiled up to take any notice.

Ellie began to massage the rigidness of her throat. She looked at her hand and noticed the small smearing of blood.

'I'm sorry Ellie.' Jenson repeated.

'It's okay Jenson. You weren't to know. Anyway, what are you doing here?'

'Davrin woke me. Tessa helped get me here. How did you get the uniforms? And the jeep?'

'Why are you here? We told you to…'
'I need to be here.'
'What about Grace? Her dream?'
'Ellie, I know what she said, but I can't let you all do this alone.'
Jenson paused. He glanced over at the Jeep.
'Where's Chloe?'
A sudden uncomfortable silence broke.
'Come on Jenson…get into the jeep before we're seen. We'll explain everything.'

~~~

The jeep drove up past the large mesh side-lines. The main gates opened. Not even an I.D. checked as they were ushered straight through.
'Over there!' Ellie directed.
A row of Stem jeeps lined the outside of this esteemed building. A charismatic 'STEM' logo hung above the framework. Six stories high, it was strong in character. A seductive spectacle, exuding power.
Henry pulled up beside the jeeps. He turned round and threw a pair of thick handcuffs back towards Jenson.
'What are these for?' Jenson asked.
'We have ta make it look convincin.'
Henry turned his helmet towards Ellie,
'Ya ready?'
Ellie's helmet was masking her real feelings. She was scared. She wasn't too sure if this plan would work. After all, they were already a man down. She didn't even know if Chloe would make it. But it was too late to turn back now. They were already too involved. She needed to do this. For Chloe. For Callum. For her dad. For Meatloaf. She nodded.
'Let's do this. Let's take these fuckers down!'

Chapter 47

The main entrance groaned as the aerodynamic doors slid open. Each side, disappearing from view, and roaring on impact. The mechanised electronics brought with it an automatic power. And a gust of wind spat out from each end.

Jenson was first in. He was shoved forward by Henry. And as the wind hit him, a chill took hold. The doors roar had matched that of a lion's breath. And the wind, carrying the warning as every hair on his neck stood up. They were now entering a 'Lion's Den', the big lion they wanted to take down.

The sleek grey interior complemented the mood of this place. Its emotionless colour produced a conservative dullness. But this neutral representation had no balance. They knew they were well out of their depths.

There were two Stem soldiers inside. Both unmasked. One of the soldiers stood behind the main desk, while the other one stood over beside the elevators. The second soldier seemed to be talking to a bald man in a white coat.
Jenson's arms were tucked in behind his back as Henry marched him in. This illusion seemed strong.
Henry and Ellie, both concealed behind their helmets, nodded politely to salute the oncoming man in the white coat. He looked like some sort of scientist. And he was just about to exit.
'Hi,' he said.
Ellie and Henry both nodded.

Ellie noticed, even with a small greeting, that he was of a foreign stature. Eastern European perhaps? She wasn't exactly sure where? She had become responsive to the many accents in her school from the different nationalities. She also detected his name tag as he walked by them. It read 'Dr. Schafer'.

Dr Shafer gave off an air of importance. His tall frame added to this. He was remarkably tall in fact, just shy of seven feet tall. And he was thin, and pale, fully bald and looked middle aged. But there was something youthful about him. His strides had given off an easiness as he passed them.

He left the building without hesitancy, even though they had Jenson in their clutches. Perhaps he didn't know who Jenson was?

'We found him trying to steal our jeep.' Henry barked. His tone seemingly angered and in the best non-Irish accent he could manage. 'Where will we put him? His name is Jenson Rose.'

Ellie wasn't sure if he sounded English or American. Maybe a mixture of both. She didn't know why he had disguised his voice. But it seemed to work.

The soldier at the front desk looked up. He quickly answered.

'Fifth floor with the rest of them.'

Henry and the others didn't hesitate. They rapidly charged towards the elevators as if they had been here before.

The soldier picked up his walkie talkie and quickly spoke again.

'We have an offender. Get a cell ready.'

The soldier's voice came echoing out from the elevator. A suited man stepped out. His walkie talkie emitting the message loudly.

'It's okay, I'll take it from here,' George called out.

They all knew George was Mr. Whites lackey and head of security. They had spoken before entering, about the people they may encounter inside. And of course, Ellie had dealt with him back at Margaret's funeral. Only this time she seemed to have an advantage. This time she was disguised. This time she was armed. And this time she was ready.

'Where have you been, and what took you so long?' George asked. 'Your orders were to simply leave the new drug at St. Anita's and come straight back here.'

But just as George got closer, he realised what had taken them so long.

'Well, well, well. Look what we have here. Twice in one day! It must be my lucky day.'

Nobody said a word. They had to stop. George's movement came to a halt as he blocked them from going any further.

'What have you been up to Mr. Rose? Causing trouble again? Did you not learn from the last time we met?'

'You're not gonna get away with this.' Jenson mouthed.

Henry tugged on him, as if reprimanding him for his sudden outburst.

'We found him trying to steal the new drug,' he said.

'Trying to help your little friends again where you?' George retaliated. 'When will you ever learn Jenson? Always sticking your nose in where it doesn't belong. Let me show you to your new cell. I'll take it from here.'

'No!' Ellie spurted.

'What?' George answered.

They all paused. Nobody knew what to say. But then Henry spoke again.

'No. We can bring him up for you. Level five, isn't it?'

George took a quick glance at Henry, detailing him behind the helmet. He then turned to look at Ellie.

'No… I asked her.'

Ellie hesitated.

'What is your name soldier?' George demanded.

Ellie's indecision had gotten the better of her. And with only a moment to think, she blurted out the first thing that came to her head.
'Collins,' she replied

'Take off your helmet Collins.'

Ellie panicked. She knew she could not pull off her helmet, otherwise their cover would be blown. She didn't know why she had spoken. A foolish move, but this was it. Earlier than expected. They all knew this was the moment that would determine everything.

George walked past Henry and Jenson. And now standing directly in front of Ellie, he gave his orders again.

'I said, take off your helmet soldier. NOW!'

Chapter 48

Ellie was scared. She looked past George. She didn't know what to do.

Henry nodded his head, an indication for her to do as she was asked.

She slowly raised her arms up. She took hold of her helmet, each hand securing itself around the concealed globe. Her palms were sweating from within, but the thick fabrics allowed each glove to grip the armour.

Henry quietly un-cuffed Jenson and slipped him a tazer gun. George was oblivious to any of this action. His attention entirely on Ellie. And her delay was working.

'Are you deaf?' He asked. 'I said, take off your helmet!'

Ellie's uncertainty was causing George's patience to dwindle. He immediately back handed the helmet.

This caused Ellie to side-step. She lost her balance. She shuffled away as the helmet toppled from her head.

'What the....'

But that was as far as George could get. He recognised who she was. But he also recognised the cold barrel of Henry's gun pressing up against the back of his head.

'I wouldn't do dat if I were you,' Henry said, watching him reach for his own gun.

George hesitated.

At this point Ellie had her gun out as well, quickly shifting its direction to the soldier emerging from the reception desk. Then suddenly the electronic doors roared again. Another soldier had just entered the building.

It was a stand-off. George and two Stem soldiers, against Jenson, Ellie and Henry.

This stalemate had only one outcome. They needed to move quickly before they were outnumbered. But before either of them could think, Geroge spoke.

'You will not get away with this.'

His daring words had allowed enough time to distract them. Within seconds, one of the soldiers had pressed forward, inching towards Ellie.

'ELLIE!' Jenson shouted.

But it was too late. Just as he had spoken, the soldier tackled Ellie to the ground.

This attack presented an opportunity for George. He elbowed Henry as hard as he could, accurately striking him in the gut.

Henry's gun fell out of his hand. George immediately lunged towards him. And as they both fell to the ground, George began to viciously assault him, throwing punches as if he were a punching bag. This was a fight Henry was surely going to lose. He was half his size.

Jenson's eyes were still on Ellie, watching her squirm under the pressure of the weighted soldier. But before he could help, he recalled there was another soldier.

The room suddenly went quiet. Jenson's senses had closed off to the destruction around him. His mind was numb. And a fight or flight response kicked in. He knew that Ellie and Henry were being trashed around by the soldiers, but he also knew that if the other soldier sounded the alarm, it was game over.

He shifted quickly. And without really thinking, he ran towards the remaining soldier. He could see him hurrying back towards the reception area.

Jenson figured in any high-tech facility, there would be a panic button. And his instinct was right. He spotted the soldier reaching down under the desk.

He sprinted. His mind focusing in on the soldier. His response was to prevent him from raising the alarm.

'HEY?' He called out.

The soldier glanced up. His hand remained underneath. He was desperately searching for the panic button. His fingers sliding along the brim of the desk. But Jenson's cry had caused his assertion to waver.

Jenson threw himself on top of the soldier, impaling him against the desk. The soldier didn't have a chance to fight back. Jenson instinctively speared his tazer gun into his neck. His aim was overbearing. The electric volts were too strong. The soldier's body shook. He dropped to the ground.

Suddenly, Jenson heard the screams. It was Ellie. His mind had reawakened his senses.

He watched on from the reception desk. He could see her being punched repeatedly on the ground. It was like watching a member of a pride wrestle to take down its prey. And like a squirming zebra in its grasp, Ellie was trying to escape. But it was no use. She would never have the strength to flee from its grasp. She was restrained just before the final blow could be administered. This was one of the lions they needed to take down. And Jenson needed to hurry.

He picked himself up and rushed over. Just as he got there, he raised his tazer gun again. But this soldier was prepared. His anticipation allowed him time to turn around and kick Jenson in the chest.

This strike sent Jenson flying across the concrete flooring. He dropped his weapon as the wind was taken from him. He struggled to breathe. The loss of air began to make him feel dizzy. He couldn't move. His senses had disappeared now, but not like before. The quiet noise that allowed him to focus had been replaced. He was now dazed. A nauseous feeling corrupted his lungs as he gasped for air. And a white noise took over his clarity.

A few yards away, Henry and George were still grappling on the ground. George was stronger, but Henry had the agility and speed.

Unlike Ellie, Henry had managed to evade George's grasp. He was now reaching for the gun. But just as he took hold, George grabbed his ankle and pulled him back. The gun had somehow slipped away again.

The soldier had now left the wounded Ellie. He had moved on to his other target. He ran over and kicked Jenson in the chest again. Jenson was on all fours. This sent him spiralling over onto his back.

Struggling for air, Jenson's whole body seized. Now a rigid form, his chest shook. And rasping coughs confirmed just how bad he was. He lay there helpless. He couldn't breathe.

The soldier stepped over his body and motioned towards the gun. It was the same gun Ellie had dropped when she was tackled to the ground. He reached down and took hold of it. Turning round, he pointed it at Jenson.

'I don't care who you are. You make one more move and I'll shoot!'

Another air of silence took place as Jenson began to realise his fate. *They had come so far but had this been his end? Had Grace predicted this bullet, the bullet that would end his life?*

With sheer determination, a whaling scream emerged from Ellie. A large rage erupted from inside her. She charged towards them, perhaps trying to distract the soldier from pulling the trigger, or the anticipated anger taking over. But either way, she had reached the soldier just in time.

Jenson heard the howl and tilted his head sideways. The soldier's body began to tremble. And as the magnitude took hold, he crumbled to the ground. The volt had forced the gun from his grasp. And in its place stood

Ellie. Her tazer gun still pressing forward. She stood there furiously. She was panting. The anger clearly showing on her face. The swelling had already made its way to her eye, and bruising would shortly follow.

Jenson caught a quick breath and scrambled along the ground. He retrieved the handgun. His lungs were still incapable of taking a full breath, but he needed to move.

Just as he looked up to see Ellie, he watched the panic on her face. She screamed once more.

'HENRY!'

Jenson followed her line of vision. He watched her dart over to Henry. He could see George on top of him, over by the elevators, punching him repeatedly.

George must have heard Ellie's scream and sensed her coming. As soon as she got over to him, he transferred his weight from Henry. And just as Ellie was about to stick in the tazer, George reached back and flipped her over his shoulder. And in one rapid combat technique, he redirected her into the lift doors. The crash was louder than any sound within this moment. Ellie was hurt.

Jenson had recovered. He began his surge toward them.

Henry must have been semi unconscious because Jenson saw George step away from him. And when he did, Henry didn't look like he was struggling anymore. In fact, he didn't look to be moving at all.

George lifted a gun from the ground. He pointed it towards Henry.

Henry's helmet had been knocked off in the fight. His face, now bare, and completely covered in his own blood.

It felt like slow motion for Jenson, watching this enfold in front of him, yet strangely, he seemed to have more time than George. Maybe instinctively faster, or just pure luck, but Jenson had his gun raised first. And without any uncertainty, he aimed it at George and fired.

This somewhat 'slow motion' altered back to a 'steady reality' as soon as Jenson heard the gun shot.

He gazed on as his bullet went airborne like a soaring missile. A small cannon, disembarking straight into George's back.

George hit the ground hard. But before he could get up, Ellie stepped across and kicked him in the head.

'That's for Meatloaf, you fucker!' She said, kicking him again, and again.

'HENRY?' She called out, eventually stopping. But Henry didn't respond.

'Henry, please wake up!'

A shallow cough trickled from Henry's mouth with a small discharge of blood.

'Henry, are you okay?'

Ellie threw herself on the ground beside him. She could see how hurt he was but couldn't quite estimate the damage with the level of blood.

'Henry, can you move?'

'I tink so,' Henry replied, slowly lifting his head. And as Ellie helped him stand, he gently rubbed her cheek bone with his palm. He noticed her beaten face also.

'You okay?' He asked.

'I'll live.'

She began to smear the blood away from his face.

'Come on quick, help me!' Jenson requested as he had taken a hold of one of the soldier's legs and was hauling him along the floor.

'What are you doing?' Ellie called back.

'Quick, just help me!'

'But Jenson, we need to go get the others. We don't have much time.'

'This should give us more time.' We need to get them out of sight. Come on, hurry!'

Ellie let go of Henry.

'Quick, you grab his other leg!' She directed, taking hold of George's right foot.

Chapter 49

After all soldiers were dragged and safely hidden behind the main reception desk, Jenson, Ellie and Henry proceeded with their plan.

They took to the stairs, instinctively knowing there could be soldiers on their way. The noise of the gunshot would have certainly alerted attention. Undercover with their helmets back on, Henry and Ellie continued, in the hopes to divert any oncoming force, sending them as far away from the reception area as possible.

They had just reached the second stairwell when two soldiers came charging out of a doorway. They scurried down the steps, their feet, clanking from the metal beneath.

'What happened?' One of them shouted.

'Dis boy managed to grab hold of me gun. He fired a shot.' Henry answered. He didn't disguise his accent this time. 'But everyting is okay now. We're just bringin him up to da fift floor.'

Henry had convincingly lied his way to this plausible truth. And his stern shove into Jenson's back convinced the soldiers he had everything under control.

'Where is George?' The soldier continued.

'He's down in reception, cleanin up da mess.'

'Okay. We'll go take a look.'

But before the soldiers could leave, Jenson released his arms from Henrys light grip. He jabbed his tazer into the soldier. Ellie instinctively did the same, using her tazer on the other soldier.

They didn't hesitate. They had no time to discard the bodies. They immediately carried on running up the stairs, leaving the twitching carcasses out on the stairwell. There were no hiding places nearby. They needed to hurry. It was only a matter of time before somebody would find the other bodies and raise the alarm.

Just before emerging out onto the fifth floor, the door smashed open, and another soldier came crashing out onto the stairwell.
Jenson didn't hesitate this time. He no longer had the patience to wait. Henry didn't have time to speak. They had no more time for conversation. Jenson instantly lunged forward and jolted the soldier with his tazer gun. This sent him wriggling down a flight of stairs.
Ellie watched on this time. Even though she knew they had to do this, she could sense a detachment from Jenson. It was like watching somebody possessed. And then she realised, Jenson had nobody here to save. All his family were safe and out of harm's way. He was doing this for them. He had made sure he was here. He had come to save her father and Callum. A surge of excitement took hold as she suddenly realised that they could possibly do this. And maybe Jenson was right. Maybe Grace's dream is nothing more than a fictitious coincidence.
Jenson kept moving. His mind wanted to feel the regret in his actions, but his heart didn't allow him to feel. He had made a promise to himself weeks ago, the day he got that phone call. The day he thought Robyn had died. He swore he would take down Stem. And now his time had finally come.

Suddenly, stepping out onto the fifth floor, a loud siren sounded overhead. It was then followed by a woman's continuous computerised warning.
'Intruder alert', was now beaconing above.

'What's happening?' Ellie asked. A panic in her voice as the lights dimmed overhead. A larger red light began to pulsate.

'Dey must have found da bodies.'
Unawares, Dr. Shafer had returned from his car. Seeing the bodies, he sounded the alarm.

'We can't stop now.' Jenson demanded. 'Come on, this way!'

He had now taken charge and was running down the corridor with Henry and Ellie trailing behind.

The doors along the corridor began to open as employees in white coats started to emerge. They stood there, watching. Bewildering looks on their faces as they began to shuffle impatiently towards the stairwells.

Then, a handful of soldiers came running towards them.

Jenson slowed down just in time as Henry grabbed hold of him. The soldiers were now approaching. Henry was ready to deliver another false statement.

'Der's about five of dem behind us. Dey're tryin ta break in. An dey're comin up da lifts. Where will we put him?'

His deliberation was flawless. Ellie watched on again as Henry yanked Jenson a little too aggressively this time, sticking his gun into the back of his head.

'That way,' one of the soldiers said, pointing and continuing past.

Ellie turned back round to see the soldiers running. They had reached the elevator doors and stopped. In unison, they aimed their guns towards it, waiting for the "so called" intruders. A fear ran through her, but again, the adrenaline kicked in. She needed to see her dad again.

They took the next turn and reached a door with an armed soldier. He stood outside, guarding it. He immediately pointed his gun at them. He had seen Jenson running out in front.

'Don't shoot!' Jenson said. He was scared to see a gun being pointed at him again.

Henry turned the corner and realised what was happening.

'Don't shoot! We have him.' He repeated.

The soldier immediately lowered his gun, but not completely. Even though he recognised the stem uniforms, he appeared to be hesitant.

'Quick, let us in,' Henry added.

'I was told not to let anybody in, or out.' The soldier responded. His gun slowly rising again.

'But ders intruder's downstairs. And dey're here ta get dis boy back.'

'I was given strict instructions. I cannot allow this.'

'But we need ta keep him safe.'

'I'm sorry, I can't.'

'It was George,' Ellie remarked. 'George told us to keep this boy safe. Mr.White needs him. Hurry up!'

This impressive interjection had taken both Jenson and Henry by surprise. And it proved effective as the soldier reconsidered. He turned round and just as he swiped his card, opening the door, Ellie reached in and stabbed him with her tazer gun.

'Not bad for a teacher!' Henry muttered.

'Not bad for a nurse.' Ellie replied. Her smile, disguised from underneath the helmet.

Stepping inside, the room seemed still. An eerie silence contradicted the exterior. And an even darker light alleviated the madness outside. There were eight doors, four on either side with pigeon-hole slots. And gaped slits, large enough to slide a food tray through.

Another big door stood facing them at the other end, a similar entrance to the one they had just entered, perhaps an exit they could use?

They quickly spread out, searching to see if any prisoners were inside.

Ellie ran to the first cell on the left. Peering in through the small opening, she couldn't see anything. It was empty.

Then suddenly, Henry called out as he ran to the opposite cell on the right.

'Over here Ellie! It's your dad.'

'DAD!' Ellie yelled, leaning her hand in, and holding onto his.

'Ellie my dear. I was worried sick about you.'

'It's okay dad, we'll get you out of here.'

With that, the main door they had just entered suddenly slammed shut. The loud beacon from outside dissolved into the eerie silence.

Turning round, they saw Jenson. He was bending down in front of the soldier he had just dragged in. He looked like he was having trouble trying to retrieve something from the pulsating body. The soldier was still rattling from Ellie's shock.

Eventually, yanking the key card from his hand, Jenson turned back.

'I think this will help.' He said, waving the key card. He then ran over and unlocked Wardy from his cell. He repeatedly did this to the cell next door, but it lay vacant. He ran to the next one.

'Callum!' He said. 'You okay?'

'Jenson, what are you doing here?'

'We've come to get you out.'

Jenson swiped the card against the automated lock. It clicked open immediately.

Callum ran out. Both boys gave each other a quick hug before moving on.

'Where's Chloe?' He said, his head, dwindling round to see if she was somehow behind. With no sight of her, he stood there staring at them.

'Where is she Jenson?' He repeated. An uncontrollable fear took over, 'Jenson?' He questioned again.

Jenson didn't know what to say. He didn't have the heart to lie to him. After everything they had been through. He just looked back at Ellie.

Ellie heard Callum's tone and looked over.

'Callum,' she said, gently squeezing away from her father. 'She's fine, she got hurt, but she's okay. You don't need to worry. We'll bring you straight to her. Let's just get out of here first.'

Ellie wasn't too sure if Chloe was fine. But she had to tell him something, and something that wouldn't upset him. Who knows what he would do?

'She better be okay!' Callum declared, looking directly at Jenson as if blaming him if she wasn't.

Then surprisingly, a low cry called out from the cell opposite.

'Jenson?'

Jenson was curious. He immediately went over, inching his way towards it. The cry did sound familiar.

'It can't be?' He thought. *'How are they even here? I told them to go home.'*

Her words, repeating over and over in his mind. Her vision of him being killed. An insane prediction, now plagued with a sudden realness. And there she was, standing on the other side of the door, peering out from the small hole. It was Grace Harper. She was looking right at him.

Chapter 50

'Grace? How are you even here?' Jenson asked. He immediately slid the key card across the panel. The door opened.

'My father?' Grace said.

'Over here,' Sterling called out, his hand, reaching beyond the cubbyhole.

As Jenson opened Sterling's door his hearth sank. He felt a big pain in his chest, as if something inside him had erupted. Grace was here. She was here in person. *'What about her vision? Had it been true all along. Am I going to die?'*

'How are you both here?' He asked.

'They came for us,' Grace replied. She then looked frightened as she turned to her father. 'What about mum and the others?'

'It's okay Grace,' her father said. His hand, stretching out to console her. 'I heard the man in the suit giving instructions to leave them behind. I think they just wanted us.'

'But why?'

'Ethan?' Jenson retorted. A flashback had resurfaced.

'Who?'

'Ethan! He's done it again. He's betrayed me.'

'Why?'

'His dad is Payton White. He was in the wheelchair, at the hospital. He came outside with me. He watched me get into your car. He must have remembered the registration plate. Stem must have tracked it to your home.'

'That makes sense,' Sterling agreed. 'They were there, ready to ambush us when we got home.'

'I'm so sorry. I didn't mean to get you involved. I figured if I sent you home, then…'

'We came to you Jenson. It's not your fault.' Sterling responded.

'But Jenson?' Grace said. 'My dream?'

'Dis will have ta wait.' Henry instructed. 'Dey're comin.'

Henry had his ear pressed up against the cold steel. He was listening from beyond the door. He could hear a commotion outside.

'Jenson? My Dad?' Callum echoed. He was standing over by the other cell door.

Jenson didn't have time to think about this revelation. He hurried over to the cell Callum was standing beside.

'Thank you.' Tom said as he emerged, stepping out of his cell, still dressed in his white lab coat. 'Come on, follow me,' he instructed, grabbing the swipe card from Jenson.

He immediately ran over to the other exit door and opened it. 'I can get us out of here, but we need to hurry.'

Everybody began to filter out through the narrow opening. But just as Jenson had stepped beyond the door, he hesitated.

A voice from the last occupied cell, which nobody had even noticed, called out to him.

'Jenson?' The voice bellowed. It was a low whimper.

'There's somebody else in there. Quick!' Jenson said.

'Okay, but hurry.' Tom insisted, handing the key card back to Jenson as the others filtered past. 'We don't have much time.'

Jenson ran back inside. He opened the cell door and immediately recognised who it was. It was Bill, the long-haired priest who had helped Davrin.

He looked rough. His hair was matted with grease, while his clean shave had turned into a scruffy stubble.

Jenson had just about recognised him. He knew he was a good guy. Ellie had told them about him.

'Come on!' He instructed, opening the cell door, and prompting Bill to follow.

Just as they reached the exit door, Bill scrambled ahead of Jenson. He pressed against the iron sheet and slammed it shut.

Jenson turned to face him. He didn't understand what had just happened.

But Bill was one step ahead of him. Within a snap second, he snatched the key card from his grasp.

'What are you doing?' Jenson questioned.

'I can't let you leave.'

Bills face started to change. He looked somewhat deranged. He seemed different. A black steam began to emerge, like a dimming shadow, emitting from his pores. Each gland releasing a black vapour, darkening with every second. And then, Jenson remembered where he had seen this before. It was back when he had first met Stephanie. The distorted images, now returning.

~~~

'WHAT HAPPENED?' Ellie shouted. The door slammed shut behind them, leaving Jenson on the other side.

'DAD.... Open the door!' Callum demanded. 'We have to get him out!'

'I know, I know....I don't know what happened?' His father answered. He quickly squirmed over towards the code panel.

~~~

'What are you doing?' Jenson said.
'I cannot let you leave!' Bill answered.

'But Davrin is safe. We'll take you to him.'
And then the black mist darkened even further, causing Bills eyes to turn black.

'You cannot leave!'
But these words were not Bills anymore. The voice, it was somebody else. It was as if somebody had taken control of him. It was a harsh rasping voice, but a female voice.

'Who are you?' Jenson asked. A chill exposed his backbone, clawing down his spine.
Bills voice returned.

'I've seen her in my dreams. Lilith. She talks to me. She told me you must die. She will give us back Stephanie if I keep you here.'

'Davrin's mother? I don't understand?'
An immediate suspicion plagued Jenson. *Had Bill gone mad?*

Just then, a sudden rupture caused them both to cower. The noise was loud. And as the metal sheet opened, Jenson could see the oncoming soldiers flooding in from the opposite doorway.

'I HAVE HIM HERE!' Bill screamed, running toward them. 'You cannot let him leave. SHOOT HIM!!'

The soldiers didn't hesitate. Presumably seeing a mad man charge at them, they began to fire.

Jenson didn't know if the soldiers had feared for their safety, as Bill abruptly approached. Or if they were taking no prisoners? But they fired into Bill's chest.

Bill dropped to the floor, his body quivering from the spraying bullets. And suddenly, Jenson began to think the unthinkable.

There, etched into the metal door, he stood back and watched on as each soldier invaded, like a scurrying crowd, stampeding their way towards him.

~~~

'DAD HURRY!' Callum screamed, his words evoking a terror as the gunfire sounded from behind the door.

'I'M TRYING, I'M TRYING!' Tom declared as the last number he keyed in opened the door. 'GOT IT!'

Callum, who was standing beside his father, could see the soldiers pressing forward. He then saw Jenson in the doorway. Quickly grabbing him, he pulled him through.

'Close it....NOWWW!' He yelled as he and Jenson had both landed on the ground.

Tom slammed the door shut just in time.

The sound of spraying bullets blasted towards them. The metal shield began to produce a rattling clank, with significant speed, giving them the protection from the mini torpedoes.

'Give me a gun, quick!' Tom requested.
Henry handed him his gun.

Tom didn't hesitate. He shot the key panel, sending sparks discharging from it.

'That should give us some time. We need to move, quickly.'

'What happened?' Ellie asked as they all began to push forward.

'It was that priest, Bill. He tried to trap me in there. He said Lilith told him to.'

'Who?'

'Lilith. I don't know what he was talking about.'

'But Bill's a good guy. He kept Davrin safe.'

'I'm not too sure, but something happened to him. I've seen it before, back in St Anita's with Stephanie, her face....'

'It's the new drug.' Tom interjected, charging down the corridor. 'They've given him the new drug.'

He then suddenly stopped. A door revealed itself. And rapidly typing in another code, he opened it. Now, standing in the doorway, he turned around.

'Quick, go down to the end and take the last left. When you hit the stairs go all the way down and it will lead you out into the car park. You need to hurry!'

'What are you talking about dad? You have to come with us.'

'I'm sorry Callum, I can't. I have to go back. I have to destroy everything. I fear this is only the beginning. And if I don't destroy all the data, then something terrible is going to happen.'

'But Chloe needs you. I need you.'

'I love you Callum. I've always loved you and Chloe. I know you probably don't understand what I did. But I did it for your safety.'

'But dad!'

'Please Callum, I need to do this. It's all my fault.'

'NO DAD!' Callum said, holding onto his father's sleeve. 'You can't do this to us! You can't leave us again!' His voice began to quiver.

'TOM!' Jenson interrupted. 'I need to find Davrin's mother. I promised him I would find her and bring her back. Where would she be?'

'JENSON!' Ellie pleaded. 'What about Grace's vision? We need to get you out of here.'

'Ellie please. I need to do this for Davrin. He has lost so much. Please just help the others escape. If you get Grace to safety, then she won't be with me. That gives me a chance.'

'But Jenson?'

'Please Ellie. I promised Davrin.'
Jenson turned to Tom. 'Where is she? Where is Stephanie?'

'She'll be on the top floor. But I would imagine she's heavily guarded.'

'I don't care! I made a promise.'

Tom paused.

'Okay. I'll help you. But once you're in, I'm gone. I have to come back and destroy it all.'

'I'm going with you,' Callum offered.

'Are you sure?' Jenson retaliated. He knew he could use the help.

'Yes.'

'No Callum!' Tom said. 'You need to leave. I'm doing this for you.'

'No dad, you don't get to tell me what to do.'

'Well then I'm coming too.' Ellie said. 'We're in this together!'

'Please Ellie. You need to help the others get to safety.' Jenson added.

'But you've a better chance with me in my uniform than you do on your own.'

Ellie turned to Henry.

'Henry, you go and make sure the others get out. I'll help Jenson and Callum. We're both dressed like Stem soldiers. It's our only chance.'

'But Ellie?' Her father questioned.

'Dad please. I need to do this. I'll be okay.'

'No Ellie!' Henry pleaded. 'You go wit your fawder. I'll help da lads.'

'I can't let you....'

'Your fawder needs ya. Please go wit him. I'll help Jenson an Callum.'

Ellie held onto his arm. She hesitated. She then looked over at her father.

'Okay. But be careful.'

'Come on! We haven't much time.' Tom instructed. 'We need to go, now.'

Chapter 51

Tom peered his head around the corner. He spotted six soldiers blocking the entrance to the lab.

'She has to be in there,' he whispered, turning round to face Jenson, Callum, and Henry.

'Wait here. I'll lead some of them away. And whoever's left, it's up to you. The over-ride code is 1096254. And please get out as fast as you can before I blow this entire place up.'

He then turned to his son, taking hold of his arm one last time.

'I hope one day you will understand why I did it.'

Callum stood there, staring blankly back at him. He didn't quite know what to say. He knew what his father was about to do, but he also knew he could lose him again.

And not getting the reaction he wanted, Tom turned swiftly. His tears began to obscure his view.

'Please look after each other.'
And that was the last thing he said. He immediately removed his arm and dashed out onto the corridor.

'THEY'RE UP HERE... THIS WAY!' He called out as he began to sprint down the other corridor with an array of soldiers following him.

Leaning back in against the wall, Jenson, Callum, and Henry watched on as four soldiers marched down after Tom. They looked hesitant at first, but once they recognised the white coat, they began to make a charge.

Jenson peered out from beyond the partition.

'That only leaves two soldiers,' he said, glancing back at Henry.

Henry nodded. He knew this was his cue. He knew they had to move quickly.

Jenson and Callum simultaneously stepped out onto the corridor. To a trained eye it would have brought suspicion, but the two guards were oblivious. Henry tipped out behind them, pressing his gun in again.

'I cot deese two tryin ta escape,' he said. 'Mr. white's order is ta keep dem alive.'

'You can't keep them in here. This room is off limits,' one of the soldiers said.

But just as they got close enough, Henry signalled.

'DUCK!' He roared.

Callum crouched down while Henry fired two bullets over him, hitting one of the soldiers.

Jenson lunged at the other soldier, stinging him with his tazer gun.

Callum immediately jumped up and punched in the numbers to over-ride the sequence.

The door swiftly opened.

The room was filled with laboratory equipment. And a pristine whiteness added to the cleanliness. A stench of chemicals hit them as they entered.

'There's no one here Jenson?' Callum remarked, looking round the room.

Another door suddenly opened as Payton White stepped in. He was holding Stephanie out in front. She looked frightened as the gun indented the side of her neck, just under her jawline.

'Did you think you would get away with this?' He asked. 'Drop the gun or she gets it.'

Henry hesitated. He looked over at Jenson. But within seconds, two loud bangs deafened the room. Payton had turned his gun and shot. Two bullets, dropping Henry to the floor.

'You all need to start listening,' Payton said, 'Now do I have to ask you to drop that tazer gun?'

Jenson didn't hesitate. The loud bangs had reclaimed his attention. He carefully placed it onto the table.

'Why are you doing this?'

'I had no other choice. You all think I'm the bad guy here. But you don't know the full story.'

'Whatever it is, there has to be another way.'

'There is no other way Jenson. You see, I had a child, another son, before Ethan. He was only two when he died. He went to sleep one night and never woke up. We found some blood in his bed, but there were no signs of forced entry. The coroner's report was inconclusive. We didn't know what he died of. But it was while he was sleeping. I swore to myself that I would never let it happen to Ethan.'

'But that's what happens to people in their dreams. You can't control it. It wasn't your fault. Your son just....'

'Jake. His name was Jake.'

'But you didn't know. Nobody can stop it.'

'Ah, but that's where you are wrong Jenson. You see, ever since that night, I've been searching for a way to stop it all from happening.'

'So that's why you take people and work on them like lab rats?' Callum interrupted.

Payton laughed.

'I have to do what is necessary. And if our rich government want to fund the work to save their families. Well then, you can understand?'

'No, we don't!' Callum detested. 'It's not fair. Just because we don't have the money like you. What did any of us do to deserve this? I bet you're not tested on.'

Payton chuckled again.

'I'm afraid that is just how the world works Callum. The rich stay rich and powerful. And the poor, well, I'm afraid they stay where they are.'

'I'm sorry about Jake.' Jenson said.

The room went silent. An element of pity took hold of Payton. This was the first time, in a long time that somebody had shown compassion towards his deceased son.

'The cure didn't work though.' Jenson added. 'It may never work.'

This deliberation caused Payton's grip to tighten around the gun. Stephanie let out a squeal as the gun pressed deeper into her neck.

'So you think you can do better?' He questioned.

'But it has killed a lot of people. These experiments are killing people. It nearly killed my sister.'

'You think I care about one little girl.'

'That little girl has a name too, just like your son, Jake. Her name is Robyn.'

Jenson's tone was cold. An anger pulsated in his veins.

'Well for Robyn, and all the others. Because of them, we have a new drug now. It has proven to be very powerful. You could call them the real heroes of this story.'

'Don't you dare call my sister a hero! Heroes choose their destiny's. Her choice was taken from her.'

'Well some heroes are chosen, Jenson. Let's just say we chose her.'

'So instead of people dreaming peacefully, you'll be controlling them like sheep?' Callum interrupted again.

'I should have killed you and your father when I had the chance.'

'Well you didn't. And now you're destroying everything.'

'Not quite Callum. This new drug is linked with Stephanie. She will be able to feed into the mind of every person who takes it. Interacting with them, protecting them from these so-called demons of the Dream World.'

'What about Stephanie?' Jenson questioned. 'Does she have a choice?'

'Or is she just another one of your pawns in this game?' Callum added.

'Well with any drug, you have to make sacrifices.'

'And what sacrifices are you making?' Callum probed.

'Do you not want to feel safe in your dreams Callum?'

'I want nothing from you.'

'Well suit yourself. We have sent the new drug to be tested in St. Anita's, to see if Stephanie has a link. All will be revealed very soon.'

'And then what?' Callum urged. 'You manipulate people and get rich?'

'Aren't you a clever little boy!' Payton chuckled, but a gravel of arrogance ruffled through the air. 'We have to make our money somehow.'

'But what will happen to Stephanie?' Jenson questioned. 'There has to be another way.'

'No Jenson. We've been searching for other ways for years. There is no other way. You could call it simple mind control. But if anything happens to her, by then, we should have her son, Davrin.'

'I wish Davrin had of finished Ethan off! You don't deserve to have children!'
Callum's words were piercing.
A cold chill entered the room.

A sudden vein rippled through Payton's forehead. His jaw clenched. And Jenson could see this statement had constructed anger. But Payton remained calm.

'I could easily finish you off myself Callum. But I may need your ability. So Jenson, would you do the honours and pick up that tazer.'

'You'll have to do it yourself, isn't that right Jenson?' Callum declared.
Payton swerved the gun. He pulled back the trigger. The barrel, now pointing at Callum.

'Do I have to ask again? I could always just use your sister Chloe. She has the ability too, no?'

Jenson immediately picked up the tazer. And without any hesitation, he jammed it into Callum.

Callum's eyes glared. His mouth hung open just before his body dropped. He felt betrayed. But a shroud of darkness encased him as his twitching body fell to the ground.

~~~

'This way!' Ellie directed as she opened the stairwell door.

No sooner had the door been pushed open, had she reached a stumbling block. She was smashed in the face by some sort of pole, cracking her helmet and causing her to drop.

'Who do you think you're up against?' George said, smacking her once more in the back. And as the pole struck again, he continued,

'That's for kicking me in the head.'

A soldier stood out from behind him, pointing his gun at the others.

Grace, who was standing right behind Ellie was immediately grabbed.

She screamed. But her struggle was short lived as George held his gun up to her head.

'Take that gun off her and search them for weapons,' he ordered.

The soldier did as he was asked. He quickly confiscated the guns.

Ellie was dazed on the ground.

'But I saw you get shot,' she said, her face now visible.

'Not well enough.' George replied, stepping over her and kicking her in the stomach. 'Ah ah....not so fast,' he continued, looking up. He noticed Sterling had attempted to come to his daughter's aid. 'I wouldn't do that if I were you. Watch these while I find the others. I'm sure I know where they are.'

The soldier followed his instructions and remained there. His gun, firmly steering at them as he shifted his glare.
'Please! Take me instead of my daughter,' Sterling begged.
George smiled.
'I think she is better leverage, don't you?!'
And with that, he grabbed Grace tightly and vanished down the corridor.

Chapter 52

'Good. At least you do as you're told,' Payton declared, watching Callum's twitching body on the ground. He then shifted his gun back to Stephanie's neck.

An air of silence took hold again. Payton was planning his next move. His eyes were scanning the room.

If this was a game of chess, Payton had just taken down Jenson's knight and bishop, snatching full control of the board. And now, only one move away from announcing 'checkmate'. But Jenson couldn't afford to wait. He needed to regain his position.

'Why don't you just let everyone go?' He suggested. 'You can take me instead.'

Payton laughed.

'Don't be silly Jenson. We don't need you anymore. I got what I wanted from your sister. She contributed very well for this new drug. You should be very proud of her.'

'Proud of what? She's in hospital because of you. She's in a coma and may never wake up.'

'Call it collateral damage. But she did help us Jenson. You should remember that. And just think of the countless lives she will save. And now, Stephanie will do the rest.'

'I still don't get it. How are you so certain this will work?'

'You see. Your sister was able to give us the consciousness we needed. Call it a blank slate if you like. And then Stephanie here, she has a deep connection to this dream world we conjure up every night. So, in our new studies and with our new scientist Dr. Shafer, Stephanie has been able to communicate with people in their dreams.

Even Dr Shafer himself. Stephanie has fixed his mindset. He is safe when he sleeps. Wouldn't you like to sleep without worrying if you'd wake up?'

'But Tom said you don't fully understand what this is doing to people.'

'That's called trial and error, Jenson. We will eventually get it right, with a little tweaking. And we are so close.'

'But at what cost? What if you do more harm than good?'

'Well, if you have to kill a few hundred to save millions then I can live with that. Since Dr. Shafer has come on board, we're closer than ever. We will eventually get rid of this realism of dreams once and for all. But unfortunately, we can't have people knowing what we have done.'

'People know what you do already.'

'Not this new drug Jenson.'

'But they will find out?'

'Yes. You are right, they will find out. But by then, most of them will have taken it. We will have the ability to control them. They won't be able to stop it.'

An uncomfortable silence loomed again. Their conversation had come to an end, both sides had no more to say. Each understanding that no sway could encourage the other. Jenson had no more fight left in him. It seemed Payton had won. And now, he was just about to call his 'checkmate'.

Suddenly Stephanie's silence broke. She began to mutter. It seemed vague, but the more Jenson listened, the more it sounded like a different dialect, something neither Payton nor Jenson had ever heard before.

'What's happening to her?' Jenson called out.

'I'm not sure,' Payton replied. 'Dr. Shafer gave her something before he left.'

Jenson could see the confusion in his stare.
'And you trust this Dr. Shafer?' He asked.

But just then, Stephanie screamed. She grabbed hold of Payton's fist. And squeezing it tight, she pulled it away from her neck as his gun fell. Payton called out for help. The pain, unbearable. And in one steady stroke, a snap sounded as she crushed his hand.

Quickly grabbing hold of his suit jacket, Stephanie tossed him across the room like a rag doll, a strength, no human could bear.

'You stupid fool. Did you think I would do all of that for you?' She rasped.

Payton came crashing down on top of a table full of glass tubing.

'STEPHANIE?' Jenson called out. But he knew this wasn't Stephanie.

'Stephanie is not here anymore,' the voice called out. 'I AM LILITH!'

These were the distorted words coming from Stephanie's mouth. Sinister and chilling. It was as if she was possessed. And this name, Lilith, it was a name Jenson had heard it before.

'Where is Stephanie?' Jenson asked. 'And who is Lilith?'

'YOU FOOLS......I control Stephanie now.'

Stephanie's face began to distort. But the black smudge could not fully change. It was as if she was waiting for a trigger, morphing into something, but not fully capable of changing.

'What do you want from Stephanie?' Jenson called out.

'I need to free her body.'

'Free it from what?'

'I was banished to the depths of my world. Now I will return and take back what is mine.'

'What world?' Jenson called out.

'The world of the Fae. The world where dreams are made of. They will all die!'

And with that, Stephanie's body began to levitate.

Jenson was mesmerised. His face watched on as she flew towards him.

'Myral was right. Evil was coming!'

He quickly glanced around the room, looking for some sort of a weapon.

Noticing the gun Henry had dropped, he ran over and picked it up. He turned and began to shoot.

Not a single bullet hit Stephanie's body. She raised her hands up, and like magic, somehow each bullet deflected off her.

Jenson ran for the door. But just as he got there, a table was thrown against it, breaking into smithereens.

He raised his hands up to protect his face as fragments flew everywhere. Shrapnel's, slicing his skin. He was trapped.

Stephanie flew towards him.

Quickly jumping to the ground, he scurried underneath the tables. He began to crawl over to where Payton had been thrown.

Stephanie clawed at each table. Her fingernails, like sharp razors, gripping tight. She flipped each one over, tossing them aside.

Jenson could feel the air at his feet, the distance between narrowing with every tossing table. He could hear her snarl; the anticipation of catching him.

Scouring under the last table, his options were dwindling.

Inevitably, the table was removed. Stephanie had catapulted it into the air. She was right above him, hovering, and her arm now reaching downwards.

She took hold of the back of his neck and dragged him up from the ground.

Jenson was struggling to rip himself free. It was no use. Her grip was too strong.

He began to feel the stinging scorch of her fingernails digging deep into his skin.

Suddenly, remembering the knife Tessa had given him, he somehow managed to reach in and remove it from his back pocket.

Opening it up and holding it tight, he sliced down on Stephanie's wrist.

The possessed Stephanie let out a howling scream. She dropped him.

Jenson fell to the ground. He turned around and held the bloodied knife out in front. It was a weak attempt to stop this creature, but he stood tall.

Then suddenly, in one quick motion, Stephanie was gone.

'What have I done?' a voice uttered. It was fragile. It was Payton.

Jenson turned round to see him lying there. He hurried over. He knew Payton was hurt.

Quickly scanning his body, he noticed the large shard of glass protruding from his stomach. He then saw the gun beside him and picked it up.

He looked over at the exit. It was free. Stephanie was nowhere to be seen. But before he could move, a wave of guilt hit. He turned back.

'It's okay Mr. White. I'll help get you out of here.'

He grabbed hold of Payton and helped him to his feet. But Payton was in a bad way. He was struggling to stand. The blood, oozing from his gut.

'Jenson. Save yourself,' he said. 'You have a better chance on your own.'

'No. I won't leave you. I won't leave anyone behind. You can fix this mess.'

They both managed to hobble across the now cluttered room.

'YOU WILL NOT GET AWAY!!' The chilling voice returned. It was behind them.

Jenson, now holding onto Payton, turned round and raised his gun.

It was too late. Stephanie was too fast. She was too strong. Lilith had taken full control.

Payton was knocked out of Jenson's hands and Jenson was knocked against the back wall.

'WHAT DO YOU WANT?' Jenson called out.

'YOU ARE THE LAST GATEWAY! YOU ARE PREVENTING ME FROM ENTERING THIS WORLD. YOU MUST DIE!'

Chapter 53

Just then, the door was kicked open. It was George. He had a hold of Grace by the hair, his grip so tight, the pain was visible on her face.

Suddenly, Grace let out a scream. She saw Payton's body lying on the floor beside them. Her cries piercing now as she noticed Stephanie's levitating body. She was flying right towards them.

George shrieked. His grip deliberately loosened as he tossed Grace aside. His instincts were not to save her, but to save himself. He raised his gun and began to shoot.

Stephanie swooped in as each bullet reflected. She grabbed him by the throat and soared into the air. It was his turn to yield the grimacing pain on his face. Her nails etching deeply into his skin.

Grace's hands had saved her fall. Each palm resting against the cold floor. She could see her reflection in the varnish. And with that, she could see George's legs being suspended above, and dangling for dear life.

Within an instance, before Grace could even cower, George's legs stopped. Like a sudden switch, the life inside them had been removed.

Grace's palms slid across the tiles from the fallen blood. She squirmed away. And just as she attempted her escape, George's decapitated head fell, rolling alongside her.

She screamed. For Grace could feel the swift wind above her. It was only moments until she would be next.

~~~

Sterling grew impatient. He knew his daughter was in danger. He had to take a chance, for her dream had now become a reality, the realness they had all wanted to avoid. And in a flash, he leaped up and jumped on top of the soldier. This sudden tussle had somehow knocked the gun from the soldier's hand. And whilst Sterling tried his best to outweigh the soldier, he wasn't a fighter. The gentle giant stature was of no use. The soldier immediately spun him.

Wardy quickly caught wind of these actions. A man in his 60's, but still, with enough response, he instinctively ran over. He grabbed the gun, and without hesitation, he fired.

Sterling could hear the discharge, the noise drumming in his ear. Suddenly, his component had stopped.

'QUICK, GO!' Wardy yelled. He stood there. His gun, pointing at the soldier. His finger, ready to pull again.

'QUICK! WE NEED TO GO NOW!' Ellie shouted, grabbing hold of Sterling.

And within seconds, Wardy was left alone in the corridor, just him and the soldier as Ellie and Sterling had vanished. They were already making tracks back to the others.

~~~

A response team had made it to the room. Each soldier lining up to shoot. But Stephanie had anticipated this. She sensed them coming.

Still levitating, she spun around aggressively, throwing George's severed body at them. And the force, so powerful, had knocked them all to the ground. She then raised her hands. And just like Davrin in his dream, she slapped them forward. This motion had somehow caused the soldiers to sweep along the ground, their wavering bodies scrambling to hold onto something.

But it was no use. They were swept along the corridor from the drifting wind.
Stephanie hovered back into the room.
  Grace, now crawling on all fours, with her head tucked towards her chest. She wouldn't look up. She was scrambling for shelter.
  Stephanie's body flew directly down. She reached out her hand and grabbed Grace up by the hair.

~~~

  Ellie and Sterling had reached the stairwell door. They opened it to see a line of soldiers smashing into the lift door. And with this impact, Grace's cries bellowed again. But this time Sterling could sense an even stronger danger.

~~~

  Grace could feel her whole-body dangling from the fibres of her hair. Each follicle holding on with sheer strength, a strength she wished would weaken. Her wild afro hair, denser, and unlikely to snap. Her hands squirming and trying to claw away at Stephanie. But she couldn't take hold. Her fate, now sealed with that of Georges.
  'OVER HERE!' Jenson shouted.
He had picked up a chair. He needed to draw Stephanie's attention. He had to save Grace.
  With all his strength, he threw it towards them.
  Stephanie let out a shriek. She had momentarily forgotten about him. She twisted her body, flinging Grace out in front, the impact hitting hard. And then, her rage for Jenson caused her to toss Grace aside. But luckily her head was intact.
  'YOU MUST DIE SO I CAN BE REBORN,' She demanded.

Jenson turned to grab anything he could. But Stephanie was too quick. She flew over with sheer speed. She took hold of him. Her sharp claws sinking into his neck as she ascended, taking them both high into the room.

'You don't need to do this.' Jenson cried.

'I do! I took over this body long ago. I have been locked up within it, waiting. If you die, I will be free!' She then began to crush his throat.

Grace could see Stephanie illuminate, as if something was happening.

Suddenly, gunshots sounded as Payton lay there, firing his gun at Stephanie; a weak attempt to take back what he had done.

Stephanie threw Jenson towards him as each bullet hit.

Her skin then began to glow, a red burning colour. And a bright light glistened. It was so blinding nobody could keep their eyes open.

Grace could feel the heat, but within seconds it had diminished. She looked up again. But this time she could see the flames beginning to fade.

Stephanie's body fell to the ground.

Ellie came running into the room. She saw Stephanie's body slowly drop, positioning itself on her knees with her back tilting upwards. Her mouth was wide open. She then, let out an astonishingly roar, so loud, the piercing thrills began to sting. They all covered their ears and watched on as a dark demonic shadow exposed itself, emerging from Stephanie's jaws.

Callum woke up. His hands were scrambling to cover his ears. The screams were deafening. And as he watched on in discomfort, he could see the black shadow appear.

'I'm FREEEEE,' the shadow declared, as black vapour dissected the room. And seconds later, all signs of the shadow had disappeared.

Chapter 54

JENSON?' Grace yelled.

The shrieking sounds had dissipated. But Grace had now managed to get to her feet. The beating she received had bruised her muscles, but she knew she had to get to him.

She scurried over and fell to her knees. Her arms cradling his back as she pulled him towards her. And as she tossed his body round, turning him over, she gasped.

'Oh no!' Ellie said as she too conceded.

It was Jenson. He was on the ground, just as Grace had described it in her dream. His lifeless body, lying beside Payton's, with a bullet hole in his forehead.

Grace stood up.
'Is he….?'

Ellie checked his body. She then held onto Grace's arm. She nodded.

Callum got to his feet. He saw Grace over at Jenson. Her face said it all. He walked over and joined them, standing over Jenson's dead body.

'What have you done?' Ellie exclaimed, turning to look at Mr. White.

A remorseful groan escaped Payton's lips.

'I'mmmm sooorry,' he said as the blood poured from his mouth. He then looked over at Jenson's corpse just moments before he too took his last breath.

'HENRY?' Ellie called out as she watched him stir.

Henry felt grateful for the Stem bullet proof uniform he was wearing. But this happiness was short lived when he saw Jenson and the destruction that was caused around him.

Suddenly a loud explosion sound came from inside the building.

'That must be my dad,' Callum said. 'We need to get out of here.'

'What about his body?' Grace asked.

'I'll get it.' Henry said. Watching Sterling cling onto his daughter.

But just as he leaned down to pick Jenson's body up, a voice spoke out.

'Where am I?'

It was Stephanie Belshaw. She seemed normal again, looking up at them. A bewilderment in her stare.

'Where's my baby? Where's Davrin?' She asked.

Then suddenly, the floor behind her blew up, sparking flames from within the room. And then another explosion hit.

'We have to go NOW,' Ellie shouted. 'HELP HER' she added as both Henry and Callum helped her up.

They all began to run out of the room leaving Jenson's dead body behind. There was no point in trying to save his remains. The explosions were getting worse. They had to move quickly.

The building began to crumble behind them. And all running as fast as they could down the stairs, they were following Tom's instruction to make their awaited escape.

Reaching outside, they all watched on, with many others, as the building floors shattered, collapsing into a burning wreckage of debris. The explosions were quickly destroying all that was left of Stem Industries.

'What are we going to do now?' Callum asked. 'Did you see the demon? It's alive.'
'Something tells me it's only going to get worse.' Ellie declared.
'Come on, we have to get out of here,' Wardy instructed. 'I'm not too sure what these soldiers will do once everything falls.'

~~~

Standing over by his car, Dr. Shafer, watched on as his dark grey eyes reflected the flames of the burning building.
'We did it my Lord. We will free the others and destroy this world,' he said, getting into his car and shutting the door.

Chapter 55

'Chloe?' Callum cried, opening the door with a cup of coffee in his hand.

He had waited by his sister's bedside all day, watching her unconscious body lying in the hospital bed. It was the first time she had opened her eyes.

Slowly lifting herself up with her hands, she moved over, positioning herself into a more upright placement.

'Go easy,' Callum instructed 'You've been shot.'

Chloe shifted further in the bed.

'I feel like I've been kicked repeatedly in the stomach. Where am I?'

'You're in the hospital.'

'How long have I been here?'

'All day.'

'They did it then. They got you all out?'

But Chloe's thrill quickly flattened. Her deep concern suffocated any celebration. Callum wasn't smiling, and she could see this. She clutched onto her stomach and shifted herself upright.

'What is it Callum? Who didn't make it?'

Callum dipped his head.

'Tell me Callum, what is it? Did you get dad out?'

'No,' Callum answered, his eye's locking onto hers. 'He never made it out.'

'But I never got to say....' Chloe never finished her sentence. 'Where's Jenson?'

Their eye's converged again, but Chloe could see the affliction in his.

'What happened?' She asked louder, feeling somewhat reluctant for him to answer. She knew something was wrong. Holding onto her breath, she waited.

'He never made it either.' Callum said.

'But we shot him with a tranquiliser dart. He wasn't supposed to be there! How is that possible?'

'He's dead Chloe. He's gone!'

Chloe's bottom lip began to quiver. She bent over, leaning into her hands. The wound in her stomach began to burn, but the sadness exceeded any pain. She began to cry.

Callum knew she had grown fond of Jenson.

'I know you liked him, so did I.'

'But we came this far Callum.'

'There's more Chloe.'

Chloe looked up as her watershed eyes glistened in the dimmed light.

'Tell me Callum. What is it?'

'Well you know that demon we saw, the one in our dream with Davrin, the one that was pretending to be his mother?'

'Yes?'

'Well it…..it's here.'

'What do you mean, it's here?'

'It's here. It came out of Stephanie.'

'How?'

'I'm not sure how, but I saw it with my own eyes.'

'Where is it now?'

'It vanished.'

'Vanished where?'

'Sterling says it's in our world now. He says small spirits come through all the time. But they are harmless. They are only small spirits roaming our world. He says this one is different. It seems to be here for a reason.'

'What reason?'

'I don't know.'

'What about the others, are they okay?'

'Yeah. A few bruises and bumps but they're all safe. Stephanie is somehow back to when she was younger. She doesn't remember anything though. She and Davrin are staying in Tessa's. Grace and her father have gone home to their family. Wardy is gone home to be with Meatloaf before he buries him. And Ellie is upstairs with Henry. They just told Jenson's mother and father what happened.'

'Can I see him?' Chloe asked.

'We didn't have time to get him out. Stem Industries burned down to the ground with Jenson inside.'

'You left him inside, on his own, to burn?'

'We didn't have time. He was already dead.'

Just then, the door opened.

'Oh, hi Chloe. Great, you're awake!' Ellie said. A smile on her face as she stood in the doorway. But her sudden appearance did not scream joy. She looked confused.

'I'm sorry, I know this doesn't seem like the time and place, but I think you guys might need to see this,' she added.

'What is it?' Callum asked.

'It's Jenson's sister, Robyn. She's awake.'

~~~

They followed Ellie up to the hospital floor but before they got to the room, they could hear the commotion.

Getting closer, they could hear a little girl's voice. And reaching the doorway they recognised who it was. It was Robyn.

'No, get off me,' she kept saying as each nurse tried to restrain her.

'Honey please,' her mother cried. She was barely holding herself together after receiving the news of her son's death. 'You need to stay easy. I'm sure it's hard.'

'But Mum, it's Jenson.'

'Oh Robyn,' her mother mouthed. She started to sob as her husband began to console her.

'Honey, your brother is gone,' her father told her.

'But dad, Jenson has to come back to us. Myral and the others need him. He is the Last Gateway. He needs to save them. He is the only one who can save us all.'

'Oh honey.' Her father said.

'But dad?'

Ellie, Callum, and Chloe stood there all staring at each other.

Could this be true? Could Jenson be brought back somehow? After seeing a demon possess a body, and then escaping through it like some sort of a portal, was such a thing even possible?

Chapter 56

Later that night, Davrin was sitting down at Tessa's kitchen table sipping a glass of water.

'How's your shoulder Dav?' Tessa asked, stepping into the kitchen.
'It's okay.'
'You know you don't have to blame yourself.' Tessa said.
'I can't help but think this is my fault. Jenson would still be here if I didn't take that dart out of him.'
'Don't blame yourself Dav. He wanted to go. I believe these things are all mapped out. The world has a plan for us all. Look, your mother is back with you, so we have to take some positives from all of this.'
'She doesn't even know who I am,' Davrin sulked.
'It will take time Dav. It's like she has been possessed all these years. She will need to get used to you, get used to having a strapping teenage son instead of a little baby. I've put her to bed. God, it was as if she was a baby herself. I would imagine it's like being in a coma for the past 15 years. She will get there. You both will. Now go on, you look tired. Go get some sleep.'
'Is she going to stay with us?' Davrin asked.
'Of course she is. You both are. To be honest, I could do with the company. We have to rebuild this family. I feel like I'm going around the bend, talking to Terry in my head all the time.'
Tessa smiled again.
'Sure, I never was fond of those places like St. Anita's. I always thought they did more damage to a person than

good. But don't you worry, we'll help get your mother back to her old self again.'

'Thank you,' Davrin said, getting to his feet. 'Thank you for everything.'

'Margaret would be so proud of you,' Tessa acknowledged. 'Sleep safe.'

'You too,' Davrin remarked.

~~~

After cleaning up the kitchen, Tessa saw the deck of tarot cards lying on the table.

Sitting down, she reached over and picked them up.

Taking the cards out of the box, she began to shuffle. To some, the tarot cards were a false approach to tell one's future. But to Tessa, who had faith in the cards, she believed otherwise. For she always relied on the cards. They always helped her in some way to obtain a perspective on the future, if even not hers.

Flipping over the first card, the Major Arcana card, it showed the 'The Devils' card.

She stopped. She got a sudden fright.

Continuing, she quickly flipped over the second card, another Major Arcana, which revealed 'The World'.

Pondering, she tried to figure out what these two had in common.

'Devil and the World?' She thought.

Slowly turning over the third Major Arcana to reveal its true fortune. She let out a gasp.

There, staring back at her from the table, beside the other cards was the card of 'Death'.

Just then she got another unexpected fright. She heard a noise out in the hallway.

Cautiously pulling the chair out from under the table, she got to her feet. She began to step over to the kitchen door.

'Dav, is that you?' She called out.
After hearing no reply, she spoke again.
'Stephanie?'
And again, nothing.

She had reached the door, drifting her eyeline out into the hallway. But nobody was there.

Stepping further out, she noticed the door leading into the garage was ajar.

'Hello?' She said, inching over and slowly leaning her arm out to push it back.

Without warning, the door pulled back as Stephanie revealed herself. Her eye's looked shadowy, black in colour, but it was too dark to make her out.

'Stephanie, are you alright?' Tessa asked as she switched on the light.

The brightened visibility disclosed just how dark Stephanie's eyes were.

Her Devil like eyes startled Tessa, and the shivers followed.

'Stephanie, what is happening?'
But that is all she could say before Stephanie raised her hand. And in it, she was wielding one of Terry's pocketknives.

~~~

Tessa's scream had woken Davrin. He wasn't sure at first, but he soon realised this was not a dream.

He quickly jumped up out of bed and ran down the stairs.

Reaching the bottom, he noticed a body lying in the hallway. The lights were off, but the front door was wide open.

A shaft of brightness from the moon gave enough clarity for him to make out who it was. It was Tessa.

'Tessa?' He cried, jumping down beside her body, and holding her upright. 'What happened?'

'Stephanie,' Tessa vaguely replied.

Davrin could see the blood coming through her hands as she held them up to her throat.

'My mum? Where is she?' He asked.

'She......she's gone'

'Who took her?'

'No one....she did this.'

'What? Why?'

'She said.....Lilith needs her.'

And these were the last words Tessa spoke before the gargled blood suffocated her windpipe.

'I'm sorry Tessa, I am so sorry.' Davrin cried.
He sobbed as he held her dying body in his arms.

A gust of wind took Davrin by surprise. The cold air came in from the night sky outside. He knew instantly what was happening. A real darkness was coming.

Author's Notes

Again, I would firstly like to thank **Jennifer Maher.** Since collaborating on 'Jenson and the Dreamers', she instantly knew what way the second book should be. And within her first attempt, she had sent me this wonderful cover for the sequel, 'The Last Gateway'. Jennifer, you are a creative mastermind, with a brilliance I could not have done without!
For any of you readers out there who have children in your life, if you haven't picked up your copy of 'The Happy Half-Moon Girl', you need to! This will send your child off into a magical sleep! And keep your eyes open for Jennifer's second book 'My Unicorn Snores', coming soon. Please check out her Author and Illustrator page – **jennifer-maher.com**

To **Phyllis, Daniela Geanta, Ross, Kesia, Trisha Patton, Jennifer007, Emma Houston, Tara L, Paul, Amazon queen, Grainne, Jen Henderson, Chrissie, Rachel Brown, Dan, Paul Kearney, Helen, Eamon, Jennifer Ryan and Derek Christy**. Your reviews were incredible! Thank you all so much! I am so grateful for the time you took to read the book and write about your experience. Each review set a light inside of me allowing me to feel the excitement all over again. And everybody else that left a rating, thank you so much!

There are also three special people on TikTok who I would like to thank,
@robgb0
@missbeehaven123
@leannevickery

I reached out to see if you would be interested in reading my book and perhaps sharing it. And the effort that was put in honestly left me speechless. Each review was unbelievable! I felt so excited after seeing them. I cannot thank you all enough!!! Please go follow these incredible influencers who are paving their own destiny's. Each one, allowing audiences into their lives, reaching out to either make people laugh, to set up their own business, or just to make somebody feel good in their own skin. You are all amazing!!!

To **everybody else who shared it**, thank you!!!

And last, but not least, to **YOU, the person reading this**. Thank you from the deepest depts of my heart! You've bought the books and have taken the time to come on this journey with me. I am forever grateful!!

Please continue to follow me on this journey,
Facebook - Alan Hendrick
Instagram - alanmhendrick
TikTok   - @alanhendrick1

I cannot wait to share the final instalment. Book 3, coming soon…..

'The Jenson Rose Trilogy'

When Two Worlds Collide

Printed in Great Britain
by Amazon